SHAKUNTALA

Utkarsh Patel is a corporate-professional-turned-mythologist, and now an author. He is a professor of Comparative Mythology at the Mumbai University and has qualifications in Indian and World Mythology. He is a founder-member of the Talking Myth Project (http://www.talkingmyths.com), an attempt to create an online repository of age-old stories lost in this modern world. Utkarsh blogs at www.utkarshspeak.blogspot.in and is a regular speaker at various forums. Follow him on Twitter @utkarshmp. He can also be reached at utkarshmp@yahoo.com

SHAKUNTALA
The Woman Wronged

Utkarsh Patel

RUPA

Published by
Rupa Publications India Pvt. Ltd 2015
7/16, Ansari Road, Daryaganj
New Delhi 110002

Sales Centres:

Allahabad Bengaluru Chennai
Hyderabad Jaipur Kathmandu
Kolkata Mumbai

ISBN: 978-81-291-XXXX-X

First impression 2015

10 9 8 7 6 5 4 3 2 1

The moral right of the author has been asserted.

Printed by XXXXXX

To my mother

Foreword

Shakuntala's story as told by Vyasa is one that needs to be told again in our times, for us.

Hers is of course the story of the mother of the man who gave this land its name—Bharata. It is the story of a heroic mother—a single woman who brought her child up not just to be a survivor in her society but to be a great conqueror, a superb leader, a brilliant emperor and the master of his times. It is the story of the mother of a man who became an ideal in leadership for all times to come, who set standards in justice and commitment to people for all times by refusing the kingdom to his own sons, because he found them incompetent, and giving it to a rank outsider. All of us are reflections of our mothers—as much as we are products of anyone or anything, if not more. And this, as Indian psychologists point out, is far truer of Indian sons than, say, sons in the contemporary West.

But more than that, much more that that, it is the story of a woman and a wife. A wife who insisted on equality and respect from her man, who reminded her husband of his duty towards her, who told him what honour is and what an honourable man should do. Such honour in men is something our own times need greatly. She had the courage to stand up for herself, to stand up for all exploited women, who are treated as objects rather than as people, for women who to this day are used for pleasure and then discarded like trash. And she showed this courage openly—by walking right into the royal court, standing there in the presence of all possible earthly power and challenging her man who sat on the throne to do what was right.

Vyasa's Shakuntala is a woman of courage—courage that knows no fear.

Shakuntala is all that a woman should be—independent, assertive, courageous and yet endowed with tenderness, capable of great love, the ability to give of oneself unreservedly, to take risks. Perhaps she imbibed all this from the environment in which she grew up after she was abandoned by her biological father because she was the symbol of his fall, his shame. That environment—the environment of the ashram of a rishi—is India's richest heritage, the ambience from which the most beautiful things Indian were born. She grew up in an environment where she felt secure—totally secure—loved and cherished. Our girl children today too need to grow up feeling secure, loved, cherished.

Shakuntala's soul belongs to the Vedic women—she is their cultural daughter. Through her we see what Vedic women were—the kind of women any culture, in any part of the world, at any time can be proud of. Women not crippled by fear, women who knew how to give and receive love, women who knew how to bend before love and how to fight it if that was what was called for. Authentic women who participated in the social, cultural and spiritual life of their times as the equals of their men. Women who were hungry for life, full of the spirit of adventure, passionate, assertive.

I congratulate Utkarsh Patel for telling her story for our times.

Satya Chaitanya
Chaitra Navaratri 2015

Introduction

Shakuntala is a well-known character made famous by the Sanskrit play *Abhijnanashakuntalam* by Mahakavi Kalidasa, written between the 1st century BCE and 4th century BCE. *Abhijnanashakuntalam* has been studied and analyzed by many authors and playwrights and has been one of the most successful and renowned plays of India.

Abhijnanashakuntalam has been translated into various Indian and international languages. Englishman William Jones translated it into English in 1789. Soon, Jones's version was translated in many other European languages. Among the translators, Goethe was one who was deeply influenced by the play and is supposed to have written in a letter:

> The first time I came across this inexhaustible work it aroused such enthusiasm in me and so held me that I could not stop studying it. I even felt impelled to make the impossible attempt to bring it in some form to the German stage. These efforts were fruitless but they made me so thoroughly acquainted with this most valuable work, it represented such an epoch in my life, I was so absorbed in it, that for thirty years I did not look at either the English or the German version. [...] It is only now that I understand the enormous impression that work made on me at an earlier age.

No wonder he modelled the jester in the prologue of *Faust* (1797) on the vidusaka in *Abhijnanashakuntalam,* as noted by Heinrich Heine. Goethe's friend Schiller wrote of the play, 'In the whole world of Greek antiquity there is no poetical representation of beautiful love which approaches even afar.'[A]

However, what is lesser known is that Shakuntala is one of the first female characters to appear in the epic Mahabharata written by Maharishi Ved Vyasa. Shakuntala's story is told in the Sambhava Parva part of the Adi Parva of the Mahabharata. The story is recited by Vaishampayana to Janamejeya. This tale from the Mahabharata was taken by Kalidasa and recreated in his own way into one of the most romantic plays of all times. Many of his other plays were also based on mythology, like *Kumarasambhava, Raghuvamsham, Meghaduta,* etc.

However, there is a big difference in the original characterization of Shakuntala by Vyasa and the dramatic representation by Kalidasa.

Vyasa's Shakuntala is the precursor of many of his later heroines in the Mahabharata—strong, decisive and fiery. She had a mind of her own and could stand her ground against the mighty king of Hastinapur, King Dushyant. Also, Dushyant is a king of little character and displays rather loose morals in Vyasa's Mahabharata, instead of someone who suffers from temporary amnesia as represented by Kalidasa in his version. The major difference, however, is the character of Sage Durvasa.

Sage Durvasa is an invention of Kalidasa, whose curse brings on the dramatic forgetfulness, leading to all the troubles in the life of Shakuntala. It also gives Dushyant the much-needed excuse to reject his wife, which, in the original version of Vyasa, is a breach of morality and a sign of his lusty escapade with Shakuntala.

Vyasa's Shakuntala knew the background of her birth and

understood its repercussions. She stood her moral ground when the king refused to recognize her and ensured that she won justice by the sheer ability of her reasoning and straightforwardness. Vyasa's Shakuntala is not a damsel in distress shedding copious tears; she fights for her right and gets her way, and does not succumb to the man, irrespective of his position and stature. She was amongst the first women in the Mahabharata to fight for her rights in a man's world and get her due.

There could have been several reasons that motivated Kalidasa to change the character. According to the tenets of *Natyashastra* by Sage Bharata, a hero cannot be guilty of moral turpitude. Kalidasa was a master of literature and language and probably sought to fully follow the tenets of *Natyashastra*, at the risk of 'twisting' the original tale from the epic Mahabharata. The curse by Rishi Durvasa could be one way to mask this moral turpitude. Another probable reason could have been that Kalidasa was a court poet during the golden period of the Guptas. As a court poet, it would not have been judicious to write a play which depicted the royalty in a bad light. To show a king as someone who does not epitomize high morals and ethics would be a huge disservice to royalty and thus, his *Abhijnanashakuntalam* resorts to the inclusion of Sage Durvasa as a creative indulgence, but stays with the dramatic elements which make the story so interesting.

Shakuntala: The Woman Wronged is a fictional narrative that represents the protagonist in the Vyasan mould of characterization of the heroine. In this, Shakuntala comes across as a smart individual like the later heroines of the epic, Satyavati and Kunti, and a fiery precursor to the likes of Amba and Draupadi. The original thread is the same as that of the story in the Mahabharata by Sage Ved Vyasa. Some creative liberties have been taken in expressions and certain characterizations to highlight the personality of Shakuntala. Certain other myths have also been added to enable a discussion and debate of lesser-known or little-debated characters from mythology. Needless to say, the misunderstood characters are females, who have not been discussed openly for any number of reasons.

This work is not to be seen as anti-Kalidasa, as he was undoubtedly amongst the best poets or playwrights India has seen. This work is only to introduce to the readers the original Shakuntala as envisioned by Ved Vyasa. Mythology, like water, has the unique ability to take the form of its container. Kalidasa had his way of interpreting the tale and making it famous, while I am only trying to recreate the character as conceived by the original creator of Shakuntala. While Kalidasa's Shakuntala made for a beautiful, lovelorn heroine inviting sympathy, Vyasa's Shakuntala is more heroic and much closer to the modern-day woman. This work seeks to reiterate that image of a woman envisioned many centuries ago by Vyasa, who has given us some of the most powerful female characters in our epics.

Mythology has been a rich source of popular literature the world over, and more so in India. The beauty of mythology is that it is ageless and can be adapted and made contemporary at any point of time, and if not, it is definitely debatable at every stage of civilization. This work of fiction takes up many other myths that are well known and hopes to spark a debate on some of the issues they raise. They are intertwined with the character of Shakuntala because the author finds it both relevant and necessary to enable a divergent viewpoint from the oft-beaten path that the 'popular' myths have always traversed. The views expressed here are of the author, but hope to strike a balance and find an echo in the present world. One also hopes that the novel will hold a mirror to what society has done to the status of a woman, from what it was in the times when the epic was authored. This is a small effort to achieve that minor error-correction.

The novel is in three parts:

1. The birth of Shakuntala—which deals with the relationship of Menaka and Vishwamitra and the early childhood of Shakuntala.
2. The youth and marriage of Shakuntala—which represents the coming of age of Shakuntala and her relationship with Dushyant.
3. Shakuntala at the court of Dushyant—which showcases her coming to terms with her status as a single mother and her final confrontation with Dushyant.

(All references to the Mahabharata have been taken from *The Mahabharata of Krishna-Dwaipayana Vyasa* translated into English from the original Sanskrit text by K.M. Ganguli [1883–1896].)

List of Characters

Following is a list and brief introduction of characters as they appear in the book:

Narada Muni

Narada Muni was a manasaputra, or the mind-born son of Lord Brahma. He was considered to be the greatest worshipper and follower of Lord Vishnu and could present himself at Vishnu's abode without prior permission. His 'non-curseable' personality made him extremely influential in the Heavens, the main arena of action, though he had access to all the three lokas. He was an expert in the Vedas and Upanishads and possessed extraordinary proficiency in Samaveda, which is dedicated to the art of music. He knew the art of articulating each syllable and was also well-versed in semantics.

Popular representations depict Narada Muni as a mischief-maker and kalaha-priya or the lover of quarrels, but quintessentially, Narada Muni is someone who is instrumental behind many an action in the world of Indian mythology.

Here, he is the carrier of information and appears at strategic points to initiate action or debate.

Lord Indra

Indra was the king of gods and also referred to as Devendra, the god of gods. The Vedic Indra was a very important god in the Hindu pantheon, but by the Puranic times the status of Indra had been significantly lowered, especially due to the rise of other gods like Vishnu and Shiva. During the Vedic times, Indra was amongst the most important gods along with Agni, Surya, Vayu and Varun. Indra was the god of the skies with thunder and lightning as his weapons. Acts of Indra's heroism and valour are captured in numerous hymns in the Rigveda. By the time the epics were written, Indra was being represented more as a titular head of the gods, without much respect or relevance. He was demoted from his position during the Puranic times and his role was limited to sending apsaras to seduce sages and even relatively minor gods could hurt his much-maligned status. But that is a subject for another occasion.

Lord Indra resides at Indra-lok and his consort is known as Indrani or Sachi.

Here his role is minimal, to the extent of sending Menaka to seduce King Kaushik.

King Kaushik/Vishwamitra

King Kaushik was a Kshatriya and a brave ruler of Kanyakubja. He is mainly known for his fight with Sage Vasishtha. When he lost the battle, he realized that it was not physical strength or prowess which mattered, but the power of knowledge which decided one's might. He undertook severe penance to become a sage and was later known as Vishwamitra—the friend of all. He was also responsible for testing King Harishchandra and his wife Taramati. The trials and tribulations of the righteous Harishchandra are well known.

He also happens to be the father of Shakuntala; the sage who was seduced by Menaka under the orders of Lord Indra.

Rishi Vasishtha

A revered sage of the Vedic times and one amongst the saptarishis—the seven great sages. He possessed the celestial cow, Nandini, the cause of his enmity with Vishwamitra.

Menaka

Menaka was an apsara at the court of Lord Indra and her role in mythology has been limited to breaking the penances of sages under the instructions of Lord Indra. She possessed extraordinary beauty which Indra used to achieve his objectives. She was also the mother of Shakuntala.

In this work, however, Menaka has been given a character and role. She has not been projected as a heartless nymph, whose only objective is to seduce. Since she stays on earth for a length of time, she imbibes the characteristics of a mortal in this book. This enables her to feel like a woman and a mother. Apsaras in literature have always been used as catalysts who have no significant role, but here she has been endowed with emotions.

Sage Kanva

Sage Kanva was one of the major rishis of the Rigvedic times. A number of hymns are ascribed to him. Sage Kanva is also supposed to have cursed the Yadava clan when some Yadava boys tried to test his knowledge by presenting a boy to him as a pregnant woman. Many years later, the piece of iron that emerged from the boy as a result of Sage Kaura's curse killed Lord Krishna towards the end of the epic Mahabharata, bringing an end to the Yadava clan.

Sage Kanva was also the foster-father of Shakuntala, after he found her abandoned, and brought her up.

Urvashi

A beautiful nymph in the court of Indra.

Shakuntala

Shakuntala is the daughter of Menaka and King Kaushik/ Vishwamitra. She is later adopted by Sage Kanva, who brings her up like his daughter, when both the parents abandon the child at birth. She is the protagonist of this work.

Anusuya

A fictional character created by Kalidasa and retained in this work as a friend of Shakuntala.

Priyamvada

A fictional character created by Kalidasa and retained in this work as a friend of Shakuntala.

Dushyant

A reputed Chandravanshi king of the lunar dynasty, and the king of Hastinapur. He belongs to the famous lineage of Puru and is an ancestor of the central characters of the epic Mahabharata.

Here he is the male protagonist and goes on to marry Shakuntala.

Amish

A close friend and minister of King Dushyant and a fictional character in this work.

Bhadrak

A close friend of King Dushyant and a fictional character in this work.

Giri

The bodyguard of King Dushyant and a fictional character in this work.

Sarvadaman/Bharat

Son of Shakuntala and King Dushyant. He goes on to lend his name to India in the vernacular, Bharatvarsha, and is also the first of the major kings mentioned in the epic Mahabharata.

Indra-sabha

'Narayan Narayan,' intoned Narada Muni, as he breezed into the intoned Indra-sabha, the court of Indra. His words echoed in the unusually quiet court as he floated near an indolent Indra. Indra respectfully acknowledged his presence, carefully concealing a 'what-now?' look. Narada, seeing through this, kept smiling and continued, 'Narayan, Narayan, how is the lord of the gods, the slayer of the mighty Vritra, Lord Indra, today?' Indra forced a smile and said, 'I am fine, O great muni. What brings you here?' Narada smiled and said, 'Well…I was returning from earth and passing by your court. None in the universe can resist entering this court, and I am no exception. So, here I am.' Indra said, 'You over-exaggerate the importance of my court, munivar, but I will accept your compliments nonetheless. Is everything fine on earth?' As soon as Indra asked the question, he had the uncanny feeling of something ominous coming his way. 'Well things couldn't be better,' said Narada, which was not the kind of response Indra had expected. But Indra knew…this was not the end of the subject.

'Tell me O lord of the gods, why is the court so quiet today? Where are all the apsaras and gandharvas of your court? Why don't I hear any music and dance, the hallmark of your court?' This was a question typical of Narada. Indra knew the muni would not come to the point till he decided to or intended to. Indra knew this was going to take time. 'Well, nothing is hidden from you,

O muni. Nothing exciting is happening here or elsewhere. Vishnu rests peacefully in his annual slumber, Mahadev is meditating and Brahmaji is working on another Veda I am told. Menaka, Urvashi and Rambha have danced to the best of celestial music, and have nothing new to offer. The asuras are looking for some new cause to fight and a leader to lead them. The humans seem to be complacent about their lives and go on living it every day. In short, I am bored to eternity!'

Narada smiled again, 'Maybe I can entertain you with a story!' 'Oh sure,' said Indra, knowing quite well that this was not a suggestion, merely a preface to the sage's pre-meditated plan! Narada said, 'However, Lord Indra, my story might not have the romantic flavour of your court or the action of celestial battles or the intrigues of heavens. Do you still want to hear it?' Indra knew these delaying tactics and said, 'Munivar, I am bored with all that, maybe it's time for something pristine and simple…just like you!' forcing the words 'pristine' and 'simple' through his teeth. The effort was visible to Narada, but he chose to ignore it. Narada was used to such snide remarks and comments; he never took them to heart. After all, didn't he always have the last laugh?

But this was just a harmless story, meant to get Lord Indra out of the woods. How could the lord of the gods be so dull and down? Wouldn't this harm the equilibrium of the heavens? What was an Indra-sabha without the usual fun and frolic, without music and dance and joyous merrymaking? It was with this in mind that Narada ignored Indra's lack of interest and extreme formality.

Narada began, 'O lord of the gods, this is not just a story. This is based on some things that I have just witnessed on earth. It also involves some of the powers bestowed on people that you favoured. I am relating this as I find the events that have unfolded very interesting. In fact, I think this will bring about significant changes in the fabric of mankind and the way they work and live.'

'This is regarding the mighty King Kaushik. Kaushik's father, the great King Kadhi was of the lineage of the famous Kusha. Kaushik turned out to be a brave and handsome young man and an able successor to the throne of Kusha. People were happy under his rule. Recently, when he was returning from one of his conquests, he decided to rest with his army at the hermitage of the great sage Vasishtha. As you know, O Indra, Vasishta's hermitage is like a small heaven on earth. The peace and tranquillity is unmatched in the human world. You can hear the birds chirping mantras and the air is aromatic from the different yagnas being performed all over the hermitage. There are no barricades to the hermitage, yet no wild animals venture in and none of the domestic animals step out. No one has seen blood being shed in the hermitage nor has one ever heard of violence or greed of any sort.'

'Kaushik was impressed by the serenity of the ashram and decided to camp there for a few days, allowing some rest to his army too. Sage Vasishtha was delighted to hear about the king's desire and decided to reciprocate the gesture by offering the best of his hospitality, befitting the king and his army. After all, the king had been kind and noble enough to provide his people with a trouble-free regime. The king and his army were treated to food and rest. However, Kaushik was intrigued by the sage's ability to muster up resources in no time for so many people, meal after meal. Just how could a sage with simple means manage such lavish and sumptuous meals for a big army?'

'Kaushik decided to satisfy his curiosity and asked the sage about it. Vasishtha told him about his treasure trove, the cow Nandini. Nandini, I am sure you remember, O Devendra, is the offspring of your cow, Kamadhenu, and a gift from you to Vasishtha. The sage went on to explain to the king that Nandini provided him with everything he needed. King Kaushik was impressed and felt that such a cow was required more by him than a simple sage. He expressed his desire to have the cow for himself, as it would be of far greater service to the kingdom.

'Vasishtha smiled but declined. Kaushik's tone changed from request to an order, but Vasishtha did not change his mind. The matter took a turn for the worse when the king ordered his soldiers to seize the cow. Vasishtha then used his yogic powers and conjured up an army which decimated King Kaushik's troops in no time. The king was then presented to the sage, who looked at him sorrowfully and said, "O King, you are the ruler of the kingdom and we are your subjects. It is your responsibility to look after your subjects. Using your powers on sages does not befit you. I am setting you free as my objective is not to rule and demean you. I am a man of few words, but let me give you some advice. Never misuse your power and, above all, never underestimate the power of knowledge."

'What the king didn't know was that when the sage saw the huge army of the king, his mind revolted against the mayhem that was about to be unleashed. He spoke to Nandini and gave her a choice of going with the king or staying back. Nandini made her choice known by creating a host of warriors, who, along with Vasishtha, were responsible for the rout faced by the king's army.

'A crestfallen King Kaushik went back defeated. A single thought continued disturbing him. He had the powers of the body, but the sage had the power of the mind. Vasishtha could conjure an army with his powers, while he had to maintain an army all the time. What was the use of such power which could be decimated by a simple sage? He realized that power lay in penances and meditation and not in armies and weapons. He has now renounced the world and is meditating…meditating to become a sage!'

The last words startled Lord Indra. 'Did you say he is meditating to *become* a sage?'

'Yes, O lord! Isn't this interesting?' asked Narada.

'Interesting?' said Indra. 'This is against the laws of mankind!'

Narada had regained his impish smile. 'Why do you say so, O lord of the gods? There is no harm in seeking knowledge.'

Indra was beginning to get agitated. 'Who said anything against seeking knowledge? That is for all. Do you not see the problem in a king becoming a sage? Let me rephrase this for you—can a Kshatriya become a Brahmin?'

Indra went on, 'I am appalled, O munivar, to see that you find nothing wrong in this. A Kshatriya is trying to become a Brahmin. One who is supposed to provide benevolence, is trying to become the recipient of the benevolence. A ruler wants to acquire knowledge and become a sage. The protector of the Vedas is going to read the Vedas and you find nothing wrong in this?'

Narada continued in his cool-as-a-cucumber demeanour, 'Aren't all human beings the same? Don't they all feel hungry, suffer pain, and have urges and needs? Don't they all protect themselves from sun and rain? Don't they all take birth, grow, marry and reproduce?'

Indra protested, 'What are you saying and whoever denied any of this? But can you overrule the laws of Manu? The earth is not like heaven. Human beings are ruled by a set of laws laid down by Manu who had the divine blessings of the gods of heaven; and trying to change them without our intervention will lead to a state of disequilibrium, which is not good for them.'

'So...are you disappointed by the lack of divine permission or just upset about a Kshatriya becoming a Brahmin?' interjected Narada.

Indra was making efforts to conceal his anger. 'How come you always get the point wrong, munivar? Don't you see that this is going against the norms? Don't you see that what is achieved by one today can become a norm for all tomorrow? I am surprised that I have to explain this to you!' concluded Indra, presuming he had the last word, till he heard 'Why?', as Narada persisted.

Indra was beginning to get angry, as he did not seem to have an answer to this. 'Why? What do you mean by why? Munivar, is there anything that you don't know? Have I said anything till now, which you didn't know already? Then why are you insisting on a discussion which is meaningless? You know that this is against the law...'

'Law of...?' Narada Muni interjected.

'Law of...of...mankind,' Indra fumbled.

Not one to give up, Narada asked 'Is it?' with his usual smile, which was unsettling Indra. Indra thought, *Just why do I have to endure this person? He is a learned sage himself and he finds nothing wrong in this, is he trying to pull my leg or just being ignorant of the rules laid down for the conduct of mankind?*

'But my lord, King Kaushik has been meditating for close to four hundred years now. I am just returning from his kingdom and everyone is talking about it. I spoke to Sage Vasishtha, but he didn't seem too bothered about it,' said Narada.

Indra was surprised, 'You mean Vasishtha knows about it and is not bothered? He didn't find anything amiss in a Kshatriya changing his caste to become a learned Brahmin?'

Narada seemed amused and said, 'Well, I don't think it matters to him, he is not feeling insecure!'

'Insecure? What has insecurity got to do with this?' Indra retorted, 'This is going against the rules laid down for mankind and I am appalled to see that neither you nor Sage Vasishtha seem to find anything wrong with it. Is it not the duty of learned men like you and the rishi to ensure that laws are not breached?' Indra continued, 'Do you see what a disequilibrium this could cause in the three worlds, if one mortal acquired power that he does not deserve to have? You can't even comprehend what a hot-headed Kshatriya—who tried to raze Sage Vasishtha's ashram and forcefully acquire Nandini—is capable of if he achieves the power. A mortal tries to transgress his status and break the barrier set for him. Today he does it supposedly in the quest of knowledge; tomorrow he will do so in the quest for immortality. What is transgression today will become transcendence tomorrow. Have you thought about what this will lead to? Man will ask for the heavens!'

Narada tried to say something, but Indra raised his hand indicating that he had not finished. 'I don't think I want to waste my time trying to impress upon you the malefic effects of such an act. If you cannot do anything, then maybe I will have to step in.'

Narada felt that the conversation was over and his staying any longer was pointless. 'Well, I guess I would like to leave now. I came in to say hello, but it seems like I have overstayed my welcome. I hope I have been able to cheer you up with what I thought was an interesting story which I witnessed on my trip to the earth. Narayan, Narayan!' said Narada before leaving.

Indra was beginning to feel better after Narada's departure. *I wonder why this person unsettles me*, he wondered. However, Indra noticed that he was not feeling bored anymore. Had he found some purpose? Or, maybe, a celestial pastime?

Indra Decides to Act

Indra parted the clouds to see King Kaushik lost in meditation. The sight disturbed him. He went back to his chambers where he met Indrani, his wife. Indrani sensed trouble and offered him a glass of somarasa. Indra gulped it down and sat motionless. Indrani knew from experience that when disturbed, Indra never liked questions. She sat next to him without saying a word, waiting for him to break the silence.

Indrani had been observing that of late Indra didn't seem interested in anything. Even in his sabhas, amidst all the revelry, he seemed to be lost. The mighty slayer of Vritra, the controller of clouds, was not his usual self. Indrani was disappointed that she couldn't do much to uplift his mood. She, who the heavens referred to as the most fortunate of all, since her husband would never die of old age; she, who won Indra after competing with many other women; she, who became Indra's beloved because of her voluptuous figure, which had Indra lusting for her always, couldn't do much. Not that she did not try.

A couple of days back, she had dressed in her most revealing finery, put celestial kohl in her eyes and applied perfume made of the celestial musk-deer—which she refused to share with anyone—and plied him with somarasa, but he didn't even seem to notice. But today was different. Her lord seemed preoccupied with something, not bored. But she did not want to pry, lest he be upset with her. She might be the queen of the lord of the gods, but she knew her limits and if he returned to her after all his dalliances, it was because she never interfered with his duties and concerns of the world, not because his apsaras couldn't hold him back!

Indra strolled into Nandana, his garden, and sat under the shade of the celestial flowers immersed in thought. Was he overreacting or was Narada Muni unable to understand the gravity of this act of King Kaushik? Even Sage Vasishtha didn't seem to be bothered. How was it that nobody had seen fit to inform him? Was that the purpose of Narada's visit?

Seeing Indra, a number of apsaras came close and bowed. Indra dismissed them, indicating that he be left alone. They were surprised, for Indra never liked to stay alone. He always wanted them to be around him, with music played by the gandharvas. It had been unusually quiet lately.

Indra was deep in his thoughts. *How can I allow this act of transgression? Today a king wants to become a sage, tomorrow a menial might want to take up arms, a soldier might recite the Vedas...where will this end? Today man is trying to break the boundaries of caste, tomorrow man would like to become God! How can this be allowed? Shouldn't man realize that we, the powerful gods, are watching and will not allow this?* Indra suddenly found his long arms craving for action. His spirits were high and he found a new vigour within. The last time he had felt like this was when he had fought the deadly demon Vritra.

He parted the clouds once again and looked at King Kaushik. The king's hair extended to his knees; his beard was touching the ground. Birds were hovering around his matted locks. Mounds of mud had settled upto his knees. His body looked emaciated, but there was a sense of peace on his face. The sight of the peaceful face unsettled Indra once again.

He sent winds strong enough to blow the king away. Everything around him was uprooted, but Kaushik was steadfast and did not move an inch. Indra then sent thundershowers and rains to distract him. It poured relentlessly till the waters reached Kaushik's neck, but he remained unmoved. Indra then parted the cloud cover from the region where Kaushik was meditating to let the rays of the sun fall on him unfiltered. The vegetation burnt to ashes, ponds dried up and birds started falling dead. Kaushik's skin started to peel, but his meditation was not disturbed. The stubborn resolve of Kaushik was now beginning to anger Indra. He debated hurling his vajra, the thunderbolt, but decided against it as that would kill the man, and he did not want to be known as the killer of a would-be sage! Kaushik was not disturbing the residents of the earth and any such act by Indra would give a chance to the earthlings to detest him. Indra liked people worshipping him and offering him prayers.

Indra did not want to do anything in haste. So he retired to his chambers to think. How strong must the resolve of this man be, that such calamitous spells of nature were unable to wake him from his penance. It was this strength that Indra had to break. It was not the man, but his strength that he needed to vanquish. Indra was beginning to enjoy this feeling, the feeling of breaking the resolve of a king who had been meditating for close to four hundred years. This was going to be fun, more invigorating than capturing the demon Vritra, which was history.

Kaushik's resolve had to be broken but not in the usual way, thought Indra. Here the rules would be different. He was a man, and Indra, the lord of all pleasures, knew what would melt this man. A king could resist strength but not sensuality and who knew the power of the senses better than Indra? How could a king resist what even gods could not resist? Indra's victory would be when Kaushik lost to the sensuality that would be unleashed on him.

Indra was overjoyed by the very thought. There was a sudden spring to his step and he began to feel better, something that he had not been feeling for a very long time. Fighting asuras has been physical joy, but this would be cerebral and Indra hoped to win…yet again!

Menaka

The apsaras were a worried lot. Sulochana, Sukesi, Vividha and the others were all huddled together, discussing the latest absence of activities in Indra-lok. Sukesi moaned that since they were not performing at the Indra-sabha, she didn't even feel like dressing up. Vividha mocked, 'You should be happy, that way you get to spend so much time playing around with Madana, the handsome gandharva!' The apsaras giggled at this. Sukesi shot her a sharp look, to which Sulochana said, 'Oh come on, stop getting angry. Don't we know about it, I guess even Indradev is aware of it!' Sukesi's angry look changed to that of fear, 'If only you girls would stop gossiping about me and Madana. You know Indradev doesn't like gossip.' Vividha continued, 'So true, Indradev doesn't like gossiping, but he sure does like hot news!' 'Vividha,' yelled Sukesi, 'quiet, you silly girl, Menaka is coming. She is the lord's favourite, please don't gossip in front of her.'

Menaka glided down Nandana. Though the other apsaras were jealous of her for being Indra's favourite, they could not deny that she was breathtakingly beautiful. Her soft feet ensured that no grass was trampled under their weight. Her gait was like a doe seeking her partner. Her body slim yet curvaceous. Her half-closed doe-eyes were a painter's delight and her luscious lips enticing enough to stop any being in his tracks. Her cheeks had stolen their colour from the rainbow...or was it the other way round? She was probably the only one who never had to rush to her personal chambers to dress, if she got a call from the lord of gods; she was always ready. While the others were jealous of her, they accepted the fact that she was extraordinary and yes, none of the gandharvas ever took liberties with her. Needless to say, even Devi Indrani acknowledged her grace and her knowledge of the art of seduction. She was unparalleled.

Menaka came and sat next to Sukesi and said casually, 'So what is this I hear about you and Madana?' There was pin-drop silence and Sukesi turned pale. Menaka continued, 'I am wondering what Madana saw in you. Just look at your uncombed hair, your dull colourless lips and eyes without kohl. Why are you looking as if you are mourning?'

Sukesi attempted to speak, but knew that Menaka hadn't finished. 'Sukesi, you are an apsara. We were *born* to entertain and charm. One look from us should be enough for mortals to give up life and gods to give up immortality! Would you achieve this by such mournful looks? Do you think Madana is going to give you a second look? What if Indradev sees you in this pitiable and unkempt condition? You would be banished to earth or suspended from all celestial duties.'

Sukesi made a feeble attempt. 'But lately there have been no activities at the sabha, so...'

'So? So what Sukesi?' countered Menaka. 'I hope you know that the lord has not gone for any war, he is very much in Indra-lok. What if he calls for a session any moment or walks into Nandana? Are you ready for him? Or would you have to go and plunge in the perfumed pool first to rid yourself of your body odour? By the way, when did you last use perfume in your bath?' Sukesi didn't know where to look. 'When did you last oil your hair? And you, Vividha, where are your ornaments? Why are your eyes not lined with kohl? I am appalled at your looks.

You girls look worse than mortals and I hope that is an insult to you all. None of you deserve to be part of the Indra-sabha, and before the lord of the gods sees you, please go and attire yourselves appropriately. What apologies for apsaras you girls are!' rebuked Menaka. The others simply ran away from there after bowing to Menaka. Menaka was angry and her face showed it.

She moved on towards the music room to meet Chitraratha, the chief gandharva. He was constantly composing new ragas and raginis and creating music never heard before, adding to the already rich Gandharva-veda, the upa-veda that dealt with music and dance. She loved to hear new tunes so that she could work on fresh moves for them. If only these silly girls understood that being an apsara was not easy. One had to constantly work on honing one's skills and mastering the arts. She was about to step into the music room, when she heard her name being called.

She turned around to see Chitralekha running towards her, 'Yes, Chitra, I can hear you, why, the whole of Indra-lok can hear you! Now calm down and tell me why you have been calling me.'

Chitralekha said, 'The lord is looking for you and wants to see you right away.'

Menaka exclaimed, 'Me? Now? Where?'

Chitralekha was still panting, 'In his personal garden, he is under the somalata canopy, and he said it was urgent.'

Menaka turned to leave when the upper part of her garment got stuck in the bushes at the entrance to the music room. She pulled at it in a hurry, and the rose-tinted garment came off the bush with a tear. Menaka felt very uneasy about the torn bit. It was a bad omen. Something inauspicious was on its way. What could it be? She tucked in the torn bit and hurried towards the somalata canopy, a favourite place of Lord Indra.

Lord Indra had a goblet of somarasa and was looking into it

with gleaming eyes. There was an impish smile on his face when he looked up at the sound of Menaka's anklets.

Menaka bowed and said coyly, 'You called for me, O lord of the clouds?'

Indra smiled and replied, 'Come sit with me, my dear.'

Menaka walked upto Indra, feeling uncomfortable with his smile. He was drunk, but not on the somarasa...*this was different*, she thought.

This place had a heady environment, something very intoxicating. The shade of the somalata bushes provided coolness which induced a feeling of warmth. Yes, it sounded odd, but then that was exactly how it felt. This was a place where even if one sat alone, everything around one seemed to be moving, as if in celebration. The small creepers of the bushes dangled in the soft breeze, teasing the senses. The breeze through the bushes whispered sensual tunes. The soma flowers were heavy with nectar, waiting to be poured out on whoever wanted to drink and revel. The slim and tender branches intertwined among themselves, as if giving sensual messages to the inhabitants of the canopy. Menaka was already lost in its atmosphere, when she realized that the lord was speaking to her.

'Menaka, my dear, it is nice to see you. When will you stop stealing the colours from my bow? The Indra-dhanush has faded as I can see the colours all over you!' Indra said with a smile.

Menaka blushed, 'You jest, my lord.'

Indra continued, 'There, I found the crimson on your cheeks!' His fingers brushed Menaka's blushing cheeks. A shiver went down the supple figure of Menaka, like ripples on a still lake. Indra continued, 'Is anything bothering you, my dear?'

'Oh no, nothing, my lord. What can bother anybody in Indra-lok, the object of reverence to mankind and envy of the asuras?'

countered Menaka, not meeting his gaze.

Indra said, 'I can understand the envy of the asuras, but what can one do when even man starts envying the gods? What is for reverence, cannot be possessed, right, my dear?'

Menaka looked up. 'I do not understand, my lord. How can man want to possess what is of the gods? Since when did the mortals develop the traits of the asuras?'

Indra smiled, 'Not mortals, my dear, mortal. A king is trying to equate himself with the rishis and if he is successful, then he may look to usurp the position of the gods.'

Menaka was puzzled. 'How can a king become a sage? I have never heard of anything remotely similar to this, my lord. Who is this mortal who wants to change the laws laid down by Manu Maharishi?'

'Do you want to see him?' asked Indra. Menaka nodded.

Indra bent and moved a few clouds and asked Menaka to look down. What Menaka saw scared her no end. She saw a feeble and hardly visible man, meditating. He was covered with long dirty locks; a skeleton of a figure with ants and insects all over his body. She noticed that the ground around him had cracked and smoke and sparks were emitting from it. The trees and plants had all burnt down due to the heat emanating from the spot. Dead birds and animals lay all around what was once a dense jungle. Oh, what a ghastly sight! Menaka could bear it no longer.

'My lord, what is this?' shrieked Menaka. Indra handed her a goblet of somarasa, which she gulped down at once.

'He has been meditating like this for close to four hundred years now. His meditation has generated so much latent heat and energy that the whole ground will burst into flames if he doesn't stop soon,' said Indra.

'So why don't you stop him, O lord of the gods? You are the

vanquisher of the deadly demon, Vritra; what is this bit of a man, an apology of a king before you?' asked an intrigued Menaka.

Indra smiled, 'Do you think this is beyond me? His meditation can be disturbed by just a flick of my finger. But would it befit my stature as the lord of the gods, to meddle with a mere mortal? Do you want the future generations of mankind to think that I became insecure by the meditation of a mere mortal?'

Menaka was puzzled but decided to keep quiet till he finished.

Indra continued, staring into the distance, 'I don't think it calls for my intervention, as this is not a matter of gods against asuras. This is regarding an insane man who is intoxicated with power. He is jealous of the sages and is trying to show them that knowledge can be achieved by anybody. Silly man! If it was as simple as he thought, then we would have as many scriptures as men on earth!' Menaka found that amusing. Indra continued, 'This does not require earthquakes or thunderstorms, which would be overkill. It simply requires the touch of the senses, the whispers of love and the breeze of lust. What do you say, my dear?' Indra looked at Menaka.

Menaka looked perplexed. 'Pardon my ignorance, O bearer of the Indra-dhanush, but I haven't quite understood.'

Indra smiled, held Menaka close and said in a hushed tone, 'You, Menaka, all he needs is you…'

'Me?' asked a shocked Menaka, 'What can I do to stop this old man, my lord?'

Indra said, 'You have it all, my dear; the looks, the skill and everything that a mortal dreams of. No knowledge is greater than possessing you, no transcendence can be greater than the feeling of your touch…am I not right, my dear?'

Menaka was beginning to understand what was coming, but couldn't reconcile herself to the idea of waking up a man whose meditation could generate such intensity.

Indra went on, 'Besides, I want to test the man for the purity of his penance. Is his penance beyond the call of flesh or is it still vulnerable, and who but you could test him for this?'

'But my lord…'

Indra's fingers were on her lips and the look in his eyes hushed her. She could not say that she dreaded the very moment he would lay his eyes on her. She could not say that she did not want to disturb a mortal who was trying to become a sage, hardly an issue of significance for her or for the gods. She could not say that she was for the gods and not mere mortals, and definitely not this man, who was barely visible! Indra's finger on her lips did not move till she knew that this was an order and not just a suggestion.

Menaka sighed and asked, 'When do you want me to leave?'

'Oh, as soon as you can, now, if that is not asking for too much, my dear.' Indra seemed to be enjoying Menaka's predicament.

Menaka continued, 'And when do I come back?'

'I will indicate the right time to you, leave it to me; just remember, his meditation has to stop. Only you can do what needs to be done—stop his meditation, disturb his singular focus and make him forget his quest to be a sage, my dear,' said a smiling Indra to Menaka.

Indra left Menaka alone under the canopy. She didn't like the idea of disturbing a human being's meditation. Is that what she was for? Wasn't she supposed to be learning the arts of dance and music and look good? Wasn't she supposed to be the 'chosen one' of Indradev, while all he chose her for was to seduce a mortal? Where did she err? What had she done to deserve a mortal who was such a ghastly sight?

Menaka Meets Kaushik

Reluctantly, Menaka left Indra-lok. Some of her friends were sad, while she knew that Rambha and Misrakeshi were happy to see her leave. Urvashi met her just as she was about to descend to the earth. She had a sad look on her face and for the first time, embraced Menaka. She seemed to be the only one who was genuinely sad, but said nothing. Menaka could see her eyes swell with tears, through she was unable to drop the pearls from her eyes. Did it have anything to do with Urvashi's relationship with a mortal by the name of Pururavas? Indradev had sent her to Pururavas and she had lived happily with him, till she was brought back, by some Indra-lok intrigue. She never looked the same again, and in all the time gone by, Menaka had never bothered to find out why. If only she had tried to understand Urvashi's sadness!

But she did like this sudden unspoken bond between them. She didn't know why, but she felt as if she would soon understand what Urvashi's silence was trying to say. She felt as if there was only one person in Indra-lok who seemed to understand her predicament, and it was Urvashi.

Menaka descended on earth and got to work. She cleaned up the area where Kaushik was meditating. She induced the rivers to flow from there, cooling the earth. Through powers that only apsaras have, she converted the desert into a small garden in full bloom. There were flowers everywhere, trees had fruits and the birds were singing. She did all this while Kaushik was still meditating. Musk deer, peacocks and nightingales added to the beauty of the gardens. She knew Indradev would be watching from the heavens, as he never trusted his apsaras completely. But that did not deter her; she had a task and she would do a good job of it. Mortals would remember her skills and her beauty.

Menaka put on her celestial make-up. She wore a single garment barely covering her well-endowed voluptuous figure. She put on anklets, bangles, earrings and necklaces, all made of flowers. She was the epitome of beauty and sensuality and she knew that if the gods were watching her, even they would not be able to resist her; this man was a mere mortal, given to the temptations of flesh.

She went down to the brook nearby and collected water in an earthen pot. A sudden strong shower drenched her completely. She was now irresistible and she knew it.

Holding her garment in place, she walked to the meditating hermit and placed the earthen pot beside him. Suddenly, the trees became musical instruments. The air was resonating with celestial ragas when Menaka started her celestial dance—the dance to lure, the dance of seduction. The drenched damsel performing bewitching dance movements to the strains of music was a sight to behold!

Menaka went round and round, inching closer to the emaciated hermit. She could see his eyes flicker, his hands shiver and his parched lips open. She went closer and poured cool water into his mouth using a leaf of the lotus. The water touched Kaushik's lips and he felt the warmth of flesh and heavy breathing over him. His eyes opened to a sight he would never forget. A woman of indescribable beauty was standing before him.

Just then, a gush of wind blew the garment off Menaka!

Oh Vayudev, this is your mischief, admonished Menaka in her mind, but pushed aside the thought when she saw Kaushik's eyes devouring every bit of her.

Menaka turned coy, tried to cover herself with the cloth which had been soiled. She hid behind the trees, but a deer was staring at her. She went into the brook and concealed herself neck-down. All the while, the hermit's gaze never left her for a second. Kaushik followed her into the brook and kept staring at her. Menaka closed his eyes with her hands, asking him to relax. Just then it started to rain. She bathed him in the brook, under the soft rain, amidst lotus flowers and music played by the birds and trees.

Kaushik had never felt such bliss in his life. The waters soothed his parched and dry body. His hair opened up to long lustrous locks. The waters had cooled his body, but inside him was a raging fire. He could not take his hungry eyes off this divine beauty. She could not be a mortal, as he had never felt so before a mortal. She was divine, she must be an apsara. Only apsaras had the power to make one feel so aroused and stimulated.

Both Menaka and Kaushik emerged from the waters and disappeared into the mango grove nearby. Kaushik, hungry for centuries, ate and drank the choicest of fruits and wine, fed by Menaka, drinking in her beauty. Menaka was aware of his lustful looks and realized that even though he looked feeble, those eyes of his still had the glow of a king. A closer look revealed that he must have been a handsome man before he embarked on this journey to become a sage. Kaushik was tall for a mortal, and even in his feeble state, had the arrogance befitting a royal. His gaze was beginning to unsettle her.

Soon it turned dark and neither of them had spoken a word. Kaushik could not take his eyes off her and she made sure that he didn't. The moon was shining bright; the stars were studded in the heavens. A soft wind was playing music and the musk deer was intoxicated by its own aroma. The parijat flowers were in full bloom and she could see the king coming close to her. His hands were over hers and before she could realize, his lips were over hers. The king had been abstaining far too long and it showed.

Menaka had never made love to a mortal and the king was adept at the art of lovemaking. In all the four hundred years, the king hadn't forgotten anything and Menaka was beginning to enjoy it. The moon and the stars hid themselves behind the clouds and the trees dropped flowers on the couple in the name of modesty.

The morning sun found two people sleeping like one, under a colourful blanket of flowers. The world had ceased to exist for the two and nakedness didn't bother them. The twitter of the birds woke Menaka and she blushed at her experience, certain that the two parrots were staring at her. She had nothing to cover her but suddenly it just didn't matter. She arose and took a bath in the brook nearby and just when she was coming out of the water, she felt the lustful sight of the king caressing every part of her. She was embarrassed and realized she had never felt like this before.

Dripping, she walked all the way to the cottage and changed into some semblance of clothing. She had to learn the ways of mortals. The king followed soon after cleaning himself, oblivious to the lack of clothing on him. She handed him fresh garments and fed him a nourishing meal of fruits and milk which he devoured in no time.

Menaka was beginning to bask in the knowledge of having been successful at her task, as the king had cut short his meditation and would have to start from scratch to reach the stage he had achieved. However, she seemed to be worried about something. Would she have to leave now? Heavens, why was she thinking this way? How come she was worried about leaving, instead of looking forward to it? Her thoughts were broken by the warmth of flesh. The king was staring at her with hunger in his eyes, and she was attracted by the looks. She was being seduced and before she could say anything, the two were locked in a never-ending embrace.

Nothing existed for the two, except food, wine, love and looks for each other. A king was in love with an apsara whose beauty was ethereal. An apsara had fallen in love with a mortal, whose touch had made her a victim of an emotion she had never known. She had heard about Kamdev's actions and had always wondered about his arrows and the pain they gave. But Menaka had never thought that one day, she too would be smitten by the arrow of Kamdev and instead of writhing in pain, she would enjoy it. The warmth of human flesh was elusive and she had never experienced it. The gandharvas were too obsessed with themselves and always preoccupied with one thing or the other. Man sure knew how to treat his woman, and this man was certainly skilled.

Life was a never-ending fairy tale. Menaka was happy that Indradev had forgotten all about her and Kaushik never alluded to his meditation. The king had regained his health and looked more like the divine Kartikeya. Strong legs, muscular arms, a perfect torso, high cheekbones, a well-defined jawline, luscious lips, deep penetrating eyes and a rich baritone. He would hunt for food, which Menaka loved to cook. The world seemed to exist just for the two of them.

The two? No. Menaka was experiencing much more than the joys of having a man beside her. She was carrying a baby, the news of which sent Kaushik to seventh heaven. Menaka was going to be a mother, the crowning glory of every mortal woman on earth. She just couldn't understand this wondrous feeling, but then decided to take it like every other joy that had come her way in the last decade.

It had been ten years and Indradev had not even looked back at her. Needless to say, she hadn't missed Indra-lok even for a day. She loved it here—her home, her man and now her child who was ready to come into the world.

Indra-sabha

'Narayan Narayan', said Narada Muni as he floated into the Indra-sabha. Everybody rose in reverence and Indra bowed to the muni. Indra indicated that the music continue to play, while inviting Narada. 'Welcome, O celestial sage! It sure has been a long time since you came this way. Tell me, munivar, what brings you here?'

Narada smiled. 'The desire to see you, O Mahendra! I was passing by, and thought of offering my obeisance to you and Devi Indrani.'

Indra smiled and said, 'O munivar, you jest. It's our pleasure to be hosts to you, the greatest of all munis in the entire universe. Tell me, what can we do for you?'

Narada continued, 'You embarrass me, O lord, just your blessings and I will leave as I am in a hurry.'

Indra was curious. 'Where are you headed in such a rush, O munivar?'

Narada was surprised. 'Hurry to go to earth, O Devendra. Aren't you aware, there has been a birth and I am going there on the invitation of the parents?'

Indra seemed puzzled. 'There are numerous births on earth, what is so special about this one, and just who are these favoured parents?'

Narada's eyebrows were raised in concern. 'My lord, are you saying you are not aware of this? I thought this had your sanction...'

Indra sat up. 'My sanction? Just what are you talking about, munivar? Can you speak clearly, I hate riddles, please!' Indra's voice and his irritation, both were rising.

Narada said, 'Pardon me, O lord, are you not aware, that Menaka, the favourite apsara of Indra-lok, has given birth to a child?'

There was hushed silence in the sabha. The gandharvas stopped playing music, the apsaras stopped dancing as everything came to a standstill. Indra was shocked. 'Menaka has...what?'

Indra gestured to be left alone. The sabha emptied, except for Narada Muni and Indra. Indra had completely forgotten about Menaka. Yes, he had sent her to earth to seduce King Kaushik, but once the work was done, he had just not bothered to get her back. But she, too, had never tried to contact him in all these years and nobody even reminded him of it. And today she had begotten the king's child. How could she do this?

He heard Narada Muni saying, 'My lord, is there a problem? I didn't realize this would disturb you so much. But wasn't it you who had sent Menaka to earth? At least that's what I heard...'

Indra kept quiet as he was at a loss for words. How could he have allowed Menaka to stay back after her task was over? How did he forget all about her? Not once did anybody even remind him of her. It had been such a long time since she was missing from Indra lok and he hadn't even realized it! Just how did this happen? He didn't want another sad apsara in his sabha, especially after what had happened to Urvashi. And bearing a child of a mortal, how on earth did this happen? He had to do something, and fast, before she got attached to a mortal's child. He clapped his hands and called an attendant. Just then he realized that Narada Muni had left already. *O this menacing muni, every time he appears, he leaves me disturbed*, thought Indra.

Indra Meets Menaka

'How are you, my dear?' Menaka was startled to hear the voice of Lord Indra. She had just given birth to a beautiful daughter and had barely begun to enjoy what mortals called motherhood.

'My lord, what a surprise! I had thought you had forgotten me.' Menaka managed to find some words.

Indra was smiling. 'How could I forget you, especially after you did such a great favour to me?'

Menaka's head was bowed. 'Favour? Why do you use such words, O lord? You embarrass me.'

'No, my dear, had it not been for you, the earth would have seen rivers flowing in the opposite direction. Earth would have spewed fire and fish would have been flying. I am indebted to you for this and have personally come to take you back to Indra-lok. Come my dear, my vimana, the chariot, is waiting for you.'

Menaka looked up. 'Go with you? Now? How is that possible, O lord?' she said, fighting tears and pointing to the newborn.

Indra looked at her and said, 'Why, my dear? What is the problem? This baby is Kaushik's, give it to him. Such things are the tasks and responsibilities of earthlings, you are celestial. Don't bind yourself with emotions that are of mortals. You were given a task, and that is done. You need to get back to Indra-lok and earn your reward.'

Menaka was in tears. 'But, my lord, let me at least speak to the child's father. Let me bid him goodbye.'

Indra was beginning to find it amusing. 'Menaka, my dear, you are crying. Why? Don't tell me you are in love with someone you referred to as "ghastly". Saying goodbyes are the norms of humans and you are not one. You don't have to do that. Just leave the child, and come with me. Matali, my charioteer is waiting.'

Menaka was on her knees. 'O lord, I have stayed with a mortal for close to ten years now and have given birth to his baby. How can I leave without meeting him once? Who will take care of this child, who has not even cried once? Be assured, my lord, I promise, I will be back.'

Convinced that Menaka would not go back on her words, Indradev left in his vimana. Menaka embraced her child and started sobbing uncontrollably.

'So you are an apsara, who was sent by none other than the crooked Indra?' Menaka was startled to hear the loud voice of Kaushik. 'I should have known! Indra sent you to disturb my penance and I fell in your honey-trap. O lord, how could I not see through this web of deception?' Kaushik had fire in his eyes.

Menaka protested, 'No, my lord, you don't understand me, I truly love you and this child is the proof of our love.'

'This child is the outcome of your deceit and my love—two unequal emotions. You came to stop my penance and I was carried away by your sweet ways and words. Had I not seen Indra talking to you, I would have never known this divine secret. Did Indra have to stoop so low?' asked Kaushik looking towards the heavens.

Amid sobs and tears, Menaka said, 'Allow me to explain, my lord. Yes, I did come at the command of Indradev, but...'

'But what, O celestial being? What do you have to say now, O destructive beauty?' Kaushik could be heard in the heavens. 'You have said enough, O servant of Indra. You have served him well, O divine maid. But I will prove to you and your lord that what has been thwarted will begin again and neither an apsara nor Kamdev can stop me now. I can't bear to spend even one moment with you. Every second will remind me of your deception and my defeat. I am leaving.'

Menaka was shocked, 'My lord, what about this child, your progeny? Who will father her? You heard Indradev commanding me to leave.'

Kaushik turned away and didn't even look back while saying, 'Ask your master, O maid! He will give you further commands and you can act accordingly. As far as I am concerned, I can't bear to even see her, who is the result of deceit. She reminds me of how you lured me from my chosen path, my scholarly pursuit, which was not wrong. She reminds me of my defeat, my lust and my craving for earthly ties. Above all, she reminds me of everything that is you...your lies, your deceit and your dishonesty.'

Menaka was inconsolable. Kaushik had left. He didn't look back even once. She had to leave on the orders of Indra. How could she abandon this smiling child, who had been a part of her for so many months now? How could she leave a child who was barely a few days old? The child was tugging at her bosom, where motherhood was spilling over. She hugged her child and prayed for a miracle which would allow her to stay for just a few days more. Just a few days, so that she could mother the child.

She looked upto see a few gandharvas waiting near the mangrove. They were there to escort her back to Indra-lok. Indradev never trusted anybody, didn't she know that? Where were the gods? O someone, please help me.

'Narayan, Narayan,' Menaka heard the familiar chant of Narada Muni. She understood that he knew all. She looked at him pleadingly to see him smiling. 'My dear, don't cry. Tears have no value for your lord and there are none to see them or value them. Keep them for the future. Give the child to me and I will find a home for her,' he said.

Menaka could not bring herself to hand over the child to him.

Narada was smiling. 'Don't you trust me?'

'If there is one person in this universe who I can trust, then it's you, O munivar, but I am now a mother. I can't part with this child, who needs me more than anybody,' said a tearful Menaka.

'You talk like a mortal, O apsara of Indra-lok,' said Narada.

Menaka looked up. 'I am, O munivar, and above all I am a woman. I served a man like his wife, I begot him a child and today I have been abandoned by him, without even being heard. I have been cast away like a soiled garment by the man I loved, while being used like a pawn by another who calls himself a god. Does that not make me a woman of the earth then?' asked a caustic Menaka.

'Menaka, my dear, I am neither a man nor a god, so I understand the methods of neither, and for once I am happy being neither. What I can understand is that you are in trouble and I can help you. If you can trust me then you can leave the child in my custody and I will find a home for her, where she will be treated like a daughter and nothing less,' said Narada Muni, urging her to leave before she earned the wrath of the god of the clouds.

Menaka knew that she had no choice and though Narada Muni was known for fomenting trouble, today she could sense earnestness in his voice. She hugged the smiling child for the last time and gave her to the celestial muni. Her tears were unstoppable when she bent to touch the feet of Narada Muni— something no apsara had ever done to anybody, at least not in reverence.

Narada Muni watched the weeping Menaka leave, wondering

why the gods were so cold. He was brought back from his thoughts by the small hands tugging at his rudraksh mala. The sage had never seen such a beautiful child who was smiling, oblivious to the fact that she had just been deserted by her parents, one out of choice and one for the lack of it.

Narada Muni knew just the right person who would make up for loss of parents for this beautiful child. His smile was back on his face, when he said, 'Narayan, Narayan!'

Sage Kanva's Ashram

Sage Kanva's ashram was like a spot of heaven on earth. It was small, amidst a dense forest, a forest where every wild animal turned tame. The ashram was built on the banks of the Malini River, which wound through the ashram, as if it was brought all the way from the mountains just to nourish this spot. Cool winds, Vedic chants ringing in the air amidst the twittering of birds gave it just the right atmosphere for communion with the Almighty.

Sage Kanva was a learned sage and considered to be amongst the Saptarishis. He had built the ashram and took care of its inmates like his family. There was not a shrub, animal or any of the sages and their families whom he did not know by name. Birds sang melodies to him, animals ate from his hand and many a time he could be seen playing with the children. Everybody in the ashram knew that children were his favourite—a boon God could not grant him, due to his vow of celibacy. Maybe God had other plans…who knew the ways of the Almighty?

It was an unusually wonderful day. He could hear the birds singing the most beautiful tunes. The sun was bright, heralding the beginning of a new day. He was accustomed to taking a walk around his ashram, meeting each and every shrub, animal and inmate as part of his morning ritual. He loved this much more than any activity. It was his way of meditating, being one with Brahma, the Creator of every living being on earth.

The creator had a taste for creation, felt Sage Kanva. How

perfect was everything? Every leaf was the same from the same tree, but differed when the type of tree changed. Every flower had a different hue and smell. The colours of leaves were all different shades of green. There were flowers on shrubs, bushes and trees and even in the small lakes. The lotus was the best, dark pink emerging to fade to a lighter shade by the time it reached the tip of the petals. The lotus leaf was in the water, but kept itself dry as if proclaiming, I am the lord's favourite and have to be dry to allow him to step on me! The animals, birds and insects had all been painstakingly and thoughtfully created. Each carried a distinct colour which seemed to have become its identity—be it the tiger with its stripes or the deer with its light spots or the parrot with its distinct green or the peacock with a palette of colours on itself. Each had a distinct trait—be it the gait of the elephant or the glide of the cat or the elegant swimming of the fish. The Almighty had taken care to ensure that the waters had fish and other beings, the skies had birds, and the earth had the best of both—the four-legged animals as well as the favourite and the most intelligent of all creations, the humans.

But credit was due to Sage Kanva for taming the birds and animals in his ashram. The parrots could sing Vedic hymns and all the birds would stop chirping during a yagna, lest they disturbed the sacrifice. The morning twitter would start with hymns and holy words rather than mindless chirping. Even animals would gather during yagnas as if they were invited to participate in the rituals. The animals would move all around the ashram, without harming anyone. The deer and the cubs of tigers and lions would move around fearlessly as if they had been taught to look for food elsewhere and not amongst themselves. It was difficult to believe that this benign Sage Kanva would hurl such a curse on the Yadavas that their clan would come to an end.

Sage Kanva was once resting under a tree when a Yadava lad, dressed as a pregnant woman, came to test his greatness. Kanva was enraged at the impudence and cursed him saying whatever emerged from the inflated womb would bring an end to the clan he belonged to. The lad was none other than a Yadava and, as ordained, a piece of iron emerged from his womb. The piece of iron was thrown away in the river, but could the greatness of the sage be undermined? Could anybody say if his curse would take effect or not? Well, another tale to tell[B]...but why talk of curses or the Yadavas here? At this point, Sage Kanva did not even remotely look like an angry cursing sage. He was the epitome of peace and tranquillity and a fatherly figure for the entire ashram.

The sage's peaceful walk was distracted by an unusual sight. A few shakunt birds seemed to be hovering around something. Stepping closer, he saw a child who was being provided shade by the birds. But where had this child come from? He hadn't heard about any child being born in the ashram!

He bent down and picked up the child. She was one of the most beautiful children he had ever seen and her smile was divine. The sage looked around and was about to call for help, when he heard 'Narayan, Narayan'. Narada Muni emerged from behind a tree, as if he was waiting for someone to pick up the child.

Sage Kanva bowed to the celestial sage, 'O great Narada Muni, what a pleasure to see you early in the morning! Welcome to the ashram.'

Narada raised his hand in blessing and smiled. 'This child brings me here, O great Sage Kanva. I have come to leave her with you.'

'Leave the child? Why, and who are her parents? Please enlighten me, O learned sage.'

Narada Muni said, 'O sage, this is the child of King Kaushik and the celestial apsara of Indra-lok, Menaka.' He then went on to tell Kanva the entire story and how he had promised Menaka that he would find a suitable home for her child. Narada Muni continued, 'Sage Kanva, I hope I have not erred by bringing the child to your ashram. I couldn't think of anybody else.'

Sage Kanva was looking down at the smiling child, marvelling at her cheerful disposition. He said, 'Your wish is my command, O munivar. You can convey to Devi Menaka that her child will be my daughter from today and I will ensure that she gets the love of both father and mother. She will make a name for herself and the world will look upto her.'

Narada Muni was glad and blessed the child, who was smiling at the world, nestled safe in her foster-father's arms, while tugging at his long beard. He took Saga Kanva's leave and the ashram soon began buzzing with activity.

Sage Kanva called for Gautami, a woman who looked every bit a mother, except that she wasn't one biologically. Gautami had never been able to conceive, but was a mother to the entire ashram.

Gautami came to the sage's cottage and was surprised to see the baby. She had never seen such a beautiful baby in her life; it couldn't be an earthly being, she thought, it had to be a divine child. She bowed to the sage, without taking her eyes off the baby girl. The sage noticed the motherly gaze and handed the baby to her. 'Here, take this child, Gautami,' Sage Kanva said. 'This is my daughter. The great Narada Muni has left her in my custody and that's all there is to know about her. From today, I want you to take care of her. Tell all in the ashram that she is my daughter and is a part of the ashram from today.'

Gautami's vision turned hazy as tears filled her eyes. God had probably not given her a child of her own keeping in mind this day. She never faulted God for her barrenness and this was her reward. Thanking the Almighty, she embraced the child. She was about to leave, when she turned back and asked the sage, 'What is her name?'

The sage thought for a moment and said, 'Shakuntala, yes, Shakuntala! Isn't that an apt name? She who was found protected by the shakunt birds, ought to be called Shakuntala, what do you say, Gautami?'

'Shakuntala it is, for my beautiful child,' said an elated Gautami before leaving the cottage.

Menaka at Indra-lok

A dishevelled and distraught Menaka was sitting in front of the mirror with a comb which hadn't touched her hair for a long time now. One look at her and everybody could tell that she was not the same Menaka who had left Indra-lok.

Is this what womanhood is on earth, thought Menaka. Did they not have a say in anything or regarding anyone? As an apsara, she was destined to do what the gods ordered, but did a woman too have to do what men told her? Didn't she have a choice? Here was she, an apsara, who did what she was told, as a task. But how did one control the heart, which was so wayward? Kamdev had ways which only he understood…or did he? Was love based on the whims and fancies of a god for whom striking love arrows was nothing more than a sport; a sport where more were left injured and writhing in pain than happy?

As a celestial being, was she any better than a woman on earth? Here she was at the beck and call of a god who used her to lure a man away from his chosen path. She achieved this using the sheer beauty of her physical attributes and her ability to make a man lust after her. Wasn't such work given to prostitutes on earth?

She lived with a man like his wife on earth—caring for him, providing for him and taking care of his every need. She bore him a child and was even willing to live on with him, till Indradev came and pronounced another order. Instead of looking back at the last ten years as probably the best years of his life, Kaushik chose to identify deceit and deception with them. The earth was testimony to her unshakeable love for Kaushik. Couldn't he overlook the divine order which had sent her to earth? Was man so naïve that he could see only a moment of deceit against a decade of love and dedication? Or was it his selfish conceitedness in perceiving what he wanted to and no further?

Menaka's tragic trance was broken when she heard her name being called out. She saw Urvashi's face in the mirror opposite her. She quickly wiped her tears and rose to welcome her. Urvashi gestured her to relax and sat next to her. 'Let your tears flow, Menaka, don't stop them. They hurt more when stopped.' Menaka did not know what to say, no matter how much she tried, the tears just rolled down her cheeks. Urvashi put her hand on Menaka's shoulder and said, 'I understand your pain, Menaka. If there is one person who can, then it's me, and why not? Have I, too, not been a pawn in the hands of the lord of rains? On earth, love is the best thing that can happen to us, and with a mortal the meaning changes altogether, which none of the gods or gandharvas will ever understand.' She went on, 'Treasure the experience, my dear, and feel proud, as you have experienced both—the love of a man and motherhood. How many in heaven can claim to have experienced that bliss?'

Menaka could no longer control herself and burst out crying. She sobbed uncontrollably, something that she was trying to hold back ever since she had returned to Indra-lok. Urvashi held on to her, giving vent to her own tears and both didn't realize how long they held each other. Menaka emerged out of her sorrow feeling lighter and composed herself. Urvashi knew how Menaka was feeling. She did not have anybody to console her when she came back from the earth leaving her love, Pururavas, behind.

Menaka got up and thanked Urvashi for being there and caring for her. Urvashi said, 'Menaka, we are our own balm and have to heal each other every time one of us is hurt. Our lord enjoys playing games with mortals, where we are his pawns. Once our task is accomplished, we are left hurt and bruised and he does not even care to find out how we are faring. At such moments, if we don't stand by each other, who will?'

Menaka realized how lonely Urvashi must have felt when she had returned from the earth, and none of the apsaras had even gone to see her. Instead, some of them actually indulged in gossip and took pot-shots at her predicament. But Urvashi did not do so and Menaka couldn't thank her enough for that.

She was feeling better by the time Urvashi left. Suddenly she had formed a bond with her, something which had never happened before. Apsaras were known for their lack of feeling and one-upmanship amongst each other. But today not only did she feel close to Urvashi, but also didn't care much if anybody took her place as the 'chosen one'; the fruits of success were sour and tragic.

The string of her thoughts was broken when she heard the familiar 'Narayan, Narayan'. She was overjoyed to see Narada Muni standing in front of her. In her joy, she even forgot the customary salutation as she rushed to him asking, 'O munivar, what news do you have of my child? Have you found a place for her? Where is she? How is she?'

Narada was smiling. 'Hold your horses, my dear. Allow me some refreshments at least. I am coming from afar, from earth, and the journey was so tiring!' joked Narada Muni.

Menaka was getting impatient. 'O Brahmarishi, why trouble me more, I am already a troubled person. Please tell me that you bring good tidings of my daughter. Please!' urged Menaka.

'Menaka, my dear,' said Narada. 'Don't you trust me? Would I leave your daughter unattended? Come; let me tell you all about her new parents.' And Narada told her all about Sage Kanva and how he was now the foster-father of his newly christened daughter, Shakuntala.

'Shakuntala? What a lovely name for my daughter!' said the proud mother amid tears rolling down her silken cheeks. 'O munivar, can I see my daughter, just once, please?'

Narada was quiet as if deep in thought. He said, 'As per the rules of Indra-lok, you cannot see any mortal, unless shown or given specific permission for the same. But let me grant you a wish, O celestial being. From today, you can see your daughter whenever you wish to. Just close your eyes and think of her. You can even visit Sage Kanva's ashram, but you will not be visible. She or any other mortal will not be able to see you.'

Menaka's face fell for a moment, but she knew she had got much more than what she had asked for. At least she would be able to see her daughter grow. She bowed and thanked Narada Muni for his blessings and apologized for not paying her respects properly when he had arrived. 'Menaka, I might have taken offence if this behaviour was from an apsara, but I can never take offence from a mother. I will now take your leave and assure you that I will be in touch with the sage and will keep bringing happy tidings occasionally,' said Narada, about to leave.

'O munivar...' And Menaka stopped mid-sentence.

Narada looked back, with an enigmatic smile on his face. 'Yes, my dear. Is there anything else?' Menaka toyed with the end of her garment, hesitating. Narada waited, knowing well what was on Menaka's mind. He persisted, 'Yes, my dear, tell me what else bothers you? I am getting late; I have to meet Devi Indrani as I have not paid obeisance to her for a very long time. Hurry up, my dear.'

'Any news of King Kaushik?' asked a hesitating Menaka.

Narada smiled, 'Yes my dear. King Kaushik, a hurt man with a broken heart, has begun his penance and this time with more vigour and greater resolve. He is even more determined this time, and nothing can stop him now. Nothing.'

With this, Narada Muni left, leaving Menaka all alone. She prayed that Kaushik would achieve what he had set his mind upon and wished he would show Indradev that if a mortal was determined, no divine intervention could come in his way. She would pray for him and hope that one day he would understand that what had started as a task for her had become rich with emotion. She loved him like no mortal could.

This brought her back to her daughter. 'Shakuntala,' what a wonderful name! She must thank the sage for christening her daughter so. It was time to see how she was faring. She closed her eyes and tried to see.

Shakuntala

Sage Kanva's ashram was abuzz with activities because of the child that was God's gift to the sage. Everybody had come to see her, especially the children who were curious to see this bundle of joy who never tired of smiling and stretching her hands to reach for everything—flower necklaces, earrings, garments, beards, et al. She was such a pleasure that nobody wanted to leave Gautami's cottage.

Gautami was having a tough time getting baby Shankuntala ready for the naming ceremony. The auspicious muhurta would pass by, if all these people did not allow her to bathe and dress this child, who seemed to revel in the presence of so many. Usually children cried with so many hovering around them, but this one seemed to enjoy all the attention she was getting.

With much effort, she got the child ready for the ceremonies and took her to the sage's cottage, where he had made the necessary arrangements. It seemed that the entire ashram had decided to stop work and attend the ceremony which was going to be a grand affair. All the hermits, sages, their wives and children were there for what was going to be a 'simple' ceremony. Even the birds, the calves and fawns, besides numerous other animals were going to attend this naming ceremony.

Sage Kanva took her in his lap from Gautami and gestured to her to sit close by. Even as a child, Shakuntala looked beautiful and the black dot on her forehead only added to her beauty.

Gautami was very superstitious and she would have never allowed the child without the black mark to protect her against the evil eye. She was draped in a white cloth and adorned with small flower bangles and anklets. She sure looked divine, thought the sage, who was every bit the proud father today!

All who were present could sense that this was no ordinary child. Amidst Vedic chants, the child was officially named Shakuntala. The ceremony was presided over by Rishi Dhananjaya, as Sage Kanva was the doting father today and not a learned rishi. At the end of the ceremony, Sage Kanva invited everyone for a meal at his cottage and it was time for celebrations. The womenfolk got together to prepare the meal, the men went their way for making arrangements for the meal and the children were hovering around the sage, who was simply trying his best to stop the children from fussing over the child. Undoubtedly, Shkauntala was the cynosure of all eyes today…and who knows, would be even later!

Tears rolled down the closed eyes of Menaka. She knew her child was in safe hands and was happy that Narada Muni had left her child with Sage Kanva. She couldn't have done this herself. She prayed for the long life of the sage and Gautami and hoped they remained as happy forever.

Shakuntala's Questions

Sage Kanva was sitting quietly and observing Shakuntala who was busy painting something for the last few days. She never destroyed any parchment which she started. She had been meticulously mixing dyes and pigments from plants and flowers and creating colours as yet unseen in the ashram. For a ten-year-old, she was extremely sharp.

It had been ten years and Sage Kanva could remember every moment of Shakuntala's growing up. As a baby, Shakuntala had seldom cried, except when she was hungry. Even later, when she started walking and playing, she would rarely cry, except when she was physically hurt. She was extremely beautiful and different from the other girls of her age. After all she was half-divine and half-royal and the sage was very proud of her. He had never made her feel different, and ensured that she got a complete education. He had taught her archery, and since the last one year, she had been learning arts and music. From this year, he was planning to initiate her into subjects like politics, law and justice. She was already quite adept at expressing her views and holding her side during an argument. Many of the hermits had come to him trying to understand how to handle some of her questions, which made them uneasy. Not because they did not have the answer, but because the questions were too intelligent for her age.

As a ten-year-old, she was asking too many questions and

Sage Kanva was well aware of it, as it was he who had to bear the brunt of the majority of her questions. Who made the world? Who put colours on flowers? Where did the rainbow take its colours from? Why didn't fish fly and why couldn't she too? Why did the animals not talk like humans? Why was it that the weather seemed nice when she woke up, but became hot later? Why were she and her friends different from the boys in the ashram? Why did they get different kinds of education? Why did they spend more time at home than the boys who seemed to spend so much time outside home? Why did the teachers focus more on the boys when it came to teaching the scriptures than them, the girls?

However, the most baffling of all the questions that kept coming in different forms was, 'Why are you so old, when all my friends' fathers are so young?'

'All my friends have mothers, why don't I have a mother?'

Sage Kanva always fumbled at these questions, wondering what to do. Could he tell her the truth about her parents? Would she be able to bear the truth? Wasn't she too young to know the reality of her parents? This had been going on in the mind of the sage for the last few years and he had begun to sense a sort of frustration in Shakuntala. He could see that she was aware of his discomfort and had started wording the questions with utmost care. But the questions had not stopped.

'Narayan, Narayan,' came the voice of Narada Muni, breaking Sage Kanva's reverie. He rose with folded hands and welcomed the celestial sage. After the initial greetings, Narada Muni said, 'I can't marvel enough at the peace and tranquillity of your ashram. It's simply amazing.' Sage Kanva thanked him for the appreciation. Narada continued, 'But I can't say the same about you, O Sage! You seem to be a trifle distanced from peace.'

Kanva understood that his face had given him away. He said, 'O munivar, nothing on earth or heaven is hidden from you. Something is bothering me and you have come to my rescue at the right time.' Narada smiled and said, 'Tell me your concern, but before that, where is your daughter Shakuntala?'

Suddenly Sage Kanva realized that Shakuntala was not in the cottage. She had left the cottage some time back and what he was looking at was the unfinished painting. He stepped out and saw Shakuntala playing with her favourite fawn, Mrigakshi. Kanva called her inside and asked her to seek Narada Muni's blessings.

Shakuntala knew Narada Muni and found him very interesting as he was always smiling. What she was unable to understand was how he appeared all of a sudden and then suddenly disappeared. There was something sinister about him, except that he looked so harmless. He confused her no end.

'What are you thinking, my dear child?' This question jolted Shakuntala out of her thoughts.

'Oh nothing, O munivar,' she blurted out. 'Please accept my respects. What would you like to have, O munivar? Can I offer you some fruits?' continued Shakuntala.

Narada was pleased. 'No, my dear. I don't want anything. Bless you, my child; go play with your fawn while I talk to your father.'

Shakuntala stepped out of the cottage leaving the two sages alone. Sage Kanva now raised the subject of his concern. He wanted to know if it was the right time to reveal the truth of her parentage to Shakuntala. Narada Muni asked, 'Is it absolutely necessary?'

Sage Kanva was clear that he did not like to hide the truth as it was unethical. Further, every human had the right to know about his or her identity. Shakutala had an illustrious parentage and she had to know about them, even if she would never get to meet them. 'Including the fact that both of them deserted her?' questioned Narada Muni.

There was absolute silence.

'That is the only thing that is holding me back, O munivar,' said Sage Kanva finally.

'But isn't hiding the truth as good as lying?' Kanva heard Narada Muni ask. Now Kanva was confused. Why couldn't Narada Muni simply give a verdict instead of asking questions both for and against a subject which was already so confusing? Narada Muni continued, 'While I do agree that I brought the child to your ashram because I knew you could give her the love of both a mother and father, and you have not disappointed me or her mother, I must say that you understand her better than me. If you think that she has to be told, then please tell her, and what better time than now? She is old enough to understand.'

Sage Kanva wasn't sure. 'Is she? I mean is she old enough to understand?'

Narada Muni laughed. 'O Sage Kanva, for a father a daughter never grows old enough for anything, so I will overlook your apprehension as part of a father's overprotective nature. Why worry? If she reacts badly to the news, then she is young enough to overcome it with your love and affection.' Sage Kanva was pleased to hear this solution from Narada Muni. 'However,' Narada Muni had not finished, 'I sincerely hope that she does not end up despising her parents.'

Kanva was surprised by the last statement. How could a child not feel resentful towards her parents, when she realized that she had been deserted by both? How could one expect a ten-year-old to understand the compulsions or the machinations of an adult world? How would he... 'Oh Brahmarishi, how do you...' Sage Kanva stopped mid-sentence when he saw little Shakuntala come in to collect her painting. Narada Muni got up and took his leave, as if avoiding Kanva's conflict. Shakuntala too, left the cottage with her painting and Sage Kanva was left alone with his problems which seemed to have been compounded by what Narada Muni had said.

Menaka

Menaka was worried about what Narada Muni had told her before he left. Usually she was very happy to see him as he always brought good news from earth for her. But today, he had unsettled her. She was concerned and wondered how her daughter would react once she learnt that she was the child of deception, at least initially. Menaka had not gone to earth out of love. She had gone to seduce a king who was on his way to becoming a rishi, a learned man. Love was the effect, but deception was the cause and that could not be denied. What would she think of her? Motherhood was revered and cherished on earth. It was an honour for a woman on earth. Would an apsara, who entertained in the court of Lord Indra, ever achieve that status? Would her daughter ever understand that she had no choice? That apsaras were there to obey and they had no right to object? Would her daughter understand that she gave birth to her as a mortal would, but she could not display the emotions of a mortal mother? Would her daughter ever understand how she craved to live the life of a mother and love like one?

She closed her eyes to see her daughter's reactions.

Shakuntala Learns About her Parents

Sage Kanva, though unsure of the outcome, had decided to take the bull by the horns. He asked Gautami to be present when he spoke to Shakuntala. Gautami was vehemently opposed to the sage's idea of revealing the truth to her, but kept her views to herself, as she trusted the sage's decisions more than her emotions.

Shakuntala knew that her father was going to tell her something important, because he had never looked so grave before. She was all ears.

Sage Kanva was saying, 'My dear, you have always wanted to know why I am older than your friends' fathers, right?' Shakuntala nodded. 'You have also wanted to know about your mother, right?' Shakuntala nodded, looking at Gautami who was avoiding her eyes. Shakuntala felt something amiss, but kept quiet as her father was speaking. 'I think it is time you knew the truth, and I trust you are old and mature enough to face the truth...' *Face the truth?* Why was her father using such a phrase?

Sage Kanva told her everything that she needed to know. How King Kaushik was meditating to become a sage, and how her mother was sent by Indradev to disturb his penance. How they fell in love and she was born. How her father came to know about the evil designs of Indradev and how he decided to pursue his path and Menaka had to leave, obeying the orders of Indradev. How Sage Kanva found her in his ashram and was advised to adopt her by the celestial sage, Narada Muni.

Shakuntala was motionless as she faced the sage. There was no emotion on her pale face which had suddenly lost colour. A few drops of tears fought with each other to roll down her face. She heard it all. She always had a feeling that she was different. Now she knew.

After a long and disturbing silence, she got up and left the cottage.

Gautami got up to follow but stopped when the sage gestured to her. 'Leave her alone, Gautami. Let her come to terms with this herself. Some battles are best fought alone'. Gautami was weeping, wondering how a ten-year-old could fight the battle of her identity. How would her little girl come to terms with her loneliness? From the window of the cottage, she saw Shakuntala walk away with her fawn till she was lost in the distance.

Sage Kanva remained motionless. He was aware of the storm within his daughter's heart. He knew it would become worse when she realized that she was an unwanted child and that her birth was an accident caused by divine intrigue. God, help my daughter now, she needs divine help and courage to battle this. If she can overcome this, then I am sure she can weather anything in the world, prayed Sage Kanva.

Suddenly he was disturbed by the chattering of Anusuya and Priyamvada, Shakuntala's closest friends. 'What happened to Shaukuntala, Guruji? She did not look at us and did not even listen to us when we called.' Both of them rambled on till they were silenced by the raised hand of Sage Kanva. 'My children, she is not feeling well and is a bit disturbed. Leave her alone, but remain close to her, in case she needs your help. Listen to her if she says something, but don't ask too many questions…'

'Why?' started the irrepressible Anusuya.

'What did I tell you, Anusuya? Don't ask questions, just listen to her. Good friends should be good listeners when their friends are not at peace. So be there for her, but leave her alone if she wants it that way.'

A confused Anusuya and a worried Priyamvada left in the direction that they had seen Shakuntala go.

'God, give my daughter some peace. Let her overcome this and I will ask for nothing. She is not at fault, and I don't want her to bear the brunt of all this. She is too young to understand all this. Let her not bear any grudge towards me and the king,' prayed a tearful Menaka.

Shakuntala

Shakuntala sat in the mangrove with her fawn, Mrigakshi. The best thing about Mrigakshi, thought Shakuntala, was that she never asked questions but understood everything Shakuntala told her. Anusuya asked lots of questions while Priyamvada seldom understood the things she told her. But still they were her best friends.

Her thoughts went back to what her father…well…her foster-father had said. She was a divine child. Her father was a king, King Kaushik, and now a well-known sage by the name of Rishi Vishwamitra. Her mother was an apsara, Menaka. *Both my parents are alive and neither of them have bothered to come and see me even once. Why? Did they not want me? Mothers are never so heartless, then why is my mother so? If she could come from the heavens for my father, then why couldn't she come to see me? Not even once in so many years? What could be the reason for her inability to do so? Or does she not care for me? Father did say that she still loved me…but how do I know that?*

How did my father, the king, forget his own daughter on earth? If the fault lies with Indradev and my mother, why am I to be blamed for this? Father says that the Kshatriyas are an honourable lot, but where is a king's honour in leaving his daughter in the care of someone else while he performs penance, and even after achieving what he had set out for, does not even bother to check on his own blood? How honourable is this? Why did all this happen to me, what have I done...

Shakuntala sat there all alone through the day. Towards dusk she got up and started towards her home. She did not notice her two friends trailing her at a distance, keeping an eye on her till she entered the cottage of Sage Kanva.

Sage Kanva was glad to see his daughter return. She sat next to him and put her head on his lap. The father patted his daughter's hand and soon a tired Shakuntala was fast asleep, her eyes still moist. A solitary tear rolled down the cheek of the father. Mrigakshi lay at the door of the cottage unwilling to leave her friend alone in her moment of distress. *Animals have a better understanding of emotions than humans,* thought Sage Kanva.

'Can I ask you something, Fa....Father?' Kanva was surprised to see Shakuntala looking up at him from his lap.

'Yes, my dear, why do you have to ask?' queried a worried Kanva.

'You won't leave me ever, will you?' asked a sobbing Shakuntala.

The father could not hold back his tears, and embraced her, 'No, my dear, I will never leave you, no matter what,' he said in a choked voice. 'You are my daughter and I am your father...'

Sage Kanva felt his hand being clutched as if she would never let go. Kanva allowed her to hold it, for he knew that she needed the assurance more than ever now. A reassured Shakuntala was now asleep and Sage Kanva was feeling much relieved having told her everything, but not sure if he could do justice to the Brahmarishi's request.

The next day's sun brought happy tidings. The festival of colours was going to be celebrated in a few days and all the children were busy making colours out of flowers and herbs. The boys were collecting wood for burning. Shakuntala had woken up a much matured and calm girl. Girl? She suddenly seemed to be a young woman, who had grown up in just one day. Kanva was happy that she was participating in the games and, as always, looking forward to the festival of colours which was celebrated with great joy across the ashram. They had not spoken about the previous day's discussion, but the sage was aware that his ten-year-old daughter had grown up many years in just one day. She seemed to have reconciled with her identity and overcome the distress. Had she? Only time could tell…Time is all-pervasive; it heals all and hides much.

Time

I am the ubiquitous time.

Had Shakuntala overcome her distress? I will tell, as I am known to be a good observer and healer of wounds. I have seen much and will see more, and by the virtue of being in such an advantageous position, I will do something…something good. Sage Kanva might not have seen as much as I have, but he had full faith in me and was hoping that I would heal all, all of Shakuntala's unseen wounds.

I am aware of being acknowledged for all good things and am proud of the goodness I distribute. I take care of things and heal…heal like no physician can.

I am also accused of being mean to youth. Why else would I rush during one's youth to change and spoil youth's looks? Why do I not honour the youthful and graceful looks of youth? Why am I so cruel to beauty?

Man is known for not being happy with anything; why else would he be selective in chastising me? If I had not passed by, would childhood make way for youth? And when it's time for youth to make way for the evening of life, why do a few wrinkles hurt man's vanity?

I observe and make note of everything. I forget nothing. I don't forget how man had wished to grow up in a hurry, rush through youth and when old, resist the hours from ticking to reach the end. I know how lovers would want me to slow down, enabling them to savour every moment of love between them. Youth was in a hurry, so I would fly for them. Old hated me, for they had too much of me. In some testing moments I tend to drag my pace, much to the discomfort of both old and young! But am I not allowed some mirth, when even the gods don't let go of a helpless one?

Man has always been selfish and demanding of me, but I wait for none. I move on, without a moment of rest. I spend not a second under the shade of a tree or bask under the sun or enjoy the moon. Since the creation of universe, I have come into existence and shown favour to none. It was for man, to make his life so eventful and interesting, that I *seemed* to fly by.

But I, Time, have been kind to Shakuntala. She needed my kindness and benevolence. Shakuntala's days passed like sand slipping through my hourglass and every passing grain of sand left a mark of beauty on her. In no time, the fawn Mrigakshi was a beautiful doe and the proud owner of the doe, a divine beauty.

Shakuntala was in the spring of youth and had inherited her mother's looks. At the ripe age of sixteen, she looked divine with a rare combination of looks and intelligence. In the last six years, she had mastered the Vedas, played the veena like Goddess Saraswati and debated on matters of administration like a courtier. She had rare oratory skills and was bold, a quality she had inherited from her father's Kshatriya ancestors. She had a mind of her own and this aspect made her seem different in the ashram. She never withheld her views, and if she did, it was only out of respect for the rishis in the ashram, who all loved her the way her father did. But this did not stop her from harbouring an opinion of her own.

I have been a witness to all this, and what better witness to these moments that were making Shakuntala what she is or what she is going to be. Today, I stand at a threshold. When I look back, I see all that Shakuntala has not seen and comprehended in its truest sense. When I look ahead, I can see what no one can.

What I have seen, not many have and not many will. For me a few years pass off in seconds and a few hundred years are just that…a few. I wait for none, but I miss nothing too. I have also noted what many in Indra-lok have not known, neither Menaka nor the other apsaras.

King Kaushik had resumed his penance, but this time with stronger resolve and determination. This was once again unsettling the king of the gods, Devendra. Lord Indra could not resist trying to break the penance of Kaushik once again. But this time, it couldn't be Menaka, as she had already been send for this task. Indra had not even called on her since her return. Seeking her services once again would be too damaging for his pride.

Lord Indra summoned Rambha, the most beautiful of all the apsaras. Rambha was the queen of apsaras, known for her skills in dance and all the art forms including the art of passionate lovemaking. But Rambha was apprehensive of following Menaka's footsteps as the entire Indra-lok was aware of her state since she returned. But Indra played on her vanity and convinced her to do the unthinkable at the risk of earning the wrath of an already-wounded Kaushik.

Rambha descended on the earth and began her sensual dance to lure the meditating ascetic-to-be. Kaushik opened his eyes and saw what he had seen many years ago. But this time, he had acquired powers and through them, he learned the cause of this performance. This angered him no end and he cursed Rambha to turn into a stone for the next ten thousand years!

I was a mute witness to this beside Lord Indra. What a pity! One more apsara caught in the web of deccit laid by a god and cursed by a learned man. Was this what Kaushik had set out to achieve? His anger was still mortal and he had a long way to go before achieving the powers of a sage. If he could not control this most malevolent emotion of the mortals, how would he ever transcend to a level above mortals? But who would bring this to his knowledge?

I can only see and observe; I am unable to comment. I wish I could speak to this man and tell him that knowledge enables man to be in control and not lose his cool at the slightest provocation. His powers enabled him to see that Rambha was a weapon to destroy his penance; then shouldn't he have spared the weapon and gone at the one who was using it? He treated both Menaka and Rambha the same way. What had he achieved? Nothing. The curse actually took away some of his achievement and he had to start afresh. Maybe the lord of the clouds was trying to achieve just this!

O what a pity that I, Time, have to see it all, but suggest nothing!

Anusuya

Anusuya loved to be with Shakuntala; she always knew the right answers to her questions. She responded to Anusuya with a lot of care and affection and, more importantly, attention.

Anusuya felt that Shakuntala had something bottled up within her which she could never fathom. A few years back, something had happened and Guruji had asked her and Priyamvada to stay close to Shakuntala. Anusuya did not know what had transpired that day, but it had changed Shakuntala a lot.

Both Priyamvada and she had tried to ask Shakuntala about it the next day, and all she told them was that she had come to know about her parents. So late? Did she not know all this while, what all of them knew? That Guruji was her father and she had no mother? So silly of Shakuntala…and why was this so disturbing? Anusuya always found Shakuntala a bit different from all the girls in the ashram, and it was one of the reasons why she liked being with her.

Unlike other girls, Shakuntala would never take no for an answer. Nobody dared refuse her anything, especially if it had to be with her being a girl. She loved to play and splash around in the water. Earlier, Anusuya too enjoyed it, but since the last few years, she was not allowed to get wet in the waters. Her parents had started objecting to it, and she wondered why? But Guruji never stopped Shakuntala from doing anything.

However, sometimes, Shakuntala would behave oddly.

Once Anusuya found Shakuntala staring at the skies, mumbling something, as if she was talking to someone in the heavens above. When queried, Shakuntala just changed the topic. Anusuya had seen this a number of times, especially when Shakuntala was alone. Wasn't it weird? She shared this with Priyamvada once, but as usual, she laughed it off. Priyamvada always laughed at everything Anusuya said, as if she never made sense. Silly arrogant girl!

But Shakuntala never treated her badly. With Shakuntala around, Anusuya always felt a sense of belonging. She did ask a lot of questions, and why not, didn't the gurujis at the ashram always encourage them to ask whatever they had in mind? So what was wrong with asking questions? Many of the girls didn't ask questions and ended up remaining ignorant, but not Anusuya!

Priyamvada

Priyamvada was a very close friend of Shakuntala and had grown up at the ashram with her. She didn't remember a time when Shakuntala was not around. Priyamvada was intelligent; a trifle sceptic about everything though, a quality which irritated Anusuya the gullible a bit too much.

Priyamvada admired Shakutala and her qualities which were very different from the others in the ashram. Her looks, her gait, her intelligence, all seemed beyond this place. Priyamvada always felt that Shakuntala was meant for bigger things as compared to her and the other girls. She still remembered the day when Shakuntala was very disturbed and Guruji had asked her and Anusuya to keep an eye on her. Priyamvada was very worried when she saw the concern in the eyes of Guruji and tears in the eyes of the ever-smiling Gautami. Something serious had taken place.

When they asked her the next day, all Shakuntala said was that she had come to know who her parents were. She had always found it strange that Guruji, Shakuntala's father, was so old. Weren't such people more like a grandfather or even a great-grandfather? She did ask her mother once who just changed the topic. This happened quite a few times, till she was admonished by her mother for asking irrelevant questions. Irrelevant questions?! She brought it up with Shakuntala once and she was supposed to have asked Guruji about it, but she never got any satisfactory answer.

She wasn't satisfied with Shakuntala's answer, but didn't pursue the matter with Anusuya around, as Anusuya never understood anything and one question always led to another. Later, when she asked Shakuntala about it, she replied, 'Father...I mean Guruji... is not my father. My parents are some other people, who are alive and living elsewhere. I have been left in the care of Guruji, but for me, he remains the only father I have ever had.' This did sound odd, but seeing Shakuntala fighting her tears, she decided not to ask any more questions, lest she be more disturbed.

Priyamvada never broached the subject again as she did not want to hurt her friend and nor did she ever reveal this to Anusuya, lest she ask more questions!

But this incident changed her friend and she suddenly seemed to have grown up. However, she did notice some tension whenever any discussion took place about parents in general. But Priyamvada also noticed one more change in Shakuntala; she had developed a lot of love and respect for her foster-father after this incident.

Shakuntala

Shakuntala was tending to the bushes and tree that she had planted along the path leading to her cottage. Her favourite was the parijat tree whose flowers had snow-coloured petals with red stalks. The parijat flowers blossomed at night and fell to the ground at dawn. However, the other reason that it was her favourite was due to the romantic allusions of the flower. It was said that Princess Parijataka was in love with the sun, but her love was never reciprocated. Having lost in love, she committed suicide and from her ashes rose the parijat tree. Since she was unable to bear the sight of her love during the day, she bloomed only at night, and shed the flowers as tears before the sun rose. Some also said that the tree shed its tears at the touch of the first rays of the sun! The flowers spread their fragrance in the entire area during the day, as a sign of undying love for the sun.

Shakuntala loved the very idea of the parijat tree and her undying love and the flowers which were perceived as tears. She also tended to the tulasi, malati, roses and the numerous flowering shrubs around her cottage. She loved the flowers and their fragrance. She never plucked the flowers from the shrubs as she did not want the flowers to be separated from the plants which had given birth to them and were nurturing them. She understood the pain of separation. She collected only those flowers which had fallen on the ground as she understood that they needed care, now that they were separated from the plants which had nurtured them till then!

The entire ashram knew that they would be inviting trouble if Shakuntala caught them plucking flowers. She felt the same way towards the animals like deer, cows, calves and goats which roamed around freely in the ashram. No one was allowed to be rude to the animals, let alone beat them for any reason. All the animals in the ashram reciprocated her love and care. The deer, however, were showered with more affection as they were Shakuntala's favourites.

Mrigakshi, a full-grown doe now, was Shakuntala's childhood pet and had been with her ever since she knew herself. Seldom had anybody seen Shakuntala without Mrigakshi, who followed her around the ashram upto the banks of the Malini river. Mrigakshi was the only one who could claim that she had been with Shakuntala through every episode in her life, that is, if she could speak!

One bright morning, when Shakuntala was attending to some deer outside her cottage, she heard voices from within. She was puzzled as she had not seen anybody go in. Who was her father speaking to, wondered Shakuntala.

She peeped in to find her father speaking to Narada Muni. Just when did he go in and how come she hadn't noticed? Seeing her, Sage Kanva said, 'Come my dear and take the blessings of Naradaji'. Narada Muni smiled and blessed the beautiful daughter of Sage Kanva. Shakuntala always felt an inexplicable bond with this muni, who looked the same ever since she remembered him. He never aged and that smile of his seemed to be hiding so many truths behind it. She had never seen him frowning or worried. It was as if Narada Muni had read her thoughts, when he said, 'You seem to have something on your mind, my dear. What is it?'

Shakuntala looked as if she had been caught; she just bowed

and nodded, indicating it was nothing. Narada Muni said, 'Why don't you join us, my dear? We were discussing something and you might be able to contribute.' Shakuntala was surprised by this invitation and looked at her father, Sage Kanva. The sage smiled and asked her to sit down. Shakuntala sat and looked at them expectantly.

Narada Muni said, 'We were discussing a point where both of us don't seem to have a proper answer. Is varna decided by birth or by deeds? What is your opinion on this?' Shakuntala thought for a while and then said, 'As you know, the word "varna" is derived from the root "vrinja" meaning "choice", and thus I feel varna is never based on birth; it is based on one's deeds and consequently, man has the choice to select his varna. Maharishi Manu had suggested the varna-pratha for judicious allocation of duty within a society. It was to ensure that every activity of a society was taken care of and no work neglected.'

Narada Muni, though pleased, seemed to have a doubt. 'What do you have to say about the varna-pratha that says that the varnas were born from different parts of Lord Brahma. For example, Brahmins from his head, Kshatriyas from his shoulder and so on?'

Shakuntala smiled and said, 'How can that be true when we all know that God is formless? The Vedas that I have been taught by my father have said that God has no form but is a superior power; the power which has created the world so beautiful and filled all the colours of nature so thoughtfully. To say that man was created from His body and the higher the birth the higher his position in society is, pardon my saying so, absurd.'

Narada Muni was now visibly pleased. 'Excellent, my dear, you have argued well. I have never heard anybody as young as you articulate this somewhat controversial topic with such skill. I can see your father beaming with pride!' Shakuntala bowed and felt good on hearing these compliments from Narada Muni, whom her father held in great esteem. She got up to get some fruits for the guest, when she heard him say, 'Just one last doubt, my dear, if you don't mind.'

Shakuntala sat down obediently and looked at him. Narada Muni said, 'Does man have the right to change his varna?'

Shakuntala noticed that the question unsettled her father, but he maintained his composure. She thought for a while and then said, 'According to Maharishi Manu, man becomes what he is based on his deeds. He states that man earns respect due to wealth, company, age, actions and knowledge in increasing order. If man's actions do not befit his status or knowledge then he does not deserve to continue in his varna. Further, if man wants to change his varna then he has to do so by acquiring knowledge. For example, a Kshatriya can become a Brahmin by acquiring the knowledge to become one, just as a Shudra can become a Vaishya by his deeds.'

There was a stony silence in the cottage after Shakuntala gave these examples. Sage Kanva and Narada gazed in silence at her. Shakuntala kept quiet for some time before asking Narada Muni, 'Would you like some coconut water along with the fruits?' Then she stepped out of the cottage.

Sage Kanva

Sage Kanva was impressed by the way Shakuntala handled Narada Muni's queries. However, his heart was heavy with Shakuntala's stoic response to the final question. The complete absence of feeling in this young girl who had been living with the knowledge of being abandoned by her parents, especially by a father who was alive and illustrious, was hurting him. He knew that she was crying inside but refused to share this pain with anybody. Tears were always good outside rather than inside, and best shed. Sage Kanva did not want Shakuntala to be like a cloud which kept its waters to itself, and burst into rains when it could hold no longer. When a cloud bursts, it loses a lot of itself too. Shakuntala was better off shedding her tears than holding them in for some other day. Also, clouds gather waters from one place and shed them in distant lands, and he did not want Shakuntala to weep elsewhere or shed tears where she ought not to. *God give my child the strength to bear this*, prayed the foster-father.

While he was immersed in his thoughts, one of his disciples announced the arrival of Rishi Gautam. Rishi Gautam was a learned sage, renowned for writing many sacred hymns.

He was returning from Hastinapur and was very happy to share the good deeds of the ruler of Hastinapur, King Dushyant. King Dushyant traced his lineage to King Puru, better known for sacrificing his youth for his father, the famous Yayati. King Dushyant had expanded his kingdom from Gandhar to the

Vindhyas and from Sindhu to Vanga-pradesh. He was not only an able ruler expanding his kingdom, but also a king who upheld the traditions of the illustrious Chandra Vansha (lunar dynasty) by maintaining the principles of karma and dharma laid down for a Kshatriya.

Rishi Gautam was on his way back to his ashram and had decided to stop by to share some of the recently written hymns and check on new developments with Sage Kanva. The sage was honoured to have Rishi Gautam as a guest at his ashram and immediately sent for Sharngarava and Sharadvata, his disciples, to inform all about the arrival of Rishi Gautam and arrange a small meeting to discuss his work in the evening. This was a practice at the ashram, so that all the other sages and disciples could benefit from the great knowledge such sages carried with them. During such gatherings, meanings of rare hymns and intricate philosophical issues were discussed.

Sage Kanva then called for Shakuntala to seek the blessings of Rishi Gautam. The sage knew all about Shakuntala and was glad to see that the little girl whom he had seen some years ago had grown up to be a beautiful lady. He blessed her and she left to arrange for his refreshments. As soon as she left, Rishi Gautam said, 'My friend Kanva, you have taken good care of Rishi Vishwamitra's daughter. Has he ever expressed a desire to come and meet her?' Sage Kanva replied in the negative with a sad expression. Rishi Gautam, too, lapsed into silence.

Soon Shakuntala came in with fruits and milk and left after bowing to the sages. Rishi Gautam then asked, 'Have you thought about her marriage?' Sage Kanva seemed surprised with the question, 'Marriage? Of Shakuntala? But she is just a child.' Rishi Gautam smiled, 'My friend, you talk like a true father! Shakuntala is no more a child, she is a young girl, and at her age, you ought to be looking for a groom for her.' The sage was amused at the predicament of Sage Kanva whom he had seen indulging this child for so many years. While all sages treated every inhabitant of their ashram as their children, none had expressed such emotion towards anyone in particular, the way Kanva had towards Shakuntala. He was amused by how a celibate sage was behaving like a grihastha, a householder. Sage Kanva was perturbed, not by Rishi Gautam's amusement, but at the revelation that his child was now of a marriageable age. Why was this thought disturbing him? Wasn't it the norm for a girl to get married and leave for her husband's home? Wasn't he beyond all these grihastha hassles? Then what had happened in the last sixteen years that he was entangled in family ties and bonds that were hard to break? After all, Shakuntala was not his daughter… or was she…wondered the learned sage. Was fatherhood simply about the act of giving birth or was it the engagement of a man with his child till the child grows up? Was fatherhood all about the blood-ties or was it the emotional strings that played every time one's child came close to one?

Sage Kanva was engrossed in his own worries, oblivious to the forthcoming discussion in the evening, which Shakuntala was looking forward to. She enjoyed such get-togethers where all the learned men sat together and discussed new hymns and philosophy. Though this was open to all, not many of her friends found it interesting. They attended these meetings only out of sheer respect for the guests who were inevitably very learned and the assumption was that at the end of the discourse they would be enriched by knowledge. Some yawned while some slept off; yet smarter ones feigned sickness. But not Shakuntala; she was always there for the discourses and sometimes even contributed to the discussions and debates, much to the acclaim of the visitors, making her father, Sage Kanva, smile with pride.

Rishi Gautam was supposedly working on a treatise on rules for living an ethical life. It involved the laws of different classes of people, their duties and responsibilities, punishment for offences and rules for the atonement of sins. Shakuntala was curious to know more about it, and the evening discourse promised to be lively. Wouldn't it be interesting to know the views of a rishi who besides being so learned was one of the Saptarishis, the seven great sages? However, there was something about him that was disturbing and she had never managed to discover what it was. Now that Shakuntala was face-to-face with this great man, she was extremely curious to know more about this disturbing aspect which no one discussed openly. Would her father tell her about it?

Rishi Gautam

From early evening, people of the ashram started gathering near the central pavilion of the garden where discourses were generally held. A raised platform had been constructed for the guests and speakers. Pitchers with cold water and some fruits were laid out for the guests. All the disciples of the sages would sit in front of the platform while the rest would sit behind them. Sometimes discourses went on till late in the evening.

When Shakuntala reached the garden, she was surprised to find nearly the entire ashram present for the discourse. While it wasn't unusual for all to attend such discourses, as Sage Kanva encouraged women and girls to participate, it was still a rare sight for so many people to turn up that evening. The only people missing were those who were unwell or mothers of toddlers; the rest were all there, waiting for the sages to arrive.

She was late as she had been busy making arrangements for the refreshments of the guests along with others. She usually liked sitting right in front of the platform, but unfortunately her friends never liked to sit so close to the guests, as it would be near-impossible to slip out when the discussion went heavy! While her eyes were looking for an empty space to sit with her friends she found Anusuya waving at her. Anusuya, Priyamvada and the others were already there, which was a pleasant surprise. She went towards them and nudged Anusuya and said, 'I am surprised to see you so early and that too so close to the platform.' Anusuya began in a hushed voice, 'I wouldn't miss this for anything, I want to see the sage who...' when she was distracted by someone calling her. Shakuntala replied, 'The sage, who, what? Anusuya, what were you saying? Please stop staring elsewhere, I am here...' But before she could finish, Anusuya headed towards the person calling her.

Shakuntala looked at Priyamvada and asked her if she knew what Anusuya was talking about. Priyamvada lowered her voice and said, 'Not here, Shakuntala, later.'

Shakuntala was annoyed. 'Why later, Priyamvada? Just what is the matter, why don't you tell me?'

Priyamvada pulled Shakuntala close. 'Don't you know what Rishi Gautam is known for?'

Shakuntala answered, 'For the treatise he is working on, what else?'

Priyamvada was surprised. 'You mean to say that all these people are here to gain knowledge about his treatise? Is something wrong with you? Is this the first sage who is working on some treatise? How many people from our ashram, especially the women, have shown so much interest in such works earlier? Have you ever found so many women attending such discourses? They have all come to see the sage, and not just to hear him.'

Shakuntala was visibly irritated to be in the dark about something that the entire ashram seemed to know. 'What is there to "see" in a sage?'

Priyamvada continued, 'Rishi Gautam is different. He is the one who cursed the lord of the gods and more importantly, he cursed his wife to turn to stone.'

Shakuntala stared at Priyamvada in utter disbelief. 'Cursed his wife to turn to stone? Why, what was her crime?'

Priyamvada narrated the incident in a hushed tone, 'Rishi

Gautam was married to Sati Ahalya, a chaste and beautiful woman. Ahalya was the manasa-putri, the mind-born daughter of Lord Brahma. Lord Indra was smitten by her looks. Once when the sage went to the river to have a bath, Lord Indra appeared in the guise of Sage Gautam and slept with her. When the sage came back, he was surprised to see Lord Indra leaving his hut. This enraged the sage so much that he cursed both Indra and Sati Ahalya and as a result of the curse, Sati Ahalya was turned into a stone while Indra was punished with sahasrayoni, a thousand vaginas, as manifestation of his eternal lust, all over his body! Of course, later these were changed to sahasraksh, or thousand eyes, by the gods.'

Shakuntala could not contain her shock. 'But why curse Sati Ahalya? If Lord Indra came in the form of the sage himself, how would she know that it was not her husband?'

Priyamvada was about to say something, when there was a sudden hush in the garden. They looked up to see the two sages enter the garden and take their seats. All eyes were on Sage Gautam, who was oblivious to the main cause of his attraction. Sage Kanva was pleasantly surprised to see such a gathering and raised his hand to silence all who had started whispering amongst themselves, especially the women.

Shakuntala was still lost in her thoughts. Why was Sati Ahalya cursed for no fault of hers, or did she know the real identity of the imposter? Could that be possible? Just why was she cursed to turn into stone, while the lord of the gods was allowed to go with just a minor curse, as the sahasrayoni was changed to sahasraksh?

The discourse had begun, and on the request of Sage Kanva, Sage Gautam began to explain what he referred to as the Dharmashastra, the treatise he was working on. He delved on some of the norms that were necessary for the seamless running of society, like the behaviour of a student who is pursuing knowledge, the conduct of people during different stages of their life, issues pertaining to marriage, property and the norms of inheritance. Some of the things weren't of much importance to the people of the ashram and many were mentally elsewhere. For many a scene of the sage cursing his wife, dominated their mind's eye.

Shakuntala, for the first time, heard nothing of what the sage had to say. She neither participated in the discourse, nor did she have any queries. This did seem a trifle odd to Sage Kanva, who always took pride in the intelligent queries of Shakuntala, as he felt that he had given the girl an education that enabled her to ask the right questions. But his daughter seemed lost today. She was staring at the sage, but seemed to be elsewhere, lost in her thoughts.

The discourse went on till late and soon the crowd started dispersing, with only the learned and interested remaining close to the platform. Their initial curiosity having been satisfied, many had left much earlier. For the first time Shakuntala also left along with her friends before the discourse was over, and this seemed very strange to Sage Kanva. He knew something was bothering his daughter and he needed to know what it was.

Sati Ahalya

After dinner was served to Sage Gautam and his disciples, they retired to the cottage reserved for the guests. Dinner was arranged early as the guests were to leave before dawn the next day. Sage Kanva noticed that Shakuntala was not as enthusiastic in serving the visitors as she had been in the morning. After the guests had retired and all the work was done, Shakuntala sat outside on the swing, with Mrigakshi playing nearby.

Shakuntala didn't notice her father approaching her. She was startled when she heard him say, 'Is everything all right, my child?' Shakuntala stopped the swing and moved aside to allow him to sit. She knew that her father had observed her confusion as nothing was ever hidden from him. Needless to say, Shakuntala never found it necessary to hide her feelings from her father.

Sage Kanva was saying, 'Something seems to be bothering you my child, do you want to talk about it?' Shakuntala looked at him, wondering if the sage would understand her confusion. She nodded but kept quiet. Sage Kanva knew that Shakuntala would speak only when she was ready and prodding would not work.

Shakuntala turned to her father and asked, 'Were you aware of the sage having cursed his wife because of the wrongdoing of a god?'

Sage Kanva's expressions changed, but he replied calmly, 'Yes, my child, I am aware of it.'

Shakuntala asked, 'Is he a good friend of yours?'

Sage Kanva was a bit surprised with this question, but said, 'I have immense respect for the sage.'

'Was it fair to Sati Ahalya?' blurted out Shakuntala, not able to hold herself any more.

'What was fair or unfair, my child?' Sage Kanva asked. Shakuntala knew that her father was leading her to something.

'Being cursed to become a stone due to the fault of a divine being,' Shakuntala spat the words out.

Sage Kanva was smiling. 'I hope you are feeling better now, my dear!' said the sage. Shakuntala did feel better after voicing her angry thoughts.

Sage Kanva said, 'Nothing can control destiny, my child. Sati Ahalya was chaste, but to see one's wife in the arms of another man might have been too much even for a sage. While Sage Gautam did curse the lord, he couldn't help being angry with his wife.'

Shakuntala was not satisfied. 'But she was not at fault. She did not know that the man was not her husband.'

'That is what you feel, my dear,' said a calm Sage Kanva to the utter surprise of Shakuntala.

'What do you mean, Father? Are you saying that Sati Ahalya was aware of the lord's identity, rather, are you saying that she knew that the person was actually not her husband?' asked Shakuntala.

Sage Kanva said calmly, 'I am not saying anything. I am only commenting. Sati Ahalya was a creation of Lord Brahma, the creator of the Universe. She was ayonija-sambhava, one who was not born of a woman. She was created out of all the beautiful things that the Supreme Creator had created and given to Sage Gautam to be raised. The sage returned her to Lord Brahma when Ahalya came of age. The Creator, impressed by Sage Gautam's ability to resist the temptation of such a divine beauty, gave her in marriage to him. It is said that the lord of the rains was very disappointed, as he was of the opinion that all beauties were made for him! My point is that here was a learned man, who had seen this lady from her birth till her coming of age. He knew her better than she knew herself? Shakuntala listening to her father felt uncomfortable with the last words—how could anybody know somebody better than the person herself? But her father was speaking, so she reserved the thought for later and paid attention.

'Chastity is not a physical aspect, my child. It has to do with the purity of the mind too. While I do agree that there was a huge difference in the ages of the sage and his wife, one shouldn't overlook the fact that they were man and wife, and at the behest of none other than the Creator Himself. Being a manasa-putri of the Supreme Creator, it seems highly improbable that she did not see through the deception of a god. Carnal pleasures are for satiation, but not with somebody who is not the rightful partner. Sati Ahalya was aware of her husband's daily routine and to expect him to crave for bodily pleasure at the brahma-muhurta when the union of man and woman is forbidden was out of character of a seer like Sage Gautam; and a woman who had spent a lifetime with a person, ought to have known that. Further, Indra was a divine being with no physical form and a bearer of divine perfume that emanates from every divine body. The presence of any divinity fills the atmosphere with an aroma that none can miss. How did she not recognise the aroma from the smell of the sage's body, both of which were very undoubtedly different? Thus, my statement, raising doubt that she didn't know that the imposter was none other than Lord Indra and not her husband. My dear, we are not talking of any ordinary mortal here, we are referring to a Brahma kumari!'

Shakuntala was not prepared to be convinced. 'So are you saying that she was a willing partner in the act?'

Sage Kanva was uncomfortable discussing the matter further, but it was important for his daughter to get the right message as she was at the threshold of life. He said, 'I am not casting aspersions on her character, as we are too insignificant to talk about it. But human blood, which flows in man, can at times come to a boil, making humans do things that were not meant to be done, leading to repentance of a lifetime.'

Shakuntala looked straight at her father and said, 'But I thought we were talking of learned men, Brahma-kumaris and gods weren't we?' The sarcasm was not lost on Sage Kanva, who perceived his inability to justify what had happened.

'Even if we overlook that aspect, what I can see is that it was only Sati Ahalya who seems to have been punished. Indra who committed the crime didn't have to undergo anything severe, except some marks on the body!' said Shakuntala, clearly indicating that she still had a point or two to make.

'Well, that might be true, and there could be a reason for it,' said the sage. 'The lord of rains made it seem that he was compelled to do so as the sage was becoming too powerful through his penances; to make him commit such acts of cursing took his virtues away from him and reduced his power to an extent. The other gods agreed with his argument and thus his curse was mitigated or reduced,' the sage continued, 'and let us not mix the standards of gods with mortals.'

'I guess we cannot, for very clearly the standards are tilted in favour of the gods, as I see it!' said Shakuntala.

The sage did not quite like her attitude, but reprimanding at this stage would vitiate the argument, so he allowed it to pass. 'Also, the stony inertness,' continued the sage, 'was not quite in the physical sense.'

Shakuntala looked up, confused. The sage said, 'What I mean is that her inertness was symbolic of the fact that she had lost her position as the only beautiful woman on earth. The beauty which was the cause of Indra's temptation, would now be spread amongst all the women on earth and would not be exclusive to Devi Ahalya.'

And probably give greater choice to the lord of the skies, I presume, thought Shakuntala, but said aloud, 'So for the crime of Indra, the lady was made less beautiful! Is this justice?' The sage was beginning to see his daughter's perspective.

Something else came to her mind. 'Isn't there something more sinister at play, Father?'

'Sinister?' quizzed the sage, wondering just where this was going.

Wasn't Devi Ahalya a pawn in this war between…' Shakuntala faltered, as she seemed to be debating the thought in her mind.

'Go on, my dear,' the sage encouraged her, 'tell me, what's in your mind?'

'I don't know, there is something else here; something beyond a simple curse and punishment,' said Shakuntala, trying to put an elusive thought into words.

'However, what I am unable to accept is the relatively lesser quantum of punishment for Indra,' she said, still unable to string the elusive thread of the thought.

'Well, don't forget that he was the lord of the rains,' said the sage. 'Antagonizing him could have led to the withdrawal of waters from earth. While Sage Gautam was furious at this transgression, he had to give in to the collective entreaties of all. The sage couldn't have jeopardized the lifeline of all the residents of the earth, for what could be construed by the world as something personal.'

'You mean the collective entreaties of the gods, right?' Shakuntala was beginning to collect her thoughts.

'Yes,' said a bewildered Sage Kanva.

'The gods...' murmured Shakuntala.

The sage waited.

Shakuntala muttered, 'Was this a simple matter of crime and punishment or was there something else to it? Wasn't all this a class conflict of sorts? Lord Indra was perceived as a warrior god and a protector. The same role assigned to the Kshatriyas. Indra lusting for a sage's wife was to be seen as a powerful person exercising his power beyond the realm of his caste. Wasn't this being used as a message to the warrior class, i.e. the Kshatriyas, that no matter how great they became, they still remained unequal to the Brahmins? Wasn't this being used to send a message to them that the Brahmins had the power to put them in place in case of any transgression?' Shakuntala had collected her elusive thoughts.

She paused for her breath and shot the last arrow, 'And if this is not the message, maybe the message was that if you don't mend your ways, we will make things inaccessible to you. If you don't stop coming to our ponds, we will dry them up and ensure there is no water in the ponds for you to drink!'

Sage Kanva was shocked. He couldn't quite believe that his daughter had put a finger on something that many would not even like to think about, forget speak. From where did she get all these thoughts? Or was this her father's rebellious blood speaking through her?

'My dear,' tried Sage Kanva, 'just where are you taking this debate?'

'You haven't answered my question. Wasn't Sati Ahalya made a pawn in a class struggle for power?' insisted Shakuntala who firmly believed that she had just unearthed something that might have been at the back of her father's mind, except that he was not willing to give it a thought. The idea had been bothering her for quite a while, but now she could see it more clearly. The whole concept of this class struggle was at the bottom of many lives, and who but she could understand it better?

'My dear,' said the father, 'why are we debating about people who are not mere mortals, but divine or semi-divine? The ways of earthlings are different; we have to draw lessons from such acts and not debate. It's late now and the moon is planning to retire and make way for the sun in a few hours. It has been a long and tiring day and we have to rise early for the departure of Sage Gautam and his disciples. Go and rest,' implored the doting father, certain that the matter was far from over for his daughter.

Stony Inertness

Shakuntala might not have had the last word with her father, but something still didn't settle well with her. Her mind was in a state of conflict and agitation. She just couldn't understand the fault of the woman in question. She was aware that she had unsettled her father with some of her arguments. While that had not been the objective, she worried about her father's probable tacit support of Sage Gautam's act. She discussed with herself what she couldn't discuss with her father the whole night.

Ahalya was brought up by a sage and given in marriage to the him just because he could resist her temptation! What kind of reasoning was that? Sage Gautam had brought her up since her birth, so it was obvious that he was a father-figure to her. Wasn't a father or a father-figure expected to shower fatherly or parental affection on the girl he had taken charge of? How could the award for being a good father be to become a husband of the same child? What sort of divine justice was this, even if it was that of the Creator?

In all this, where did the little girl, now a woman, fit in? Just what must have gone through the mind of a woman when a man whom she respected as a father ended up being her husband? Didn't the Supreme Creator find it necessary to ask her if she wanted a husband who had been a father-figure to her? A supremely beautiful woman given in marriage to a much older ascetic, given to the pursuits of knowledge and at a stage when worldly pleasures were unimportant; wasn't this unfair? Father had always held that man had duties and responsibilities at every stage of his life. Man had a responsibility towards his wife during the stage of a householder; it was his duty to keep his wife and family happy. If that was so, was Ahalya happy? Did anybody ever find it necessary to understand what she may have been going through? Could a man for whom the act of sex was nothing but a ritual, satisfy the cravings of a youthful maiden? At the prime of her youth, she had to live with an old man, whose attention was elsewhere. A man who found satisfaction in books and treatises and not in the youthful arms of his divinely beautiful wife.

It was said that Lord Brahma created Ahalya to crush the pride of the apsaras, especially Urvashi. None had seen such divine beauty in a mortal other than Ahalya. Did the Supreme Creator take pains in creating this beauty to let her wither in the dry desert of an ascetic's ashram? Was she destined to wait for a husband whose priority was something else and whose age-imbalance led to a sense of deprivation in this young flower? When the owner of the flower neglected its bloom, wasn't it obvious that bees would swoon over this beautiful flower? And in such a state of momentary adulation, if the flower did allow the bee to have its nectar, was this unnatural? After all, the Creator had created both the flower and the bee, or was it that the only objective was to create something to counter Urvashi and once done, the Creator couldn't care much for the existence of his own creation? *Is that how fathers behave?*

If, for a moment, Ahalya knowingly gave in to the advances of the most handsome of all gods, was it a crime? Shouldn't this have been a reminder to the husband, that he had probably failed in his responsibility or was it too hard on the ego of a learned man? Was this a crime, and if it was, then why refer to her as Sati Ahalya, when Mahabhaga Ahalya, the most unfortunate Ahalya, would have been more appropriate! Was the act of giving in to the craving of the body a single time an act of adultery or was the act of sleeping with a man who was a father-figure for a woman since childhood so? Was this not an incestuous idea, even if there was no blood relation? Were relationships only of blood and not of mind?

Wasn't the curse of becoming a stone ironic in itself? She, who was known as Ahalya since birth, became unploughable only after the curse! She was cursed to be barren and lifeless like a stone only after she felt the most fertile in her life. She was made inert only after she was made to feel like a woman for the first time and probably the only time. How had the inertness changed after the curse, since, prior to that she was no different from a living stone? How had her life changed, except that in the current stage, she didn't have to breathe and due to the lack of feeling, she didn't have to undergo the trauma of a husband who was neglecting her and confining her in the moral clutches of matrimony? A lifeless matrimony where her husband was pursuing Goddess Saraswati and she was being pursued by Kamdev! A pain that could only be felt by someone bearing the burden of divine beauty, who had the blood of youth running in her veins and who had the ability to think that she deserved pleasures that were designed by the same Creator who created woman!

This might not be acceptable to people at large, but my sympathies are with the woman, who, I still feel, did no wrong, but bore the maximum brunt of the 'crime'. She was punished by a man because she exercised her individuality. Her single decision to yield to sexual curiosity was seen as an assertion of her femininity which was a threat to the patriarchal double standards where the co-offender male goes away with a minor punishment and the woman is punished for eons.

A message being sent to the world at large, I presume!

How would I have reacted if I never got an opportunity to express my feelings? Would I have resisted an unsuitable match, even if it was arranged for me by my father? Would I give in to the advances of a man who treated me like a woman, instead of a life of inertness in the wilderness of an ascetic? Why do I not feel guilty about such thoughts, when I know that my father might not approve of such ideas? Why do I feel that I need to take charge of my destiny before it does of me?

If the Creator can make mistakes with His daughter, could mortals not make bigger mistakes? Father sympathizes with Sage Gautam; could he end up committing such a folly or worse? Would I keep quiet and accept it as destiny or would I stand up and reject what my father proposes, whatever it is?

Lord, is this some sort of a test for me or am I just imagining? If such things happen to people who accept life as it comes, what would happen to people like me, who cannot accept such things as designs of destiny? If such things happen to chaste women like Sati Ahalya, what could happen to the likes of ordinary women like me?

These were clearly the last thoughts before sleep enveloped the tired Shakuntala.

Menaka was listening to the conversation of her daughter and her foster-father and was amazed at the clarity of thought of her daughter. She had grown up not only to be a lovely maiden, but was also the owner of a strong conscience and mind. Sage Kanva had fostered in her a sound ability to debate and express her mind. 'This is one quality that you will need on earth, my dear,' thought the teary-eyed Menaka. Men, though benevolent, were narrow-minded, when a woman expressed her views. To be able to defend herself in a world dominated by norms made by men was an ability her daughter would need. For a daughter, whose mother could be of no help and a father who never looked back, the world would be cruel. 'Oh lord, take care of my girl; she is a bud about to bloom.'

Priyamvada

The next few days saw a visibly changed and disturbed Shakuntala. There were hushed discussions about the visit of Sage Gautam, but nobody spoke of it openly. The inmates of the ashram were in awe of the treatise that he was writing, at least those who heard his discourse. The womenfolk went back to their usual life, their curiosity settled by his very sight. Everything was back to normal and soon, Sage Gautam was just another sage who had visited the ashram, like many others.

But not for Shakuntala. Something in her had changed, and she had suddenly grown up, or rather matured overnight. Sage Kanva could sense the change and decided to speak to her once again and see if he could help.

One morning, Shakuntala was watering the plants and shrubs around her cottage. Her doe Mrigakshi was trailing behind her, something that she did the whole day, no matter where Shakuntala went. Just then, Anusuya and Priyamvada came with their pitchers to take Shakuntala with them to fetch water from the river. Shakuntala stopped watering the plants and went in to fetch her pitcher and reappeared to find Anusuya giggling about something.

Shakuntala gave a questioning look, but just Anusuya couldn't stop giggling. On Shakuntala's insistence, she started to say something, but a stony look from Priyamvada stopped her. Shakuntala knew it was something to do with Priyamvada. On prodding, Anusuya said, 'Someone's coming to ask for

Priyamvada's hand in marriage.'

Shakuntala was all smiles. She looked at Priyamvada who seemed to be unhappy. Shakuntala asked her, 'Aren't you happy that you will be beginning a new life, something that you have been waiting for?'

Priyamvada did not reply. Shakuntala knew something was wrong and she continued, 'Is it because you have to leave us? Where is your husband from?'

Anusuya replied, 'He is from Hastinapur and is a priest in the palace temple. She is going to the big city of Hastinapur and is still not happy. Silly girl!'

Tears were beginning to fill Priyamvada's eyes and Shakuntala knew something was amiss. 'A priest at the palace temple? How old is he?' asked Shakuntala.

Priyamvada burst into tears uncontrollably. Anusuya was taken aback and realized that Priyamvada was quiet not because she was shy, but because she was sad. Shakuntala knew that she had to get to the bottom of the problem.

By now the three of them had reached the riverbank. They sat under a tree, one of their favourite places, till Priyamvada regained her composure. Between sobs she said, 'He is more than four decades old, a widower with daughters who are married. His fourth daughter was married just last year and now that he is lonely, he has decided to get married again. He earns well as the royal family of Hastinapur are religious and perform many yagnas and other rituals regularly.' After a pause she added, 'The old priest is already bedridden and after his death, my husband-to-be will become the chief priest. My parents are feeling honoured to receive the offer and have accepted it. Our marriage will take place after a few months as the rainy season is fast approaching after which the harvest will keep people busy. So, in all probability, the wedding will be after the winter season.'

Shakuntala was extremely agitated and stood up in anger. She didn't know how to react. Priyamvada's *own* parents were making mistakes? Could parents, one's own or otherwise, mortal or divine, never take a correct decision? Getting their daughter married to a man fit to be her father? Was this a marriage of love or was it just for satiating needs? The priest had daughters who were older than Priyamvada; how would she feel when they came to their father's place? How would they treat Priyamvada when they saw her in place of their mother? Would they be able to give her the same respect they gave to their mother? Was this fair?

Was the old priest looking for a partner or a maid...a nurse for his old age...?

Shakuntala was distressed and confused. Just what was the status of a girl in her ashram or even outside? Priyamvada was beautiful, she knew her scriptures well and was an extremely intelligent girl. She could have got married to a young and handsome man from the city and that would have made her happy. Did anyone care for girls and their happiness or were they just a responsibility to be executed, however and in whatever form? Shakuntala said, 'Have you expressed your disappointment with your parents' choice?'

Both Anusuya and Priyamvada looked at her in shock. Shakuntala maintained her poise and repeated, 'Have you expressed your disappointment? Have you told your parents that the person selected by them is as old as your own father? Just what are they thinking...trying to marry you to a much older, already married man?'

With an air of surety she suddenly said, 'I think I will speak to your father about this.'

Priyamvada implored, 'No please, don't even think of it. They have already informed everybody and, by the way, they have even discussed this with your father and he seemed quite happy with the match!'

Shakuntala looked at them in disbelief. 'Father knows about it and he has agreed to it? This is unbelievable! Let me speak to him!'

Priyamvada begged her, 'No, no, please don't say anything. Nobody will say anything to you but I will get into trouble. I think this is what is destined for me. God had this in store for me, what can you and I do?' and she started crying again.

The girls returned in silence sans the usual chattering. Priyamvada was resigned to her fate as it would be unthinkable to even speak to her parents about it, who had started celebrations for having found such a great match. Anusuya was apprehensive about her future and hoped she would get married to a young, well-to-do man. Shakuntala was beginning to lose faith in the older generation. She was worried about her future and keen to know what was in store for her. Would she be given as a gift to her own father? Would she be married off to an old man or would she be left with a curse all her life?

The future looked bleak. The following days saw the girls steadily losing all joy and mirth. There was no spring in their gait. There were no giggles and hush-hush conversations. The three met, but were lost in their own thoughts. Mrigakshi too could sense something amiss, but couldn't express herself. She would nudge Shakuntala, but fail to get the usual pat all the time.

One morning, a messenger arrived with a message for Sage Kanva. On reading the message, Sage Kanva called all the elders of the ashram. He explained to them that he had to travel to the ashram of Sage Gautam for some discourse which was to be attended by many seers who were working on a treatise together.

He had been invited to help Sage Gautam arrange the works and interpretations of different seers and collate them to form a final draft. He wanted Sharngarava and Sharadvata, his close disciples, to accompany him. He requested the other sages to take care of the hermitage in his absence as he wasn't sure how long he would be away.

Before leaving, he called Shakuntala and spent the entire evening with her. He spoke to her very softly sensing turbulence in her mind since the last conversation they'd had during the visit of Sage Gautam. Sage Kanva did observe that she was lost and tried to probe the reasons, but she was elusive this time and not as forthcoming as she usually was. He could sense the distance, but couldn't fathom the cause of it.

Sage Kanva decided to leave it there; he did not have much time to debate and discuss as he had to leave the next day. Shakuntala was arranging all that her father would need and he was busy with his documents, which he had been working on lately. Sage Kanva told her that he wouldn't be long and definitely not more than a month. Shakuntala had never stayed away from her father for so long. Sage Kanva had asked Priyamvada's parents to allow Priyamvada to come and sleep over at nights, as Gautami was old and not keeping well lately.

Sage Kanva left before dawn along with his disciples. Shakuntala rose to see them off along with quite a few of the members of the ashram. The rest of them left, but Shakuntala kept looking at the boat getting smaller and smaller, till it was just a speck on the horizon. Soon the horizon had the sun emerging as if to herald a new beginning. Well…every morning was a new beginning, wasn't it? Mrigakshi was getting edgy and tugging at Shakuntala's garment, which brought her back to ground. Mrigakshi was hungry and seeking her meal, thought Shakuntala, just as all the birds which must have assembled in her courtyard.

Shakuntala got up and walked towards the ashram. She turned around once to look at the rising sun, wondering why it seemed to be smiling at her. She had never seen the bright orange sun look so majestic and beautiful as it did today. The rising sun seemed to brighten up the gloom and darkness prevalent inside her for the last few days. It brought a kind of cheer in her and, before long, she was smiling. Mirgakshi welcomed this change with a spring in her gait, which Shakuntala realized she had seen after a long time.

The Peahen

With the sage gone, Shakuntala began to feel lonely; she didn't have much to do except for household chores which did not need too much of her attention. Suddenly, life seemed like a drag. Priyamvada and Anusuya had turned a trifle serious; Priyamvada due to her impending doomed matrimony and Anusuya due to her unknown future.

One afternoon, Shakuntala decided to go to the forest with Priyamvada and Anusuya to collect flowers for the evening aarti at the ashram. The idea was to get out of the ashram as all three of them were feeling stifled there. Out in the forest, it was beginning to cool and soft winds were blowing, heralding the onset of the monsoon, something the girls looked forward to.

After collecting the flowers that had fallen from trees, they decided to sit under a banyan tree for some time when they were disturbed by the sudden shrieking of peacocks. A couple of them started making mewing sounds. Both of them were getting louder by the moment, each puffing out its chest and strutting around shaking its tail. One lifted its train of feathers in a beautiful display showing off its plumes. Seeing this, the other lifted its train to offer an even better plumage. The array of colours on display was unbelievable and the view simply divine.

Both the peacocks started dancing as if to some divine tune. It was simply breathtaking. As soon as one lifted its train and turned around to show its full self, the other would follow suit and try to better the first one.

It was not that the girls had never seen peacocks dance in full regalia, but Shakuntala sensed that this was different. Somehow this wasn't the usual dancing of peacocks, as she felt that each was trying to outdo the other. It intrigued Shakuntala no end. A brilliant array of colours was splashed in front of them in a dazzling show of one-upmanship.

Suddenly, she sensed a movement behind the tree on her right and noticed a peahen sitting and observing the two. While the peahen seemed to be foraging, something told Shakuntala that she was also keenly watching the two. While the peacocks were busy outdoing each other, the peahen left the place disdainfully, as if she couldn't care to be a witness to such a brazen display of male vanity! As soon as she left, the peacocks stopped dancing and one of them flopped down, while the other followed the peahen.

Priyamvada understood what was happening and blushed. When Shakuntala asked her the cause of her smiling and blushing, Priyamvada explained amidst giggles, 'The two peacocks were dancing to impress the peahen. Each was trying to outdo the other, and the one who managed to impress the peahen got to "marry" her!'

'Marry?' blurted out Anusuya.

Both Priyamvada and Shakuntala laughed and said together, 'Yes, Anusuya, marry!'

They got up giggling to make their way back to the ashram and were a little distance away when it started to drizzle. By the time they reached the cottage it was raining heavily. All the children of the ashram had come out of their cottages and were dancing in the rain. Shakuntala and the girls too, decided to enjoy themselves in the rain, but Priyamvada's mother came and took her away.

This annoyed Anusuya and Shakuntala, but both didn't say anything.

Shakuntala sat on her swing and kept soaking in the rain. This rain was different; while the drops were hurting her skin, the cold winds seemed to burn her from within. What was this weird feeling? She had never felt like this before. Further, the burning sensation was not a painful experience, it was quite soothing! Suddenly she remembered the peacocks dancing. The thought made her feel something and she went inside her cottage.

She caught herself blushing when she saw her face in the mirror, and wondered why the rain and the peacocks dancing for the peahen had made her feel so.

When Priyamvada came at night, she wasn't as sprightly as she had been in the evening. She looked subdued and demure. 'What happened?' asked Shakuntala.

Priyamvada kept quiet and did not say anything. Finally, on Shakuntala's insisting, she said that her mother had scolded her for getting wet in the rains—she was not a child anymore. She was engaged to a priest and she had to behave like a lady now.

Shakuntala was furious. 'Just what does this mean? Shouldn't a girl enjoy nature's bounty just because she is engaged? Just where is this written and who has issued these diving restrictions? Father says that when there was nothing, the earth and the sky were in an eternal embrace. Their love for each other made them inseparable, till the gods separated the two to make space for other creatures of the world. Rains are an expression of the love of the sky for the earth. When earth is supposed to rejoice in the showering by her lover, why are girls not supposed to enjoy?' Priyamvada shed a few tears and said, 'I guess a lot more is going to change...who knows?'

The thought disturbed her, but Priyamvada did not seem to

mind and was beginning to align herself with her parents' plans for her future.

In her bed at night, Shakuntala thought, if a peahen had the choice of choosing her partner, which the peacocks had to work for, why had God not given this choice to mortals, who were supposedly the chosen ones? Why was a woman not considered to be intelligent enough to choose her partner, especially since the parents were prone to errors of judgement, as had been evident lately?

Her last vision, before she went off to sleep, was of the peahen walking off disdainfully.

King Dushyant

King Dushyant was in his vyayamshala, where he exercised every day. Only the king and a few of his chosen friends were allowed to exercise here. He possessed a well-toned body which had been worked upon meticulously. A look at him in his vyayamshala could entice any apsara from the heavens—a perfectly shaped body, with a broad chest and a narrow waist. The upper torso was supported by strong arms which could lift opponents in wrestling bouts with ease. He had long, lean, powerful legs. His muscles were bulging and his taut skin was glistening with sweat from the exercise.

The king never missed his exercise routine as he felt that a Kshatriya should never let his body loose; one never knew when one could be called to battle. If the Kshatriya was also a king then it became all the more imperative, as a good king was expected to lead from the front. Dushyant was trained in exercising his body and mind since early youth. Besides, he enjoyed the strict regimen, which he found a manly pursuit.

As Dushyant paused during the mace workout to shift sides from the left to the right, he caught his friend Bhadrak, the handsome prince, taking a break. Dushyant joked, 'Bhadrak, you have been resting ever since we walked in here!' much to the discomfort of Bhadrak and to the amusement of the rest. Bhadrak got up in a huff, gulped down some water straight from the pitcher and began his sit-ups. Dushyant smiled and said, 'When will you take a liking for this most important aspect of life, my dear Bhadrak?'

Bhadrak stopped and sat down. The rest of them laughed. Amish, the pure one, was observing all this with a smirk on his face and commented, 'O King Dushyant, why don't you spare him these morning rituals? It is not easy for him to rise in the mornings, especially after the hard work he does for the kingdom till late in the night!'

Bhadrak shot an irritated look at Amish and said, 'If you don't enjoy at this age, then when will you, my dear purity-personified Amish?'

Dushyant smiled and said, 'Well Amish, I do agree with Bhadrak on this. This is a time to enjoy and you are too far from merriment. I too work, but I never compromise on my entertainment. A tired and bored king cannot do justice to his subjects and I am sure you will agree with that.'

'But you do take time out for exercise, no matter how late you have been working or entertaining, right, my lord?' asked Amish while looking at Bhadrak. All were done except Bhadrak who was not going to complete what he had never begun!

Giri, the mountainous bodyguard of the king, stepped forward and wiped off the sweat from his body. The king then proceeded to a chamber, which was infused with aromatic and herbal fumes. He spent some time there, allowing the fumes to permeate his body before heading for a bath while Giri waited outside.

Next, the king met his friends for breakfast where they discussed all the matters which needed the king's attention. It was during a break that Bhadrak said, 'It has been a long time since we went on a hunting expedition. The clouds have begun to hover in the skies and if we don't start in a day or two, then we won't be able to go for the next three to four months as the chariots will get stuck in the slush and mud from the incessant rains.'

There was general agreement on the idea and soon plans were made to go on a hunting expedition. Court would be held on the fifth day from then and the king and his friends would leave for the hunt the next day. Generally the hunt lasted for about a fortnight, but this time, since the clouds had already appeared on the skies, they planned to return in a week.

The Rajguru, or royal priest, was not happy to learn about the expedition, especially as he felt it was ill-timed. The rains had already made an appearance and many animals would have just given birth. In such a situation if a cub or a mother got killed, then it would bring ill-fortune to the kingdom. Also, many a female species would not be able to run fast, giving the humans an unfair advantage. All in all, it was an inauspicious moment to leave the kingdom. Amish tried to reason with Dushyant, but the king had made up his mind and no one could stop him from venturing out on the expedition, which was his favourite pastime. Besides, Dushyant felt that the Rajguru had a pathological dislike to hunting which he termed as a blood sport. For him, all times were inopportune for hunting.

Dushyant felt very strongly towards hunting. According to him, such skills were an integral part of a Kshatriya. Besides keeping one away from the sin of idleness, it served as a useful means of preparation for war, especially when the kingdom had not been at war for quite some time. Hastinapur's fame as a powerful nation was leading to lack of war. Such manly pursuits and challenges which tested a Kshatriya's true blood was something the Rajguru would never understand. He was an expert in scriptures and other matters of wisdom; the art of warfare and preparation for the same was not his forte and Dushyant preferred to maintain this difference just the way it was.

On the decided day, the entourage left the capital city of Hastinapur, the land of elephants, for the forest on a hunting expedition.

The Hunt

Preparations for the royal hunt had begun. Along with the king and his friends—Bhadrak, Amish and few others—would be Giri, the bodyguard, and some foot soldiers. There would also be cooks, ration for a week or two, musicians and people needed to set up tents, etc. A couple of carts loaded with bows and arrows, spears, etc. were also part of the entourage, besides small bait like ducks, partridges, etc. It was quite a retinue that travelled with the king on a hunting expedition; though much smaller than what other kings took with them.

Dushyant found too many people a bother—a large group restricted movement and occupied too much space. The retinue had left a few days earlier than the king and his friends, so that the royal team could start hunting the day they arrived or early the next day.

Dushyant and his friends reached by dusk, and it was decided that they would venture out the next day. Abhay the fearless, who had gone ahead, had studied the area during the last few days. His prime responsibility was to track the prints and marks of different animals and understand their movement. He was an expert and seldom wrong in identifying the near-exact location of animals.

He brought in good tidings that evening. According to him, there were a few cubs and tigresses in the area besides wild boars, neelgais, deer, sambars, etc. Dushyant was especially fond of wild boars who were big and violent and did not tire easily. They were ferocious, and if wounded, jumped back at the attacker. Dushyant also had a weakness for deer—he loved chasing and catching them unawares, a skill in itself. Deer with antlers were his favourite, he used them as trophies; needless to say, he found hunting the male species more fascinating than the females, though he also understood that the female deer ran far swifter than the male as she did not have the antlers to hamper her speed.

An excited Dushyant was looking forward to the sunrise heralding an eventful day. More than the kill, he loved the adventure and the chase. He did not like to hunt if there was no chase. Unlike others, he would never kill an animal if it seemed too easy. To the surprise of many, he would leave his prey and then chase, giving the just-escaped animal a false sense of security and then hunt it down after a chase. It was his way of giving the animal a fair chance!

Unlike the others Dushyant ate light and drank little. He did not like a heavy head or an unsteady stomach on the day of the hunt. Food and wine could wait, the hunt could not. He also felt that hunters should have some discipline. An akheta had its own rules and could not be diluted in royal trappings.

Dushyant slept in his tent, with Giri stationed outside the tent. The soldiers had burnt green-grass with a concoction prepared by the royal vaidya, to ward mosquitoes and other such insects.

Dushyant woke up to the morning sounds of the forest which were music to his ears, so unlike the palace bustle that he was used to. He found Giri up and alert as usual. Dushyant had never found Giri unprepared for anything. He was always ready and agile, something which had been noticed by all. Giri was never found wanting in his duty, which was guarding the king. Dushyant always treated him like a friend, especially after Giri had saved his life from a ferocious tigress during a hunt. Had it not been for him, Dushyant would have been dead.

Dushyant kitted up and sent a soldier to round up the others. Soon all assembled for light refreshments before they left for the hunt early in the morning. Meanwhile, Abhay returned with the news that he had found some pug marks in the eastern end of the forest.

Dushyant made the plan. Six of them would go on horses, two each from three sides: Dushyant and Giri, Abhay and Amish and Bhadrak and Agneya. They would not gallop until they found the tracks. Accompanying each team would be four foot soldiers. Once the team had found the tracks, two of the foot soldiers would be sent to inform the other two teams to converge at the spot.

Dushyant never used baits to lure the animal, nor did he like to use the battle-technique of scaring the animals with noise towards the hunters. Such aids were a lazy man's way of hunting. Hunting, in his view, had to be akin to wild animals—without any undue advantage, except that of the human brain.

All were in agreement and soon preparations were afoot. The soldiers carried additional bows and arrows, spears, sticks, ropes, shields and some basic medicines prepared by the royal vaidya as first-aid for minor scratches or cuts and some antidotes for snake bites, poisonous plants, leeches, etc. A mild drizzle at night had made the ground soft, but it had also made the atmosphere a bit warm, as the earth was releasing all its latent heat. But none of this was bothering the hunters.

The foot soldiers were all dressed in green as it was good camouflage. The riders wore tight green shirts, which were specially designed for the hunt, and dhotis tied tightly instead of the usual flowing manner. Dushyant, however, wore nothing except a dhoti as he loved the feel of leaves and the rays of the sun on his body. He found the tight shirts an encumbrance and avoided them. His opinion was that his rugged body could easily bear such minor brushes with nature.

The teams left soon after sunrise as this was the time when the animals usually came out in search of food. They headed in the general direction that Abhay had pointed out before splitting from a particular point. Dushyant and Giri rode steadily to enable the foot soldiers to follow them at an easy pace. If they tired, then they would be not be able to run back to inform the others. The team of foot soldiers was a different lot; they were fit and healthy and were also experienced in hunting expeditions. They were treated well and if they were injured, they received full benefits till they recovered.

The weather seemed unusually hot and humid and they could see no signs of the marks on the ground spotted earlier by Abhay. After what seemed to be more than an hour, Dushyant was convinced that going ahead was a waste of time. Since they had started from the camp, they had seen no pug marks, nor any animals worth hunting. He did come across a few nilgais but was in no mood to hunt them as his mind was set for a tiger. Nilgais were an easy hunt and a delight for the entire team, as one nilgai was enough to feed them for a night. But, right now, Dushyant was not thinking about dinner. Dejected, they decided to turn back.

They had hardly covered half the distance back to camp, when they saw a foot soldier from Amish's team coming towards them. Amish and Abhay's team had seen fresh pug marks. Dushyant could sense his heart beating faster. He asked the soldier to double up with Giri and the three rode in the direction from where he had come. The others followed them.

They soon caught up with Amish and Abhay and fell to

discussing the strategy. Amish and Abhay were already carrying spears and shields. Dushyant and Giri also armed themselves with similar shields and spears. Bhadrak and Agneya were nowhere in sight. They decided not to wait too long and began following the trail. Dushyant's face mirrored Amish's and Abhay's excitement. They were trotting as softly as possible with the soft mud under the hoofs absorbing the noise, except for the occasional crackle of a dry leaf which had not got wet in the night's drizzle.

The trail had been going on for quite some time, but after a point the marks went missing. The sun was soon at the top of the head, a clear sign that the animals had retired as they seldom ventured out in the afternoon. The teams had gone deep into the jungle and so it was decided to abandon the hunt and head back to the camp.

While they were returning, they could hear the screams and shrill calls of birds, but nothing could lift their morale as they had not managed to kill anything. When they reached the camp, the mood was very upbeat, which surprised Dushyant and Amish.

They found Bhadrak smiling from ear to ear. He had killed a nilgai and the entire team was looking forward to dinner. An animal killed and cooked immediately always made for a sumptuous dinner, more so forest animals, as they had not grown fat in captivity. Their meat was taut and fat-free, always tastier than what was available back in the kingdom.

Dushyant couldn't hide his smile when he noticed the smirk on Bhadrak's face. Bhadrak was boastfully telling his story of how he chased the nilgai and kept shooting arrows till it fell down. A wounded nilgai usually doesn't give in easily and this one supposedly ran a few metres with two arrows stuck to its sides. Bhadrak allowed it to run and gave chase till it could run no further before shooting the final arrow, which felled the nilgai.

Dushyant had heard such tales before and was happy that at least the team was not dejected, and even if it was, dinner would lift their morale and keep them in good spirits the next day.

The lack of a hunt had dampened Dushyant's mood but he did not want to show it as it would reflect on the morale of the entire team. He did partake in the fun and frolic around the sumptuous dinner thanks to Bhadrak. The revelry would have continued for long, but for an unexpected shower that cut short the celebrations. Everybody retired for the night.

Dushyant was glad that the too-early celebrations were done, as it gave him enough time to rest for the next day. Lying on his couch, alone in his tent, he could feel the rain making him uneasy. He realized that he had never felt like this before. It was a feeling of loneliness and though the weather was turning cool, he found he was not being able to sleep well. Was it the lack of a hunt today? But that was not unusual as there had been times when he had not been able to hunt for days; what then was causing this uneasiness?

Some of the soldiers were playing music for entertainment. He realized that they were singing some folk song. The voice of the singer was floating across the breeze and the sounds of the rain. He strained his ears to listen, though the voices were occasionally muffled by the rain. From what he could hear, it was the song of a man who was lonely; a man pining for his beloved whom he missed during the rains.

The sky and earth were one
       Like you and me
They embraced each other
In love and never parted
   Like you and me

But the joy of lovers
Is never tolerated by the world
They separated the eternal lovers
The sky and earth were not one any more
Like you and me today

The need of bread has separated us
But today, today, I miss you
Like the sky does for his love

Rains are the sky's expression of love
Rains are sky's tears due to their separation
Rains are his way of releasing his emotions

But I?
I can't shed tears of sorrow
The sky's tears are absorbed by his love
The earth revels in joy and springs buds from her self
But you?
You don't even know I am pining for you
You are burning there as I am for you
Both are burning in the fire of separation
That this world has thrown us in

Earth and sky have been separated
But they meet through rains
We too have been separated
But when do we meet?
How do we meet, my love?
How do we meet?

Dushyant had never heard such a soulful rendering of a love song. At first, the song made him feel lonely. He was the king of mighty Hastinapur, the land of elephants, but had never felt powerless like this before. Was he pining for a partner or was this momentary? The rains intensified one's loneliness, but the song was not just about loneliness; it was about love. The man's song brought gloom among the listeners. Soon the clapping and cheering stopped and it was just the soulful voice of the singer, laced with the melancholy of loneliness. He sang on and every line seemed to emphasize the singer's love for his lady and how the cool raindrops and the moist winds were only lighting a fire within the lover.

Dushyant lay awake for a long time listening to the love song and did not know when he dropped off to sleep.

The Second Day

Dushyant woke up early to realize that the sky had shed tears the whole night. The weather was unusually pleasant and when he stepped out of his tent, he could see nature in all its brilliance. The leaves, bathed in raindrops, were showing different shades of green, and the birds were out chirping animatedly as if to tell each other to hurry up and get some worms before the rains came back. The earth seemed gentler than yesterday, as if she was content after meeting her lover, but only for the moment. The clouds were still clinging to the sky, as if unwilling to part.

While all this had made the atmosphere cool and beautiful, it gave an idea to Dushyant. He had made up his mind that this was the right time for…he decided to wait till he met the others.

He was ready long before the others who were surprised to see Dushyant in unusually high spirits early in the morning. Amish knew that something was afoot in Dushyant's mind the moment he saw a glow on his face, which he had seen before.

As soon as they settled down, Amish said smiling, 'So what is on your mind, O mighty king?' Dushyant smiled back, biding his time. The others waited while a soldier brought in some fresh fruits and juice and left it in the centre. Dushyant asked about Bhadrak, only to be told that he was not feeling well. Everybody laughed out loud as they all knew that his hunt was over with just one kill. Bhadrak loved the outing more than hunting, and if he had a kill on the first day, then he would just laze around for the rest of the days, basking in the glory of his early hunt!

The laughter ceased and they all looked at Dushyant, waiting for him to speak. Dushyant smiled and said, 'All right, let me tell you what I have in mind. Today we will hunt deer.'

Amish looked surprised, 'Deer?'

Dushyant replied, 'Yes, my friend, deer. Today is the right day for deer-hunting. As you know, deer have very sharp hearing and a strong sense of smell. But the rains have made the ground soft, so there will be no crackle of dry leaves to alert them. Also, the moistness in the air and the light wind will keep our smell from travelling well. Deer are also quite confused in the rains due to the unfamiliar sounds that crop up, like raindrops falling on the leaves and ground etc. This is the right time to hunt deer.'

Dushyant continued, 'Don't forget that the cool weather will have hordes of them out in the morning as they sense weather change must faster than many other animals. Deer don't like the sun much as the sunlight hurts their eyes, due to the odd placement of their eyes on their heads. The chances of the sun burning bright today seem to be less, which will give us more time to hunt them.'

Abhay nodded in agreement and said, 'Also, this place is full of sambars and as we all know sambar males have antlers!' He said this looking at Dushyant—all of them were familiar with his craving for antler-heads as trophies.

Agneya added, 'And the females run swifter than the males, which makes it a more thrilling chase!'

Dushyant could see that all were in agreement, except Amish who seemed to be lost in thought. They all looked at him. Amish knew that they were asking him for his opinion and he said, 'While I am not in dispute with Dushyant's reasoning, I want all of us to remember that this is also the time when some of the females give birth or have given birth. Hunting deer at this time is not fair as we deprive both the mother and the fawn of each other at a very young age. Don't forget what the Rajguru had said, killing a mother or an expectant mother is not a good thing.'

Dushyant could sense a change in everyone's mood. He immediately said, 'While I am not sure if that old man knows much about hunting or animals beyond their names, we can do one thing. We will not hunt the females but go only for the males who are easily identifiable by their antlers. That should not be much of a problem, as the males don't stay in families.' While the others regained their boistrous spirits, Amish was calmly content as he could not agree more with Dushyant's reasoning. He was glad that they would not be hunting doe but just stags.

Soon everybody was dressed to leave. This time, there was a change in teams, as Bhadrak was not even awake. The sun was just beginning to make its presence felt as they were leaving. The team composition was more or less the same, Dushyant and Giri with a couple of foot soldiers, Amish and Agneya with two soldiers and Abhay with four soldiers. Abhay set out first with his team to spot the deer out in herds. On sighting, his team would send out a signal by blowing a whistle and the others would follow in the direction of the sound. These whistle-like instruments were to be blown in a particular tune, recognized by the teams, which did not disturb or alert the other animals. In the meantime, two soldiers from Abhay's team would head back for the other teams just in case they missed the whistle-message for any reason. However, Dushyant was sure that each team would find herds by themselves as he expected many to be out in the morning, and he was generally not wrong in his judgement on such matters.

Dushyant was excited and filled his quiver with arrows and

hung it on his shoulder. On Giri's insistence the foot soldiers carried a spear as the tigers would not know that the warriors were out to hunt deer only and that they would be spared for the day! Dushyant knew that it would not be out of place to expect a tiger or any other ferocious animal while they were on the lookout for deer.

The teams ventured in different directions in search of their hunt. Dushyant and Giri were followed by two foot soldiers and they were treading with caution. The horses were made to trot slowly, so that they made minimal sound, as any noise was high enough to alert the deer. Generally the soft ground due to the overnight rains had made things easy but precaution was important for all hunters. The soldiers proceeded slowly as they were carrying a load of arrows, though the quivers of both Giri and Dushyant were full. Dushyant was scanning the forest, keen not to miss the sight of a deer or a stag, while his ears were trying to hear any sound that would give away the presence of the hunted animals.

They had not gone very far when Giri noticed some deer scat. Dushyant's face lit up. He immediately got off his horse and bent down to take a closer look. It seemed fresh, which meant that the deer were somewhere close by. Dushyant also knew that deer were prone to return to the same place they had crossed earlier. By now, Giri had also alighted from his horse and all of them were looking around to find some more signs of the deer or a herd. Since there wasn't too much of scat to be seen, they concluded that it was not a herd, but just one or two deer. Dushyant was keen to know if it was a deer or a stag and wondered if it would be an antlered one, but alas, such things could not be concluded from mere deer scat!

Seeing Dushyant treading cautiously, all of them did the same.

One of the soldiers was left with the horses, as Dushyant wanted to scan the area by foot. Dushyant, Giri and the other soldier started looking around and headed in different directions, keeping a keen watch on the other members of the team. Giri, however, was keeping a watch on Dushyant more than the deer, as he never mixed duty with recreation. The only reason he ventured to look for the deer was to ensure his master got the kill and also to ensure that there were no dangerous animals lurking nearby.

Dushyant could see more scat in the direction he was heading and was sure that he was going in the right direction. He could hear his heart beat louder, sweat was beginning to trickle down his temples and his muscles were responding to the excitement signalled by the brain. He was ready for a chase and was looking forward to his trophy, the antlered head of a stag!

Dushyant went in the direction his instinct drove him. Soon he heard some movement to his left. He stopped and waited quietly. He knew it was important to be patient and not react to the slightest sound. Time had stopped and he didn't know how long he stood motionless, except for his eyes which scanned the area ceaselessly, till he heard the sound again. He was sure there was an animal nearby. After some time, he saw something emerge which seemed like the ear of a deer. A deer's ear rotates towards the direction of the sound, and Dushyant could see something similar in the direction that he was standing. He resisted the temptation to shoot as it would be of no use till the deer emerged from of the bushes. It was important to understand the size of the deer and ideally, the deer had be shot in its breast, the most vulnerable spot. But a fleeing deer could be hit anywhere to immobilize it. While he was thinking all this, Dushyant could see some movement behind the bushes and a slight glance upwards brought the antlers into vision!

Dushyant knew that an antlered deer was a full-grown deer. He took an arrow and slowly aimed about a foot behind the head, to get a shot at the body. No sooner had the arrow left his bow that the deer surged ahead. The arrow had missed its target and the stag was calling for a chase. Dushyant sprang from his hiding and chased it on foot. Chasing an antlered stag was not the same as chasing any deer, as the antlers were a huge hindrance and thus restricted its movement in a dense forest like this. Dushyant shot a few more arrows while running, something that he had mastered when he learnt archery, but the deer was a formidable runner in its own right. A tough chase was a hunter's delight and Dushyant was up to it.

The chase continued for a long time, and Dushyant didn't even realize that he was all alone; he had left Giri somewhere behind, the least of his concerns then. The stag hid behind a heavy bush and then there was no sound. Dushyant stopped, and felt for his dagger in its sweat-drenched holder at his waist. He trod softly towards the bushes, with his hand firmly on his dagger. Just when he reached the bushes, the stag dashed off towards an opening right behind the thick bushes.

Dushyant jumped over the bushes and bruised his back, but he was in no mood to give up the chase. Soon the stag was lost, leaving Dushyant blaming himself for being hasty. He was walking towards the opening, when he saw a deer under a tree, oblivious of the hunter. Dushyant was in two minds whether to shoot or not, when purely by instinct, he began to ready his bow. He rubbed his sweat-laden hands on his garment which was none too dry, and tried to hold the bow from slipping. He drew an arrow and was about to shoot, when he heard, 'Stop!'

Shakuntala

'Don't shoot,' shouted Shakuntala. Dushyant saw a girl standing next to the deer and guarding it while looking at him angrily. She was a girl of unbelievable beauty, dressed in white. Her face was glowing in anger, her eyes flashing fire and her expression raining contempt and disgust towards Dushyant, who had not moved an inch and was still in the same position when his arrow was about to leave the bow. Dushyant had never seen such a fiery beauty in his life. While the deer did not move an inch and felt absolutely secure in the presence of the girl, Dushyant was both angry and amazed at the scene unravelling in front of him.

Shakuntala patted the deer and poured some water from her pitcher which the deer drank naturally. She still had a look of disgust and anger. Dushyant was transfixed and realized that he had been in the about-to-shoot position for a bit too long now and lowered his bow and arrow. He tried to say something, but was too shocked to have been stopped in such a manner.

'How dare you hunt in this area?' asked Shakuntala angrily, and added as an afterthought, 'for that matter anywhere?'

Dushyant was now beginning to feel angry and retorted, 'How dare you stop me from hunting?'

Shakuntala shot a sharp look at him, and said, 'How dare I stop you, or how dare you hunt here? I asked you a question first and this is not an answer to my question, young man!'

Dushyant could not believe his ears. He had never been

rebuked by someone like this before. His face, already glowing after the chase, was now turning red. Just when he tried to answer, he heard, 'While I normally don't offer water to hunters, you look as if you could do with some. Would you like to drink some water, now that the life of a harmless deer has been spared and she has had her fill?' Dushyant's amazement just didn't cease. He bent down to drink. The water that Shakuntala poured into his cupped hands. Dushyant felt for the first time, that if there ever was nectar on earth, it must have tasted like the water he just had. All this while, he had not managed to take his eyes away from her.

She was not just beautiful, she seemed celestial. Her slender figure, draped in white, loose long black hair falling gracefully over her shoulders, her doe-like eyes, shapely nose and luscious lips over a long slim neck—she just didn't seem to be from the earth. She surely had to be what they called a forest-nymph.

After drinking the water, Dushyant stood up and said, 'Devi, you have no right to stop me from hunting.'

Shakuntala shot another look at him and said 'O, so the hunter has found his voice after drinking water! Do you lack basic gratitude? The least you could have done was to thank me for the water…what a waste of my decency!'

Before Dushyant could say anything, the sternness was back in her voice. 'Anyway, just who are you to teach me my rights, young man? I would have stopped even the king of Hastinapur, if I found him hunting in this area.' Dushyant's anger was now turning into amusement.

He said, 'Devi, how on earth could you stop the king of Hastinapur? This area belongs to him and no one can stop him from hunting in his own region.'

Shakuntala looked at him. 'This place does not belong to

him, it belongs to my father. My father has nurtured this entire place like his personal garden. In this forest, you won't find even a tiger hunting for deer or a lesser animal. No one sheds blood here…' and added, '…at least not animals!'

Dushyant decided to ignore the sarcasm and said, 'Just who is your father, if I may ask?'

Shakuntala looked at him and replied, 'My father is Sage Kanva.'

'Sage Kanva?' asked Dushyant. 'I didn't realize I had come so far'. He suddenly realized that he was alone, without his soldiers or Giri. He was sweating profusely but the cool breeze from the opening where they were standing was beginning to refresh him.

Shakuntala was still patting the deer, which was comfortable around her and had not once tried to run away. Dushyant asked, 'Is the ashram of the sage close by? I would like to meet him.'

Shakuntala replied, 'Why, what can a hunter have to do with my father?'

Dushyant smiled and said, 'Not a hunter, but a king maybe.'

Shakuntala looked up, startled. 'King, what king?'

Dushyant smiled. 'King of Hastinapur, devi. I am Dushyant, the king of Hastinapur and it would be my pleasure and honour to meet him.'

Shakuntala was both shocked and surprised. She let the deer free and was about to leave, when she heard him say, 'Don't leave, devi, I don't want to get lost in this jungle. Please lead me to your ashram, lest I kill another animal on the way, after all humans can't be trusted, right?' Shakuntala was blushing and tried to mumble an apology, but his eyes disarmed her and she blushed, which said it all.

She gestured to him to follow her. Dushyant could see the deer jumping all around the daughter of the sage. He was walking behind her and watching her every move. Her gait was coy and reminded him of a fawn. Her hair was flying in the breeze defying her constant efforts to hold it together. At last she managed to grab the unruly locks and make a knot, as if to say, they had to listen to her and not do what they pleased!

Soon Dushyant could see small huts and people at a distance. Some girls saw them approaching and came close to the daughter of the sage. She whispered something to them, and they all rushed back to the ashram. Within no time some old men, who looked like rishis came out to welcome them. In all the chaos, the daughter of the sage was lost and it was then that he realized that he had not even asked her name.

The eldest rishi welcomed him and he was soon ushered into a simply-furnished cottage. Soon water and some fruits were brought in. The rishi introduced himself as Rishi Dhananjaya and asked the reason for the king's arrival. Dushyant said that he had heard a lot about Sage Kanva and had thus come to meet him and seek his blessings. He also wanted to invite the sage to Hastinapur for a discourse at his court. There was immediate appreciation amongst the crowd that had formed miraculously. Rishi Dhananjaya informed the king that Sage Kanva was out of the ashram for some time but was expected soon. However, they would be honoured if he could stay at the ashram for a few days and be their guest. Dushyant's eyes were scanning the crowd ceaselessly for the daughter of the sage, but could not find her.

He immediately accepted the invitation and decided to stay back for a few days. Rishi Dhananjaya asked some of his disciples to make arrangements in the cottage for the monarch, while expressing his inability to provide royal arrangements. Dushyant was amused by his apology and said, 'Please treat me as one of you. I am tired of the royal arrangements and it would be my pleasure and honour to live the life of learned men like you. I would also be glad if I am not treated as a king, but just as another guest of Sage Kanva, less learned, though!' There were murmurs and smiles amongst the crowd, which was requested to disperse by the sage. Dushyant's humility was well appreciated by all who felt honoured by the visit of the king of the region.

Dushyant suddenly realized that he had no clothes, except the soiled ones he was wearing. He said, 'May I make one more request? I have left my clothes at the camp far away in the forest and don't intend to go back there for a few days! Perhaps I could be given one or two dhotis from the ashram for my stay here?' Rishi Dhananjaya was amused and smiled in acknowledgement.

Dushyant's eyes kept looking for the sage's daughter, but could not find her. It was rather strange, that she should go missing as soon as they entered the ashram.

Shakuntala

'You shouted at him? I can't believe this,' exclaimed a shocked Anusuya, to the utter embarrassment of Shakuntala.

'But I didn't know he was the king…and you know I don't like people who hunt in our region or anywhere for that matter,' said Shakuntala.

'But he is no ordinary hunter, my dear,' said Priyamvada who found the entire episode quite amusing.

Anusuya continued, 'I am told he is planning to stay for a few days as a guest of your father,' looking at Shakuntala.

Shakuntala was confused. 'But Father is not here, then what is the use of staying back?'

'Go tell him!' said Priyamvada, smiling at Shakuntala's confusion.

Anusuya giggled, 'Go tell him, Shakuntala, after all you have already scolded him once!' Shakuntala was beginning to get annoyed.

She got up to leave. 'Yes, I will tell him, I will tell him to leave and come back when Father returns and…'

Dushyant was standing right in front of her, 'And?' he repeated. He was looking nice and tidy, wearing a white dhoti with an upper garment which was worn like a robe, covering one arm and exposing the other. Obviously he did not know how to drape it the way rishis did. His long hair was touching his shoulders and his dark moustache gave him a distinct manliness.

Though his attire was from the ashram, his overbearing persona made him look different and definitely like an outsider.

The girls stopped giggling. Shakuntala was staring at his face, which was incredibly handsome. Dushyant again said, 'And?'

Shakuntala realized that he had heard it all, and she was embarrassed. She fumbled, 'No, well, I er…well I was only telling them…'

Dushyant, aware of her embarrassment, added to her troubles by repeating, 'Telling them what, devi?'

'Shakuntala…' prompted Anusuya from behind.

Dushyant's face lit up, 'Shakuntala? What a lovely name!' Once again there were giggles, as Shakuntala lost her temper with the naughty Anusuya.

Dushyant repeated, 'Shakuntala, what a beautiful name. I am honoured to meet you lady, I mean Shakuntala, and I hope I am not causing you any trouble by staying at your ashram.' Shakuntala nodded.

Dushyant continued, 'It has been my desire since long to pay my respects to the great Sage Kanva and visit his ashram, which is truly a heaven on earth. However, if I am not welcome, I would like to leave.'

'You are more than welcome, sire, and we too are honoured to have you as a guest in our ashram,' Priyamvada said quickly. 'We are at your service and please treat this ashram as your own. We might not be able to offer you palatial comfort, but will ensure that this place is an experience for you.'

Shakuntala was surprised by Priyamavada's words. Dushyant was pleased to hear this and gave her a questioning look. 'I am Priyamvada, this is our friend Anusuya and you have already met Shakuntala, the daughter of Sage Kanva,' said Priyamvada.

Dushyant replied, 'It's a privilege to meet all of you and yes,

I have met your friend Shakuntala. It was she who chastised me when I was hunting.' Shakuntala immediately said, 'I am sorry, I didn't know who you were.'

Dushyant smiled and replied, 'It's all right, Shakuntala, and I am not at all offended.' Her name coming from his rich, deep voice sounded so different.

The girls left and Dushyant went on. He was pleased to have met her, but suddenly something struck him. Sage Kanva was not married and this was known to one and all. Then how could Shakuntala be his daughter? He had to get to the bottom of this. He moved on, exploring the scenic beauty of the ashram. This sure was heaven on earth. He reached the riverside and soaked in the unearthly beauty. A gentle breeze passed through his coarse clothes making him feel cool and wonderful. The sun was about to set in the distant horizon, as his mind kept going back to the lovely Shakuntala. He had never seen such divine beauty in his life. As a king he had come across many maidens in his life, but none were comparable to this girl who had such a vibrant personality. In this ashram, she seemed to be one of a kind, someone who stood apart from the crowd. She seemed... well, words simply couldn't do justice to her beauty...

Dushyant saw the sun setting behind the river and realized it was getting dark; any later and he could get lost again, and this time, he did not want to get lost outside the ashram. He got up and retraced his steps towards Sage Karva's ashram.

The Camp

'It is getting dark and the king is missing. Giri, how on earth did you lose him?' asked a disturbed Amish. Giri explained that on seeing the deer scat, they had alighted from the horses and handed them to one of the soldiers to take care. Then, on the instructions of the king, they spread in three directions, though Giri kept a watch on where the king was going. Suddenly there was some rustling in one of the bushes and it seemed like a big animal. Giri immediately took out his spear and stopped, waiting for the animal to move from the bushes. His main concern was that whatever it was should not attack them. It was during this time that the king went ahead probably chasing some stag. When the movement ceased in the bushes, he decided to go closer. As soon as he did so, the animal dashed in the opposite direction. It was a huge nilgai. Giri was relieved, but when he turned, the king was missing and so was the soldier, who had headed in another direction, oblivious to the instructions given to him that he had to always remain close to the king.

Giri, frantically searching for the king, looked for foot marks, but could find none, no signs which could take him on the trail to the king. In this he must have lost a couple of hours, and when he realized that he had probably lost the king, he blew the whistle. Soon the other teams assembled, only to realize that it had nothing to do with the herd of deer, but that the king was missing. All of them spread out searching frantically but there was no sign of the king. It was getting dark, so they decided to go back to the camp, just in case Dushyant had returned.

When they reached the camp, they found Bhadrak in good spirits, awaiting the day's kill. But seeing everybody's face, he knew something was amiss. When he heard what had happened, he was concerned, too. Giri was feeling miserable and guilty and wanted to go out once again and look for the king. Everyone pacified him and convinced him that it was futile and dangerous to go looking for the king at that late hour. Dushyant could have strayed away somewhere but hopefully he was safe, at least that's what everyone was hoping and silently praying for.

The camp wore a concerned look. Amish took charge and made plans to send search teams in all directions the next day at dawn. Amish, Giri, Bhadrak, Abhay and Agneya, each would head in a different direction with one soldier each. The rest of them would stay back. Each of them would alert the others on receiving any news of Dushyant.

There were no celebrations that evening and everybody retired without a word. Giri stayed awake outside the tent of Dushyant till late and prayed silently that no harm had come upon the king. He was hoping Dushyant was safe and would be found hale and hearty the next morning. Giri could not sleep till he had some news of the king.

Dushyant

Night had fallen and Dushyant had just finished the most simple meal of his life. People were going their way and he longed to see Shakuntala once again. From the time he had returned to the ashram in the evening, he had been surrounded by men and old women of the ashram. All of them displayed concern and care, which he appreciated.

When Sage Dhananjaya left him at night, he wondered if it would be decent to ask for Shakuntala. Soon he saw the girl who was giggling in the morning and beckoned her. She came close hesitatingly and asked him if she could be of help.

Dushyant asked, 'Where is your friend, Shakuntala? I haven't seen her since evening.'

Anusuya smiled. 'Are you looking for her?'

Dushyant replied, 'I was just enquiring. After all, I must thank her for all that she is doing on behalf of her father.'

Anusuya was amused and said, 'Well, you should…after all she has been busy all evening preparing your meals, and ensuring that your stay is comfortable.'

Dushyant was pleased to hear this and said, 'So can I meet her now, or would that be out of place?'

Anusuya said, 'Why should it be out of place? She will be coming by before you retire for the day, else I will tell her that Your Majesty wants to see her!'

'Oh please, don't say that and please don't address me as

"Majesty," said Dushyant. Anusuya left, giggling.

Dushyant found her giggling slightly irritating, but knew that he would have to put up with such silly characters, as the people in the ashram were not used to his kind. But he hoped she would pass on his message and he would get to see Shakuntala. *Oh what a pretty name*, he thought.

Dushyant sat outside his cottage enjoying the solitude. There was something in the environment which made everything seem so undemanding. People here were simple and so was their lifestyle. No one bothered about protocol; men and women were going about with their tasks. Even animals seemed to be a family here. The ashram had cows, calves, peacocks, deer and all sorts of animals who moved around without bothering anybody, just as no one bothered them. The ashram was clean and the evening aarti was uplifting. He had attended many such aartis in the royal palace, but everything there was so elaborate and ostentatious. Here, everything just flowed, without any major chaotic scenes preceding such events. And above all, the singing was divine. The aarti sounded very different here, and it probably had to do with the clear pronunciation of each and every word. It seemed everybody understood each word of the aarti and sang with true devotion, instead of the ritual singing which he was so used to.

Though people kept reminding him that he was the king of Hastinapur, on his request, they were also trying to be normal. When he had arrived at the ashram, all sorts of people had come to his cottage to see him as if he was on display. Sage Dhananjaya tried his best to make light of the whole situation, but it took time to settle. However, by the evening Dushyant was feeling much better. It sure had been a tiring and eventful day. He wondered what his friends must be thinking of at the camp.

Just then he heard the voice he had been longing to hear,

'Did you call for me, Your Majesty?' It was Shakuntala. Dushyant stood up and said, 'Dushyant…my name is Dushyant, please call me by my name.' Shakuntala was standing there looking even more beautiful than she did in the morning.

He continued, 'Well, I did not quite call for you, but yes, I have been longing to meet you, er, I mean, I did desire to see you.' Shakuntala was amused to see the king of Hastinapur fumbling.

Both eat quietly for some time, till the call of a peacock broke the silence. 'Will you not sit for a while?' asked Dushyant.

She sat on the steps of the cottage and looked up at him. Dushyant sat on a higher step maintaining a safe distance. He said, 'I must thank you for all that you have been doing for me and I hope I am not being a bother by coming here in such a manner.'

Shakuntala nodded. She noticed that Dushyant was hesitating about something and asked, 'Is something the matter, Your Maje…I mean King Dushyant? You look a bit disturbed. Can I be of some help?'

Dushyant said, 'I have a personal question, but I don't want to seem invading into private matters.'

Shakuntala insisted, 'Please feel free to ask, and if I have an answer, I will do my best.'

Dushyant said, 'I was told that Sage Kanva was a celibate, but everyone here refers to you as his daughter. I am unable to make sense of this.'

Shakuntala's smile left her face and seeing the change in her expression, Dushyant said, 'You don't have to answer that, and let me apologize for asking the question. I am extremely sorry if this has disturbed you in any way.'

Shakuntala regained her composure and said, 'No, King Dushyant, let me answer your question. It is no great secret anyway and there is no cause for you to feel so sorry about it.

Sage Kanva is my foster-father. I am actually the daughter of King Kaushik, now Sage Vishwamitra and the apsara Menaka. I was found *abandoned* by my foster-father and since then he is the only father I know.'

Dushyant felt as if the word 'abandoned' was spat out of her mouth as if it was some bitter thing that had crept in, something unpalatable. However, there seemed to be no sadness in whatever she said, rather, he could feel a tinge of stoicism in the word. He was surprised to know that Shakuntala was the daughter of such a great king who was now a sage and understood where her looks had come from. Dushyant couldn't believe that the girl standing in front of him was the daughter of Sage Vishwamitra. The same sage who was well known and credited with the composition of the Gayatri Mantra, an incantation recited twice a day by every Brahmin. To think that this mantra was composed by a Kshatriya whose turning into a sage was a matter of huge debate and discussions!

Shakuntala was staring at him. 'Does that answer your question?'

Dushyant said, 'Devi, I am sorry if I have upset you with my question, but I nevertheless thank you for sharing your story as that question had been bothering me.' He found her smiling back at him, as if she already knew this and it was the only reason why she had answered his question.

There was a lull and Dushyant didn't want this to be the cause for her to leave. He said, 'So when is your father expected?'

Shakuntala replied, 'I don't know. He did send a message a couple of weeks back that he would return soon.' Silence reigned again. How could a conversation go on with only one party asking questions, wondered Dushyant? He was about to frame another question, when he saw a doe nudging Shakuntala. She looked at it and then glanced at the king and said, 'This is my doe, Mrigakshi.' There was a sudden tightening of her facial expressions, as she continued, 'And this, Mrigakshi, is the king of Hastinapur. Stay away from him, as he doesn't quite like your kind!'

Dushyant didn't like the barb, but decided to overlook it. He smiled and looked at the doe, and replied, 'No Mrigakshi, that is not the case. Your mistress is talking about a hunter she met in the morning, I am not him! I am a changed man now, experiencing peace!'

Shakuntala looked up, bewildered, and then looked at the doe and said, 'So, ask the humble man, Mrigakshi, does he not know the hunter I met in the morning?'

Dushyant looked at Mrigakshi and said, 'Of course, I know the hunter. He was only doing what he had seen the gods do. Hunting has divine sanction and I was only following the path laid down by the gods.' Shakuntala threw a questioning look at Dushyant.

Dushyant continued, 'If according to you, hunting is a crime, then let me remind you that Lord Rudra is worshipped as the god of hunting amongst other things, besides being referred to as Mrigavyadha[C]. While this should not be seen as comparing myself with the lord, isn't it an indication that the lord approves of humans doing the same? After all if lessons are derived from their actions, I am not wrong in taking a cue from him, and why me, many others do it too. O Mrigakshi, what do you have to say to that?'

Shakuntala looked impressed and glancing at Mrigakshi said, 'Well Mrigakshi, the king is right in his information, but erroneous in its interpretation. Yes, Lord Rudra is known as Mrigavyadha and is depicted shooting a deer. But tell the king that the Mrigavyadha form of Lord Rudra was not about the justification of hunting, it was something else.'

'O Mrigakshi, it would be kind of your mistress to tell me more about it, at least my misunderstanding, if any, would be cleared,' urged Dushyant.

Shakuntala smiled and began, 'Lord Prajapati had created the universe all by himself. He then created his daughter, Rohini. Soon he fell in love with Rohini, much to her embarrassment. She tried to avoid his looks and took the form of a doe. When Lord Prajapati spotted her as a doe, he took the form of a deer and started chasing her. The other gods were shocked at the sight of a father chasing his daughter out of sheer lust. This was the most heinous crime that could have occurred at the beginning of mankind and civilization.

'All the gods got together and brought forth their most frightening aspect in the form of Lord Rudra to stop the act. Lord Rudra immediately shot an arrow through Prajapati, thus stopping the heinous act that could have occurred at the very foundation of civilization. Prajapati as the "mriga" or the deer, and Lord Rudra as the piercer or the hunter of the "mriga", is referred to as "Mrigavyadha".' Shakuntala looked at King Dushyant, who was staring at her, visibly impressed. She continued, 'O Mrigakshi, I hope the king would not misinterpret words of wisdom to suit himself the next time!'

Dushyant was beginning to enjoy this. He looked at the doe and said, 'Mrigakshi, a king is entitled to some entertainment. Hunting however, is not pure entertainment, it is a test of one's knowledge, concentration, patience and judgement. No test in life can give all this together. An able ruler of a vast kingdom like ours has to pass, or rather excel, in all of the above qualities. Would you like to have a king who is neither good at nor has no experience in any of the above? Tell me, Mrigakshi, speak up, O beautiful doe!'

Shakuntala shot a look at him, knowing that the last statement was not directed at Mrigakshi, but decided to overlook it. She said, 'Alas, times have come to such a state that kings have to practice killing mute and harmless animals to test their skills. Can't the royal class, who have access to so much of learning, devise new methods of testing their skills? Is wasting a life the only way to save more lives? What are we discussing, my dear Mrigakshi? What then will be the difference between a hungry tiger and a human being, except that the former hunts to stay alive, but the latter hunts to kill!'

Dushyant was taken aback by the vituperative statements that found their mark like arrows. He looked at Shakuntala and said, 'Hunting has a social cause too. We don't hunt everywhere. We hunt specific animals at specific locations. At the forests adjoining your ashram, we hunt deer and stags. Do you know why? Due to various reasons, there are no wolves in this region, which are the natural predators of deer. This leads to excessive deer population which spills over in the fields of the nearby villages and destroys their crops. To curb the wastage caused by them, we hunt and keep their population under control. Sometimes tigers and similar cats that turn man-eaters, need to be eliminated from the forests as there are many villages in the vicinity. Do you want children and women to become food for such animals? Do you want the agricultural produce of the farmers to be spoilt by a few over-populated members of the deer community?'

Shakuntala was quiet, she had never thought from that perspective. Dushyant continued, 'Just because I come with a team and hunt doesn't mean all hunts are for pleasure. Even so, if pleasure and task can be combined, what is the harm? While I do agree that I enjoy hunting, I don't hunt animals that are harmless. I don't hunt expectant animals or mothers with their cubs. Also, hunting is a sport which brings out aggression, a quality much needed during battles and wars. As a king, I have to kill men, if they are soldiers who belongs to the enemy camp. Such hunts make battle killings easier; else, I would be saddled with too much guilt in my mind and heart, making me a soft target for my enemies and a weak king.'

Shakuntala was not prepared for all that she heard. She tried to say something, but broke off when she saw a stern look on Dushyant's face. The initial impish look at the beginning of the conversation was long gone.

Shakuntala got up in silence and left with her doe following her.

Dushyant sat there till late.

Shakuntala couldn't sleep that night. She kept staring at the sky with the king's words reverberating in her mind. She had never thought beyond her ashram when it came to such things. She had never seen animals become a nuisance to the outside world. The fact that a harmless deer or a stag could cause a farmer so much harm was unconceivable for her. That a tiger could stray out of the forest and end up becoming a man-eater had never crossed her mind. Come to think of it, she had never ventured out of the ashram. She knew so much, but all her knowledge was something that had never been tested beyond the ashram. A king had varied duties. To keep himself ready to wage a war, he had to keep himself fit. Which king, who was a human first, could enjoy the sight of blood? But which king could avoid bloodshed if he had to be the saviour of his kingdom? If the subjects of a kingdom were feeling unsafe and insecure, the human within the king had to take a backseat. As a child, he must have been trained to get used to the blood and gore, so that when he grew up, he wouldn't turn his face away from his birth-duty, that of waging a war and if need be, taking human lives.

Shakuntala felt sorry for being unnecessarily sarcastic with someone who was so honest in his views. He seemed like a gentleman, who was both sincere in his apologies and appreciative of simplicity. As a king, he was enjoying the lack of royal trappings and was making all efforts to live the life of the ashram. He respected the elders and was equally at ease with the womenfolk. In the absence of her father, she ought to have resisted being so rude. *But how else would I have seen this sensitive side of the man, I mean, the king?* thought Shakuntala, blushing till she finally fell asleep.

As soon as she woke up in the morning, the first thought Shakuntala had was to make sure she apologized to the king for her rude behaviour of the previous night. The sun was yet to rise, but the birds were in a hurry to catch the worms that had stepped out of the earth. In their hurry, they were chirping animatedly as if discussing who would go first and get the most! Shakuntala gathered fruits and some fresh milk before letting off towards Dushyant's cottage.

On reaching there, she found the cottage empty. She looked around and wondered if Dushyant had left. Had she upset him so much? She was beginning to get worried. If Father came to know that she had upset the king, he would be very angry. She left the fruits and milk in the corner, covered them and set out to look for him.

She looked around the ashram, just in case he had ventured out for a walk. Soon she was out of the ashram, visibly disturbed by his absence. She hoped and prayed that he had not left. *Why was she so sad on his leaving?* Oh well, who would like a guest to leave abruptly, especially after being so rude to him the previous night? *Was that the only reason?* Oh come on, what else could it be? Her expressions were changing from blushing to worrying, all in varying degrees.

She was distraught by the time she reached the river, when she heard some splashing. She noticed it was Dushyant, swimming in the river and hid behind a banyan tree and watched him. He was the owner of an athletic and strong body. She had never seen anybody swim so well, with such swift yet smooth movements. He was at ease like a fish in the water. She must have been watching him secretly for a very long time, for by the time he stepped out of the water, the sun was out of its hiding and the rays lit up his wet body.

Water was trickling down Dushyant's body. She had never seen a man like this before. He had nothing on him, except for the dhoti which had been wound tight on his lower half, shortened to give him flexibility. The cloth seemed too short for his majestic frame. His long hair was pulled back and tied. His muscles were taut after the exercise in the water. She was surprised to see that though she was feeling shy she still wanted to keep watching him. There was neither guilt nor fear of any sort. Besides, she had never felt like this before. This man was different; he evoked some feelings in her which she was unable to understand.

Just then she saw that Dushyant had noticed her. He was a trifle embarrassed and immediately walked behind the bushes where he dried himself to emerge wearing fresh, dry clothes. Dushyant walked up to her and smiled, with the wet clothes in his hand. He had untied his wet hair and water was still tricking down his temple and shoulders. Shakuntala noticed that he was wearing small earrings which glittered. She also noticed that he had golden bands on his arms, which encircled his bulging muscles. There were golden bangles on his wrist too. Around his waist was a heavy yet elegant waistband. She also noticed thick anklets on his ankles, which were plain but seemed to be of gold. They betrayed his royalty in the plain white attire, besides the way he walked and smiled.

Dushyant was smiling at her. 'Is this the time that you also come to the river every day?'

Shakuntala had lost her voice; she was still staring at the man in front of her. Dushyant repeated his question, closely observing her discomfort. Shakuntala was embarrassed and said, 'Well no, actually I thought you had left and I came...' She knew she should not have said so the moment she did.

Dushyant persisted, 'In search of me? You came in search of me?' Shakuntala looked down at her feet, not knowing what to say.

'But why would I leave without informing anybody at the ashram, especially after enjoying such hospitality?' asked Dushyant.

Shakuntala blushed, but tried to explain, 'No, actually, I was worried that you might have been upset with my rude behaviour last night. I shouldn't have spoken to you the way I did and I wanted to apologize. You must...'

Her voice was muffled by his hand on her lips. 'Don't say it, devi, don't...' urged Dushyant. Shakuntala stepped back and Dushyant immediately withdrew his hand, realizing what he had done. He continued, 'You didn't say anything wrong. You said what was on your mind, and I appreciated your forthrightness. Maybe you were right...about killing animals. God made all of us the way He wanted to and didn't provide for anybody to take the life of a living creature uselessly. So who am I to kill a mute animal?'

Shakuntala was glad that she had managed to convince the

mighty king of Hastinapur to change his views on hunting. She smiled and looked down. Both stood there for sometime, till they realized that it had begun to drizzle. Shakuntala said, 'We should leave, as it is about to rain.'

Dushyant looked at the skies and said, 'Then I might want to stay back. I have never been able to enjoy the rain as a king.' Shakuntala smiled back and said nothing. 'Don't you like rain, devi?' he asked.

Shakuntala smiled and said, 'Shakuntala, please call me Shakuntala, I am no goddess. Yes, of course I love the rain, this is my favourite season. I love the sweet smell of the earth when raindrops fall on it. It reminds me of the longing of mother earth for the sky, I...' Dushyant was immediately reminded of the song he had heard in the camp last night, or was it the night before? Camp! Giri! Bhadrak!

'Is anything the matter?' asked Shakuntala on seeing the sudden change on Dushyant's face.

Dushyant said, 'You see, I came here all of a sudden. My friends and the soldiers would be worried about me. Is there a way I can send a message to my camp? Can someone deliver a message, if I give directions?'

Shakuntala smiled and said, 'Of course. I will speak to Rishi Dhananjaya and have someone deliver a message. But in that case, you will have to forego enjoying the rain for the moment!'

Both headed back to the camp.

Camp

Amish was pacing up and down inside his tent, looking extremely agitated. Giri had gone on search since the morning, a ritual he had been following since the previous day. The sun was out and there was no sign of either Giri or Dushyant. 'Just what could have happened is beyond me. No sign of Dushyant, and not a word from Giri. Have the heavens swallowed him or the earth? How can such a strong man vanish? More than twenty-four hours have passed and not a word from him. This is simply beyond me.'

Bhadrak and the others were sitting amidst a pall of gloom. Bhadrak murmured, 'What will we tell the royal family, what could have happened...'

'Oh please, Bhadrak,' yelled Amish, 'Dushyant has only gone missing, he is not de...' the word didn't escape his mouth. They all looked at each other and fell silent.

Bhadrak had been in a self-crucification mode since the previous night. He couldn't stop blaming himself for their predicament, as the hunting expedition was his idea. Giri hadn't uttered a word and nor had he eaten a morsel since he realized that Dushyant was missing. Everybody knew that Giri was feeling very guilty, as he felt it had happened due to his negligence. Amish was the only one who was holding fort and keeping some semblance of calmness, though this morning, it seemed to be eluding him too.

The soldiers were sitting idle, worrying and directionless. One of them had gone with Giri, but there was no news. The sun was peeping through the cloud cover, indicating that it was noon, when Giri returned drenched in perspiration due to humidity and stress. He sat down, quietly brooding outside Dushyant's tent.

They all stood staring at him, but none said a word. There was a deafening silence, which no one wanted to break.

'Is this the camp of the king of Hastinapur?' a voice startled everybody.

They all looked up to see two young boys with shaved heads who seemed to be students from an ashram. Giri sprang up as Amish went towards them, and said, 'Yes it is, but who are you?'

One of them replied, 'I am Shravan, and we have come from the ashram of Sage Kanva, which is a long distance from this place. King Dushyant has sent a message for Shri Amish. Can you please take us to him?'

Everybody's face lit up. Amish said, 'That's me,' extending his hand for the message. Shravan handed a parchment to Amish.

Amish courteously said, 'Please be seated, Shravan. Can somebody please offer them something to eat and drink? I will be right back.' He vanished inside Dushyant's tent with the others following him.

Inside, Amish unrolled the parchment and read aloud, 'Dear Amish, I wish to inform you and the others that I am staying at the ashram of Sage Kanva. I had got lost yesterday while chasing a stag. I will be staying here for a couple of days, since the sage is not in the ashram and will be back soon. I don't want any of you to come here, not even Giri, as these are very simple people and I don't want them to be overawed by our presence. More people would mean more arrangements for them, and I don't want to burden them anymore.'

'Please wait for me. We will return to Hastinapur together.'

All of them found their smiles miraculously, though Giri was not very amused. Amish patted Giri and said, 'Relax Giri, Dushyant is safe and from his letter, it seems he is happy. Sage Kanva is very renowned, and if Dushyant has decided to spend some time at his ashram, it will only do him good. Also, nothing can harm him in the ashram, so you needn't worry.' Giri forced a smile and kept quiet.

They all stepped out and headed towards Shravan and his companion, who were resting under a tree. They had not touched the refreshment offered to them and wanted to leave. Amish insisted that they at least drink something but the boys declined, saying that they were fasting. 'Is there a message for the king?' asked Shravan.

Amish said, 'Please tell him that we will wait till he returns, and we thank you for taking care of him. Please offer our respects to the sage on his return.'

The boys left and everybody at the camp felt relieved. Giri was not very happy, though he was relieved that the king was safe.

Ashram

At the ashram, Dushyant had been sitting outside his cottage after his meal. Sage Dhananjaya and the others had come and spent some time with him. They invited him to come in the evening for the aarti. They hoped that the food was to his liking. In the ashram, they always prepared simple food. They never had elaborate and spicy cooking. Celebrations were always marked by worships and yagnas or havans. Meals were always cooked by the womenfolk of the ashram, ably supported by the men. All workload within the ashram was shared by everybody. Only heavy things like moving and carrying were done by men, the rest of the work was shared by all.

Sage Dhananjaya said apologetically, 'Your Majesty, we never have guests who are royal like you. Our guests are generally sages and people who are the worshippers of Goddess Saraswati and thus we have never had to worry about their comfort beyond what they themselves were used to. But your case is different; thus we are confused when it comes to offering you meals, clothes, etc.'

Dushyant smiled and said, 'Please don't worry about me. I am very happy with everything and enjoying the simplicity. The royal comforts seem quite meaningless to me as here at the ashram, I feel so close to nature, something that I had never had the opportunity to appreciate. To see a bird perched on a branch from the window of my palace is far different from seeing it here at such close quarters. There the birds hardly sing, but here I have heard heavenly birdsong. Let me assure you, revered sage, if I were not a king and was not obliged to live in a palace, then I would definitely live here, amongst all of you.'

Sage Dhananjaya and the others were moved by the humility of the king. They left feeling reassured that the king of Hastinapur was comfortable and happy.

Dushyant's eyes started searching for Shakuntala. He had never seen anybody like her. Last night, after she had left, he found himself staring at the sky thinking about her. This morning, she seemed worried when she did not find him at his cottage. He was definitely surprised to see her at the riverside and embarrassed to find her staring when he stepped out of the water.

Why was he thinking about her? Since yesterday, from the time she had stopped him from shooting the doe, it was only her on his mind. Had he stayed back to meet the sage? What would he achieve by meeting him? Just then a shower brought him back to reality. He allowed the rain to drench him. The cold water running down his face seemed to make him uneasy. Something was wrong with this rain. It was making him anxious. Strangely, the cold water seemed to be burning him from inside. He stood there, without realizing that the shower had become heavy and he had not moved at all.

Suddenly he stepped off at a brisk pace, much to the amusement and curiosity of a few onlookers. He did not even notice when he walked right into a puddle, or when some children playing in the rain wished him. He was too preoccupied with his own thoughts. Now he found himself running and wondered what he was running from. He reached the river and jumped into it hoping that the water would cool him. He sat immersed in the river, with the rain splashing on him, but neither the rain nor the river could extinguish the fire within him, the fire called Shakuntala.

During the last two days, he had not been able to think of anything but her. He could not forget the way she had looked at him when she stopped him from shooting the deer; the way she looked at him when he spoke about the need to hunt for a king; the way she had stared at him when he stepped out of the river in the morning; the way her eyes searched for him when she passed by his cottage. Her doe-eyes seemed to have so much to say…those deeply penetrating but slightly melancholic eyes, which seemed to have their own story to tell. O, what eyes, what looks…if there was beauty on earth, then all of it was in Shakuntala. Her looks were celestial, divine.

Every passing moment was lighting a new fire in Dushyant. With every thought, he was getting more and more anxious. He was fighting with himself. A woman from the ashram had captivated him like never before. No one had ever managed to occupy his mind for so long and it seemed that the battle had just begun.

Dushyant didn't know how long he spent in the river, but the rain had become a drizzle. The sun was going to set soon. The waters had calmed down, and the sky was smiling at him. The birds were staring at him from the branches and chirping for the last time before they retired for the day. But they seemed to be telling him something.

On his way, drenched to the bones, he felt that the leaves and flowers were all smiling at him. They too seemed to be saying something to him. He entered the ashram, looking no different from the children who were returning home after enjoying the rain. A few students noticed him and looked amused to see the king of Hastinapur, shorn of all finery—except for his athletic build—look and behave like one of them.

Dushyant hurried towards his cottage. As soon as he entered, he found a fresh dhoti and upper garment with some additional clothes kept neatly on one side. Someone had noticed him getting wet, and knew he would need fresh clothes. Had she seen him leaving? What must she have thought of him?

Shakuntala

Shakuntala was picking flowers that had fallen to the ground for the evening aarti. But she seemed to have collected both flowers and leaves from the ground…she was lost elsewhere.

She realized that she was thinking of King Dushyant ever since she had seen him come out of the river. That majestic frame, those strong shoulders, that long black hair, the confident gait and the enigmatic smile, she had never seen a man like that before. The way he looked straight into her eyes always disarmed her. Every time they met, she felt as if he had taken away something from her. Every time she came back after meeting him, she felt she had lost something to him but didn't regret it at all.

She wanted to be left alone, to think only about this man. Why was she not feeling guilty about these feelings? Though she had never seen such a man or even felt like this about any man, she didn't sense anything wrong about it.

Her reverie was broken by a sudden shower. She stood there allowing the rain to soak her. She loved the rain but this time it were different. She stood there with her eyes shut, trying to feel every drop on her. The rain seemed to be telling her something… indicating something to her. She felt it trying to touch her, wake her up and open her eyes…telling her to see…

She opened her eyes. The shower was heavy and she saw the king walk by at a distance. Yes, that was King Dushyant. What was he doing in the rain, and where was he going? He didn't seem to have seen her or for that matter anyone around him.

She stood there staring into the distance. There was nobody around. She must have been standing there for too long and she felt the need to sit. She sat at the steps of her cottage and kept staring in the direction of the king.

What was the matter? What was she so preoccupied with the thoughts of a single person? She had never felt like this before. She had never let anything or anybody ever take such predominance in her mind. Then why was she making an exception for him. He was the king of Hastinapur, and who was she? A resident of an ashram, the daughter of an ascetic…well, not exactly…

These and many unasked questions disturbed her. Mrigakshi was nudging her, indicating that she was hungry. She shot a sharp glance at her and said, 'Stop disturbing me, Mrigakshi. Can't you see I am busy?' As soon as she uttered the word 'busy' she realized that she had been sitting there for long, doing nothing.

Mrigakshi had never seen Shakuntala shout or get irritated with her. She gave her a look of disappointment and went and sat to one side resting her head on her forelegs, staring at Shakuntala sorrowfully. Shakuntala realized that Mrigakshi was upset. She went close to her, but Mrigakshi turned away.

Shakuntala took her in her lap and said, 'Don't be upset with me, my dear. At least you need to try and understand my condition. I have never felt like this before and am not sure how to react. Should I be happy or should I be sad? Should I speak to someone or keep it to myself?' Mrigakshi gave her an understanding look. Shakuntala felt better that Mrigakshi was not hurt anymore and got up to fetch food for her.

She realized that the rain had stopped and looked in the direction where she had seen Dushyant go, but couldn't remember seeing him return. She saw Shravan carrying some wet wood.

She called him and gave him some instructions. He nodded and left the wood to return with some fresh clothes, neatly piled. Shakuntala gave a nod of approval, and Shravan went towards Dushyant's cottage to leave them there.

She realized that she hadn't prepared for the evening aarti. She had to change and make the garland for the aarti.

Aarti

Not too many people attended the evening aarti as it was drizzling. Also, many of the men were busy salvaging wood which had got wet in the shower, moving it into sheds as the sky seemed overcast and more rain was expected. It had to be done before it got completely dark. Some of the women were also busy helping the men, drying the cattle sheds where rain water had seeped in due to the downpour. Sage Dhananjaya was at the aarti along with some senior sages and they expected King Dushyant to come for the aarti too.

Shakuntala was present as she never missed the aarti. Anusuya was with her, though she had work and didn't want to come, but Shakuntala dragged her along since Priyamvada's mother would not let her go till her work was done.

Shakuntala and Anusuya were busy arranging everything, when Shakuntala noticed the king walking desultorily. He had dried himself, but was looking anxious. Was he unwell? Sage Dhananjaya approached him and enquired if he was feeling well, to which Dushyant answered in the affirmative.

The aarti began with Sage Dhananjaya leading them all. Anusuya noticed that Shakuntala was excessively fidgety. She could barely keep her eyes closed, a huge surprise for Anusuya. Right from childhood, she had always lost to Shakuntala in how long she could keep her eyes closed. During the aarti, Shakuntala's eyes seemed to be searching for something. Or was it someone?

She could feel a sense of tension.

Anusuya also noticed King Dushyant's anxious looks. He left as soon as the aarti was over after exchanging pleasantries with the seniors. Shakuntala stole a glance at King Dushyant but as soon as Anusuya caught her looking, she changed her direction. Anusuya smiled and caught her arm. Shakuntala shrieked, 'Anusuya, you are hurting me!'

Anusuya loosened her grip and said, 'Is it me hurting you, or is it someone else, Devi Shakuntala?' mimicking the king.

Shakuntala blushed and started to leave. Anusuya stopped her and said, 'Come with me, I have some work.'

'Where?' asked Shakuntala.

Anusuya said, 'Just follow me. Gautami Ma was enquiring about you and has asked me to bring you in the evening after the aarti. Let's go.' Shakuntala realized that she had not visited Gautami since the king had come to the ashram, but she didn't want to go now, as she wanted to find out if the king was unwell. *Anusuya was a stubborn girl*, she thought, as she followed her.

Anusuya's non-stop giggling was irritating Shakuntala but she kept quiet. On the way to Gautami's cottage, Anusuya suddenly took a turn and before she realized, they were standing outside King Dushyant's cottage, where the king was sitting outside, lost in thought. Anusuya's giggling alerted the king and he stood up. Shakuntala wanted to meet him, but was not prepared for this sudden encounter.

Anusuya bowed and said, 'Sage Dhananjaya asked us to enquire if there was anything specific that you would like to have for dinner.' Shakuntala was surprised by the question.

Dushyant was staring at Shakuntala. 'No, devi, nothing in particular. Please tell the sage not to worry about me, I am fine and I appreciate all his courtesy and attention. Please express my gratitude to him.' Thankfully, Anusuya had stopped giggling. She then nudged Shakuntala to say something who seemed to be at a loss for words.

Dushyant was staring at both of them wondering what they were there for, wishing Shakuntala had come alone.

Shakuntala found her voice. 'Is the king feeling well?'

Dushyant said, 'Yes, devi, I am fine. Why do you ask?'

She replied, 'Well, I noticed…I mean I saw Sage Dhananjaya enquiring about your health, so I was wondering…'

'Don't worry, devi. I am absolutely fine. In fact, I have never been better, and today…'

Anusuya picked it up. 'What is so great about today?'

Dushyant was caught off guard. 'I mean the rains, the river and the ashram's environment…it's all so different. I have never felt nature at such close quarters. It's not easy for a king to enjoy these simple pleasures in his palace, nor can he go swimming in rivers so naturally. That's what I meant by today.'

Anusuya smiled and looked at Shakuntala whose eyes were locked with the king's. They remained like this for some time while Anusuya kept switching her gaze from one to the other, without either of them noticing her. A call of the peacock disturbed the pair and Shakuntala and Anusuya bowed and excused themselves.

As soon as they left the king, they headed for Shakuntala's cottage. Anusuya kept turning back to see if the king was watching them, and she was amused to see that he was.

Her giggling resumed as soon as they reached the cottage, and she, said, 'Weren't we supposed to go and see Gautami Ma?'

Shakuntala realized that she had completely forgotten. She retorted, 'Why did you stop at the king's cottage then?'

Anusuya looked at her and said, 'Well, I wanted to see him. However, was I the only one who wanted to see him? Tell me, devi.'

Shakuntala was blushing, her cheeks had turned red.

Anusuya shrieked with laughter. 'So Devi Shakuntala is in love with King Dushyant!'

Shakuntala rushed to her to shut her mouth with her palm. 'Quiet silly, don't you dare say that aloud'.

Anusuya said, 'All right' and then whispered in Shakuntala's ear, 'Devi Shakuntala is in love with King Dushyant!' and started dancing in the middle of the cottage. Shakuntala hushed her again and slapped her on her shoulder. Anusuya yelled in pain but kept prancing around the room.

Shakuntala gained composure and requested Anusuya to sit quietly and listen to her, 'Listen to me, you silly Anusuya. You are wrong, there is nothing to it, at least from my end. And definitely nothing from his end too. After all, he is a king. There will be many princesses waiting for him…why will he fancy me?' Anusuya came close to her and said, 'You are silly, Devi Shakuntala. Can't you see? He is in love with you. He can't take his eyes off you, just as you can't. Have you seen him looking at you? During the entire aarti, he was watching you. The elders might not have noticed, but I did. You mean to say that he has no work in the kingdom and is here just to take a break? A king is enduring an ashram's lifestyle just to experience simplicity? Is something wrong with you? He is staying back just for you. And you, my dear…one look at you is enough to know that you are in love!'

Shakuntala explained to Anusuya that even if she accepted this theory to be true, it would lead her nowhere. A king could never marry a girl from an ashram. While she had also noticed what Anusuya had mentioned, she feared it was a temporary infatuation. He would overcome it as soon as he left the ashram and went back to his royal life. And above all, the two had nothing in common. He was of royal lineage and used to royal lifestyle and protocol, whereas she was a commoner, ignorant of the ways of life outside the ashram. She had never met anybody who led the life of a non-ascetic. She had never even stepped out of her ashram, leave alone dream of a palace. So, it just didn't seem practical at all. For all one knew, he was actually waiting to meet Sage Kanva!

Anusuya saw Shakuntala's point. Whoever had heard of a king getting married to an ordinary woman, even if she was as beautiful as Shakuntala? What if whatever she had said or observed was incorrect? Wouldn't they all land in trouble for even thinking such things? However, she couldn't help but ask, 'But tell me, dear, are you in love with him? Be honest and tell me, I promise, I will tell not tell anyone.'

Shakuntala blushed and avoided Anusuya's eyes. 'I think I am in love with him. He is so different...'

'Are you mad?' came the harsh voice of Priyamvada, who had walked in just when Anusuya had asked Shakuntala if she was in love.

Both Shakuntala and Anusuya looked up startled to see Priyamvada staring at them. She closed the door of the cottage, bolted it from inside and sat next to them. 'Are you mad, Shakuntala? Do you know who he is? He is the king of Hastinapur. The king! If he even gets to know about this, you could be put behind bars. It is sheer madness to think that he would ever reciprocate.'

Anusuya tried to explain the situation to Priyamvada, citing all that she had witnessed, but Priyamvada didn't believe her. A king would never fall for a commoner. Kings got married to princesses and these were not just marriages, they were alliances. Even if he agreed, the royal family and the people of Hastinapur would never agree to such an alliance. Priyamvada was always practical, in fact too practical for comfort. She had become more so after she had accepted her engagement as destiny.

Priyamvada continued, 'Everyone has been talking about his humility and simplicity, which are rare qualities in a king. He is used to royal lifestyle but is equally at ease with the austere lifestyle of an ashram. While all this is true, it is too much to believe that he has fallen in love with someone like Shakuntala. Don't get me wrong, Shakuntala. You are beautiful and his life would be blessed to have you as his wife, but this is not reality. Reality is different. Girls from ashrams go to ashrams or to simple dwellings. They don't go to palaces as queens.'

Priyamvada realized that she had been too harsh and direct, but she knew Shakuntala didn't like diplomatic statements. She preferred frankness. However, Priyamvada did stop in her tracks when she saw Anusuya giving her angry looks. After a while she asked Shakuntala, 'Has he said anything to you which gives you the feeling that he might be in love with you?' Anusuya tried to intervene but Priyamvada stopped her, 'Let Shakuntala speak. You see romance even between two leaves if they are close enough!' Anusuya did not like the comment, but decided to keep quiet. Priyamvada looked at Shakuntala and repeated her question.

Shakuntala hung her head dejectedly in answer. 'There,' said Priyamvada, 'then how have both of you arrived to the conclusion that King Dushyant is in love?'

Anusuya said, 'May I speak now, Devi Cold-water? Have you seen the way he looks at Shakuntala? Even a blind person could tell that he is in love with her.'

Priyamvada replied, 'Only a blind person or someone with a fertile mind like yours can say it…no one else.'

Shakuntala was feeling uneasy. She had to stop this. She said, 'I think Priyamvada is right. Perhaps I am seeing stars on a dark cloudy night. I could be wrong so please keep this amongst the three of us. Let us not discuss this again, or ever.'

Anusuya was very angry with Priyamvada, but she agreed with Shakuntala. Anusuya and Priyamvada left, and just before leaving Priyamvada said, 'Shakuntala, I might not be able to come over tonight, as mother is not feeling well and I will have to stay back at home. Will you manage? Or should I ask someone else to come over?'

Shakuntala hastened to say, 'No, don't bother, I'll be fine.' She wanted to be left alone anyway.

Shakuntala grappled with her thoughts. Wasn't Priyamvada right? There was no match between her and the king. Hadn't she assumed too much? The king had not said anything which expressed his love; simply looking at someone in a particular way could not be concluded as love. What if she was wrong? However, she could not deny that she was definitely in love. What about that? Well, what about that? If she had fallen in love with the king of Hastinapur, it was not his fault and he didn't have to reciprocate. This was like the child crying for the moon!

Dushyant had been pacing up and down, unable to sleep. He had not been able to concentrate during the aarti too. When Shakuntala had come after the aarti, he was disappointed to see her with her friend. He had to tell her about his feelings. This couldn't go on for long...but would she reciprocate? Why not, what was wrong with him? After all he was the king of Hastinapur. But this girl was different...

Dushyant had been debating this since long and was now very tired. The rain, the walk to the river, the turmoil within him...all of this was making him weary. He tried to sit down, but every time he would sit, a new thought would make him get up and start pacing again. With every passing moment, he found himself wanting to see her alone. With every passing moment, his longing to see her again only increased. Dushyant had never felt like this before, and he realized that he was in love.

Was this love? Love and Dushyant? Oh yes, why not? Didn't kings fall in love? Was that such an obscure idea? Well not exactly, but Dushyant and love had been alien to each other till now. Couldn't this be different?

But what was the use of being in love and not proclaiming it to the person concerned? He got up and nearly said it aloud, 'I am going to tell her that I love her and propose marriage to her today.' He was already feeling better.

But what if she turned down the proposal?

Turn down the proposal of King Dushyant?

Well, if she did?

No she can't, I love her and will convince her of my love.

His thoughts were disturbed when he saw Shravan seeking permission to enter the cottage. He had brought dinner. Dushyant was disappointed to see him instead of Shakuntala and asked, 'Where is Devi Shakuntala?'

'She is not well, so she asked me to bring your dinner. Would there be anything else that you might require?' asked Shravan as if he was repeating a well-rehearsed text.

Had he been coached by Shakuntala? Was she avoiding him? Had she sensed his feelings for her? Oh lord, why did the mind have so many questions on matters of the heart? Why was this conflict between the mind and the heart tougher than wars on battlefields? Why was he unable to resolve this? Why was it so tough for him to speak to her about his feelings? But come what may, Dushyant decided he was going to speak to her.

On an impulse Dushyant got up and walked out of his cottage and soon found himself standing outside Shakuntala's cottage.

Having reached her courtyard, he developed cold feet. He decided to turn away, when he saw Shakuntala about to blow out the flame of her lamp. She must have noticed him as she came out of the cottage and said, 'King Dushyant? Is there something you need, anything I forgot?'

Dushyant hesitatingly said, 'Yes, I do…may I come in?'

Shakuntala stepped back and invited him to come in. She offered him a small stump of wood with a soft cover as a seat in the open space of her cottage and stood near the steps. Dushyant sat down in silence. Shakuntala stood nearby like a statue, without uttering a word, her mind in turmoil. He sure looked worried. Was he planning to leave for his kingdom?

'Won't you sit, Shakuntala?' asked Dushyant. She liked the way he uttered her name. She sat at a distance on the steps, waiting for him to say something.

'I need to speak to you about something,' said Dushyant. Shakuntala looked up and saw his worried face. He was still looking as radiant and handsome as he was in the morning, though she could sense something troubling him deeply.

'Shakuntala, I don't know how to say this as I have never said this to anybody before. I am not good at such things because I have spent more time with weapons than with a pen, but I still need to say this today.' Shakuntala's heart was pounding so loudy that she was worried that he would hear it. She held her breath and waited quietly.

'Shakuntala, I think…no, I am sure, yes I am. Shakuntala, I am in love with you. I have never seen a lady as beautiful, as radiant and as charming as you. You are beyond the princesses I have met and you are very different from all the royal women I have known. Please, will you marry me?'

Shakuntala's heart missed a beat. She was right. He was in

love with her. Her joy knew no bounds, she was about to look up, when she remembered Priyamvada's admonitions. How could a king marry a commoner? She remained silent.

Dushyant was expecting an answer. 'Say something, Shakuntala? Don't you like me? Wouldn't you like to marry me? Say something, dear.' Shakuntala loved the way he said *dear*.

Shakuntala found her voice and said through quivering lips, 'Let me tell you a story.' Dushyant was puzzled and was about to repeat his question, when he stopped. Shakuntala was looking into his eyes, her hand gesturing him to wait. She was going to tell her story. Shakuntala began…

Once upon a time in a forest, there lived a handsome deer. The deer kept to himself and never mixed with others. The others, too, left him alone.

One day, he heard something unusual—a beautiful song— something no one in the forest had ever heard before. He followed the direction of the song to find that it was being sung by a very beautiful nightingale, perched on the branch of a tree in full bloom. It was tough to decide what to appreciate more, the song or the singer.

This went on for a few days, but the deer never approached the nightingale, for he was not the only one watching her. The entire forest was there to listen to her and everyone seemed to be admiring her, though he came to listen only to the songs. The nightingale had seen the deer on the very first day and was flattered to have impressed such a young and handsome deer by her singing. While the others praised her singing, the deer never did. Days passed, but not once did the deer come close and say a few words.

The deer's arrogance and pride were beginning to irk the nightingale. She was beginning to feel that if the deer was young and handsome, then so was she beautiful. Then one day, she could take it no longer. She flew over to him and displayed her anger in no uncertain terms. She accused him of being arrogant and lacking the basic decency to appreciate something that was acknowledged by the entire forest.

The deer, with his head high, left without a word. The next day, when she sang, the deer was not there. He did not turn up for many days and the nightingale realized her folly. Her songs, too, seemed to have lost their beauty. When she could take his absence no longer, she set out to look for him. She found the deer near the brook. She apologized to him for her rude behaviour with tears in her eyes. The deer smiled and the smile said something to her. She knew that her anger and tears were relating the state of her heart. She was beginning to fall in love with him. The very idea made her blush and then she sang the song that mesmerized the whole forest. The song was simply divine.

The deer and the nightingale met every day near the brook and spent hours together. Time would stop during those hours and nothing else seemed to exist for them. She was madly in love with the deer and so was he. They would play near the brook, where the nightingale would flutter her feathers to sprinkle water on the deer. She loved the way he would shy away. She loved everything about him, his looks, his royal stride, his every move, his deep, penetrating eyes, except for one thing.

The deer had never professed his love for her. They spent hours together and she spoke of love, but he never spoke of his love for her, not once. This was beginning to worry her, though her friends told her that there was no doubt about the deer's love for her. It was visible in every move and every gesture of his. She had no reason to doubt. The nightingale also knew this to be true, but longed to hear him profess his love for her. She wanted to hear him say what the entire forest was talking about. She wanted to hear him say what she knew. She wanted to hear him say what *his eyes had been saying.*

Days became months; buds became flowers. Dry branches had grown leaves again, and there was romance everywhere. But the deer had still not said he loved her. The desire to hear him profess his love for her was eating into the nightingale and she could take it no longer. Though many found this too trivial, it was not so for the nightingale; for her it was a sign of the deer's arrogance and she was not willing to put up with it.

On the fatal day, she flew up to him and with her head high, displayed her anger in no uncertain terms. She chastised him for his arrogance and pride and declared that she wanted to have nothing to do with such a stubborn creature. The forest was shocked at the display of anger. It was not just the forest; it seemed as if even the gods were shocked to see the lovers part this way. There was an earth-shattering sound of lightning and darkness enveloped the earth. The deer stood there, watching the nightingale leave for the last time. He thanked God for showering raindrops to hide his tears from the world. Looking in the direction where the nightingale had flown away, the deer thought—'Go my love and go in peace. I love you and will love you all my life. But I hope you find someone in your life who can sing praises of your beauty, of your songs and confess his love for you. I hope you find someone who is not speechless since birth like me...go my love, go!'

There were tears in Shakuntala's eyes as she looked up at Dushyant who was moved by the tale. He had never heard so profoundly sad. The tale touched his heart. But Shakuntala had related this in response to his proposal of marriage, something he couldn't fathom.

Dushyant said, 'I have never heard such a profound tale, Shakuntala. It is sad but beautiful nonetheless. But what has this tale got to do with my desire to marry you, my love?' Shakuntala smiled to herself and thought, *The king is proficient in the art of warfare and administration, but not in the ways of the heart!*

She said, 'King Dushyant, you are the king of Hastinapur but who am I? An ordinary girl from an ashram who has not stepped out of this small world ever. You are a royal and are well-versed with royal lifestyle and mannerisms. I just don't belong there. I would stick out like a sore thumb next to you. I am…'

Dushyant stopped her, and said, 'Shakuntala, I am talking about you and me. I am talking about my love for you. Where do royalty and other such things come in? I love you and you love…well I don't know that. What is important is whether you love me or not. If you don't love me, then there is nothing to talk further. Tell me Shakuntala, do you love me?'

Shakuntala hesitated and continued, 'King Dushyant, a child can crave for the moon, but can the moon descend to the earth for the child? The deer in the story may have loved the nightingale, but could they have been together? They were two different individuals from two different worlds. Even if the deer loved the nightingale, it would not work…'

'You are not answering my question, Shakuntala. Do you love me? I have understood your story. We are not two different animals. We are both human beings burning in the same fire of love. I am not mute and can reciprocate your feelings, but only if I know them. O tell me, Shakuntala, please tell me, do you love me?'

Shakuntala looked at him, smiled and said, 'Yes, I do,' and then hesitatingly added, 'but…' Dushyant got up and said, 'Then there are no buts. I only wanted to hear this from you.' There was silence for some time, as if time had stopped. King Dushyant's face lit up in the dark room. He looked at Shakuntala and said, 'Marry me, Shakuntala. Let's get married.'

Shakuntala was taken aback by this sudden urgency. 'How is that possible? How can we get married? We haven't spoken to any elders—neither yours nor mine.'

'I am a king and don't need permissions and you are a grown-up girl with a mind of your own. Where is the need for permission?' asked Dushyant.

Shakuntala shot him a look of disapproval. 'That doesn't sound fair. Our seniors and parents need to know about our choice as it is a choice which affects our lives...in fact, their lives too.'

'You are right, Shakuntala,' agreed Dushyant. 'It pertains to our lives but we have to agree with it first. And once we agree, and know in our hearts that we are committing no crime, we can get married.'

'Nonetheless, how do we get married without approval from the elders?' asked Shakuntala.

'Gandharva vivaha,' said Dushyant.

Shakuntala repeated, 'Gandharva vivaha?'

Dushyant elaborated, 'Nothing can stop us from getting married, except our own will. We are not going against the norms laid down by our elders and society at large. A man and a woman can get married under eight circumstances—brahma, daiva, arsha, prajapatya, asura, gandharva, rakshasa and paishacha. Brahmya marriage is when the parents of both families agree to the wedding and wedding vows are exchanged in the presence of all. In a daiva marriage, if the girl's family has not been able to get a suitable groom for their daughter, the girl is married to a priest during a sacrifice. In the arsha marriage, the groom gives a gift of cattle to the girl's family, since the latter is unable to afford the marriage expenses. The prajapatya wedding is similar to the brahma, except that in the former, there is no kanyadaan ritual, i.e. the ritual of handing over the bride to the groom.' Dushyant stopped to catch his breath, while Shakuntala stared at him, awestruck by his knowledge.

Dushyant continued, 'The asura wedding is similar to the arsha wedding, except that in this case the groom is not of the same status as that of the bride, but slightly inferior. The gandharva wedding takes place when there is love between the bride and groom and parental consent is not required. In the rakshasa wedding, the groom forcibly takes the bride away since the parents of the bride are against the alliance. Finally, the paishacha wedding takes place when the bride is not mentally stable and is married off against her wishes and awareness.'

Dushyant continued, 'The last two are out of the question, since they are not prescribed for Kshatriyas. Amongst the first six, brahma and prajapatya weddings are not possible, since both sets of parents are not present. Arsha is ruled out since a wedding through a gift of cattle implies that your parents can't afford our wedding, which is unfair to your father. Also, exchange of monetary benefits degrades your status as an individual. In the same way, an asura wedding is out of the question and so is daiva. That leaves us with gandharva vivaha.'

Shakuntala was listening with rapt attention.

'Gandharva vivaha,' continued the king, 'is a wedding where the bride and the groom get married in a temple with God as their witness. Where there is love, one only needs God, no rituals, no people. My love, let us get married according to the gandharva tradition. We will have God as our witness and what else do we need besides that to consummate our love?' In the dark, Dushyant's frame seemed to be larger than life and the shadows on the walls even larger. His eyes were endearingly true and love was pouring out of his words. He seemed to be pleading as well as commanding and Shakuntala was unable to judge which was stronger, the pleading or the command.

'But isn't gandharva wedding considered aprahasta, an undesirable marriage?' asked Shakuntala.

'Amongst the learned, i.e. the Brahmins, yes, but not amongst Kshatriyas,' pat came the reply from Dushyant.

Shakuntala wasn't clear about the connection between the Kshatriyas and it not being aprahasta. Sensing her confusion, Dushyant continued, 'Trust me, Shakuntala, it is not aprahasta amongst Kshatriyas and like me, you too are a Kshatriya. You told me you are the daughter of King Kaushik. Sage Kanva has raised you, but you can't deny your Kshatriya lineage.'

After pausing for some time, he continued, 'If you had been brought up as a princess in the house of King Kaushik, you would have selected your husband through the practice of swayamvar. How different is this, except that there aren't any other kings to choose from, but you marry the person you love?' Shakuntala was speechless at the well-rehearsed and thought-through argument of Dushyant. He seemed determined when he said, 'Trust me, Shakuntala, this is not improper, and rest assured, the learned Sage Kanva too would not find this against the norms. In case he gets upset about our wedding, I will take full responsibility of this decision. Leave it to me, Shakuntala. I will not let any harm come to you; I love you and that's my word.'

Shakuntala was suddenly aware of his presence and that the flame in the lamp was beginning to flicker. She was not sure if she needed to add more ghee to the lamp or allow it to extinguish. It was surely very, very late, as there were no sounds in the vicinity, except those of the night.

Shakuntala suggested, 'King Dushyant, I think you should be leaving now. It's already very late.'

Dushyant realized that this was an ashram and if anybody

saw them alone in the dim-lit cottage of Shakuntala, it would not be good for her reputation. He gave her one last look and left. 'I will be waiting for your answer, my love,' said Dushyant while leaving. He was smiling and now there was a spring in his gait—an absolute contrast to the man who had walked in earlier.

The lamp was flickering and was soon out. Shakuntala stood smiling to herself in the darkness. She was happy. But there was still something that was unsettling her. Why couldn't happiness come without an accompanying sense of sadness and doubt? Why was this sense of ominousness gathering around her? Why was she feeling so anxious? Could she find an answer to that?

There was a striking similarity to her story and another. Dushyant was of royal lineage. Could he be trusted? What if she ended up being just another queen in his palace? What if she was a temporary fascination and meant nothing to him once they were married? What if she was a misfit in the palace and the king buried himself with courtly affairs? What if…oh please! Who could she speak to about her worries? If only her father was by her side to help her.

However, what if her father didn't approve of Dushyant? What if he had something else in his mind? Whoever had heard of a girl from an ashram to have married any Kshatriya, leave alone a king? Whoever had married someone as powerful as Dushyant? What if her father had selected someone like Priyamvada's husband for her? What if she ended up being the wife of another ascetic and found herself going from one ashram to another, never knowing what existed outside ashrams? Was she destined to live a life of scriptures or was she destined to make it big and live in palaces? What if she had grown up in the home of her biological father? Wouldn't life have been very much different? Wasn't Dushyant offering her that life, which was her birthright? Then why was this worrying her?

Life had lately shown her different faces of men, and she couldn't say that she liked what she saw. In Dushyant's proposal, she could see a promise of that image changing. She felt that life was giving her a chance to live it on her own terms. Shakuntala could change things in her life and this was an opportunity to do so. She could make a difference and not just exist.

Also, what if her father declined the match completely? What if he didn't like the match, would she then be able to go against his wishes? Wouldn't it be safer to simply go ahead and get married, leaving no chance for objection, except some disappointment, which could be taken care of? After all, what was wrong with Dushyant? He was young, handsome and above all, a king. He seemed to care for her genuinely.

Dushyant was in love with her and she loved him too. She couldn't have asked for more from life and this was going to change her destiny. But, did he love her dearly, dearly enough to promise…promise…?

Shakuntala got her answer. She was not going to be left in the lurch and was not going to fall for love only. There was more to life than sweet romance; after all she was the fruit of romance! And what had that brought her? Today neither her father nor her mother were even aware of her existence. She wouldn't allow this to happen to her.

She was going to ask for a promise and she knew what to ask for.

The Promise

Dushyant couldn't sleep the whole night. He was in seventh heaven as his love had been reciprocated. He would be marrying her, but when? He wanted to marry her right away and hold her in his arms. He wanted to feel the warmth of this woman, who had brought out a strange desperation in him. The daughter of an apsara and one of the most renowned Kshatriyas had to be very special and it was evident in the beauty called Shakuntala. He was desperate to marry her. Had it not been for her, he wouldn't have even stepped into this ashram. But she had bewitched him from the moment she stopped him from shooting the doe in the forest a couple of days back. A couple of days, or had it been more than that...but how did it matter?

He was awake all night and got up at dawn. Armed with some dry clothes he headed for the river, walking so briskly that the sweat poured down his face. At the riverside, he placed his clothes at a dry spot, tied his dhoti high and short and plunged into the river. He kept swimming till his body would move no more and his muscles. His skin was tight, holding on to his exercised muscles and his mind was more relaxed. The sun was rising on the other side of the river and spreading a bright orange hue. Birds were chirping animatedly and flying around making it look like a beautiful painting. The sky was much clearer and the few clouds only served to make the whole world look beautiful. The light breeze was caressing his locks and massaging his skin to arousal.

Dushyant had not been able to keep Shakuntala out of his thoughts since the moment she had acknowledged his love. He couldn't wait any longer to hold her in his arms. He was desperate as never before. Was this love?

He realized he had been in the water too long and got out of the river to find Shakuntala sitting under a tree watching him. He stood there with water dripping from his clothes, but today he was not embarrassed. He could feel the breeze and her gaze on him and seemed to enjoy both.

Shakuntala was staring at the tall and manly frame of Dushyant. She could not take her eyes off him and surprisingly, she too was not embarrassed about it. She was in love and this man had proposed marriage to her last night. But she had not come to appreciate him. She had come to speak to him.

She took her gaze away from him and looked down. Dushyant realized that he had been standing there for some time. He went behind the bushes and emerged dry and fully clothed to find Shakuntala at exactly the same spot. She seemed preoccupied with something and he wondered what it was. *Had she changed her mind? No she couldn't have,* thought he.

As soon as he approached Shakuntala, she looked up and said, 'King Dushyant, whatever you said last night, did you mean it?'

'Of course, Shakuntala, every word, I can repeat everything if that would make any difference,' he replied.

'Will you marry me and make me your queen? Me, who has been born and brought up in ashram?' asked Shakuntala.

Dushyant was beginning to get worried, 'Yes, my love, of course. I am a king, and my promise is the royal word. Why do you ask? Is there any doubt in your mind? Please tell me whatever is on your mind, but please do not say "no".' Dushyant was surprised by his last sentence. He didn't want his love to be perceived as desperation.

Shakuntala hesitated and then said, 'I have a condition to the marriage.'

'Anything you say, Shakuntala,' hastened the king.

Shakuntala looked at him and said, 'You haven't even heard me, King Dushyant. Do you commit so easily?'

Dushyant was surprised to hear that and also at his ready acceptance without listening to her condition. He decided to wait for her next statement.

Shakuntala measured every word of her statement, 'My condition is that my firstborn son will be your heir-apparent and the next king of Hastinapur.'

Dushyant was not expecting this. While he was surprised by the condition, he was also impressed to hear this from the mouth of a commoner. Such sense of maturity befitted her personality, he thought. She was revealing her Kshatriya lineage, and such boldness only added to her charm and made him want her even more.

'Why is this so important for you, Shakuntala, if I may ask before I reply?' asked Dushyant.

'It is extremely important for me, King Dushyant, and I don't mind explaining,' said Shakuntala. 'You were right when you mentioned that I am a Kshatriya since I am the daughter of King Kaushik, but I have not forgotten the fact that I was not born out of love, be it of my mother or my father. I am the product of lust and nothing more. This is the truth and I can never forget this, no matter how hard I try. You don't know what it is like to grow up with the awareness of being a product of lust.' Dushyant was shocked to hear these words and surprised to see the stern face reeling out the words.

'What happened to me should not happen to my child,'

continued Shakuntala. 'Tomorrow, I don't want my child to grow up feeling that he was the result of the infatuation of a king and the gullibility of an ashram girl. I would want my child to know that he or she was the child of love and there was no deception of any sort in his or her birth. I can ensure this by seeing to it that my son is recognized as the rightful heir to the throne of Hastinapur. That will give a sanction to our wedding as well as our relationship, even if we wed according to the gandharva tradition.'

Shakuntala continued, 'Even though this is my condition to our marriage, I want you to understand that there is no compulsion. If you decline, my emotions towards you will not change, yes, but I will not be able to marry you. You are a king and the king in you has to decide.'

Dushyant had never heard such clear articulation of thoughts from a lady and was absolutely taken aback by the harsh truth in her words. He was impressed and immediately took her hands in his and said, 'You have my word, Shakuntala, I promise. Our son will be the heir to the throne of Hastinapur, and you my queen.'

Dushyant took off his signet ring and put it on Shakuntala's finger, 'This is the signet ring of the king of Hastinapur. I leave it for you as a sign of our having met and married. This ring is yours from today.'

Shakuntala was happy and the two headed for the temple nearby.

The tears in Menaka's eyes were making her vision misty. She heard what she was worried about the most. Her daughter had grown up with a scar, under which the wound had never healed. If only she could tell her that even though it was lust initially, later it was love and nothing less than that between her and King

Kaushik. Unfortunately, she was sent to deceive, but somewhere during the deception, love had blossomed. 'My daughter, you were abandoned, but not out of choice. I did not want to leave you alone yet I could not live with you. Imagine my state, my dear. I had no choice, both during the deception and thereafter. My destiny was to obey an order and suffer. Perhaps you are lucky to be born human. Humans have the option of a choice, unlike me and the likes of me.'

Menaka was sad to learn what her daughter thought about her parents. What she heard was not absolute untruth, but what she knew was not the absolute truth too. If only Menaka could put forth her views and tell Shakuntala her side of the truth. Even if it didn't change the reality, but she would feel better. But alas...

Gandharva Vivaha

Shakuntala and Dushyant stood facing each other. She was the epitome of beauty while he was nothing less than Kamdev, the god of love. Shakuntala garlanded Dushyant and said, 'I promise to be loyal to you, your family and your kingdom. I promise to take care of all related to you and now us, and also bring up our children in the best possible way, befitting your status and the culture of humanity. From today, I am your friend, partner in life and mother to your children.'

Dushyant placed the garland around Shakuntala's neck, and said, 'I hereby take you as my wife, and now onwards the queen of Hastinapur. I promise to keep you happy and healthy and will take care of you for the rest of my life. Our children will be the royal children of Hastinapur and your family is now my family. God is witness to my love for you and this wedding.'

Both bowed in front of the idol. Dushyant then took some sindoor kept at the foot of the idol and put a dot on the parting of Shakuntala's hair. The red dot was the only colour on the fair Shakuntala who was dressed in a white saree with flower ornaments on her arms, wrists, neck and hair. The parijat flowers seemed to have grown on her branch-like frame. She looked divine and Dushyant, the king of Hastinapur, looked magnificent. The smiles on their faces were revealing the joy of the couple.

They returned to the ashram together, looking absolutely divine. Soon the word spread and people started following them.

Both were heading for the cottage of Sage Dhananjaya, who had already been informed of the events.

When they reached his cottage, he stepped out and both of them bowed and touched his feet. Sage Dhananjaya, though flustered initially, blessed both of them. He looked at Shakuntala and smiled, to which she responded happily. Sage Dhananjaya could see no sign of guilt in what she had done, and was glad about the surety that she demonstrated through her body language. He had always found Shakuntala to be sure of the what she was doing and in all the years gone by, he had never seen her doing anything that she would regret. He also knew her background and understood that it was in her blood to take bold decisions and needless to say, Sage Kanva had always maintained that she would do something different and great in her life. Sage Dhananjaya could see her destiny unfolding right in front of him.

'Go seek blessings from Gautami,' said Sage Dhananjaya. Both headed towards the cottage of Gautami. On the way, Shakuntala was stopped by Anusuya, who had come running from a distance to embrace her. There were tears of joy in her eyes and her happiness could just not be contained. On reaching the cottage, both went in.

Gautami was sitting up in her cot beaming from ear to ear. She was looking frail but her face was suffused with joy for her beloved Shakuntala. They touched her feet and after blessing Shakuntala, she gestured to Dushyant to sit next to her as she couldn't look up and see the entire frame of the king. Dushyant obediently sat next to her. A teary eyed Gautami said, 'O King, Shakuntala is a very good girl; please do take good care of her. I am not her mother, but I have tried my best to be one, and I don't know if I have succeeded or failed. But you are now her husband. Do give her time to learn your ways as she has never

stepped out of this ashram, but she will learn, after all, she...'
and Gautami stopped there amidst tears.

Dushyant took her hand in his and said, 'Don't worry, Ma, I
will take care of her and never let her shed any tears because of
me. From now onwards, she will remain with me, as the queen
of Hastinapur.' There was a sudden gasp of joy amongst all who
had assembled at Gautami's cottage on realizing that one of them
was now going to be the queen.

Gautami was overjoyed and blessed him silently. She gestured
to Anusuya, who went to the corner of the cottage and fetched
something for her. Gautami gave it to Shakuntala saying, 'This is
a bracelet that my mother had given to me, the only thing she
could afford and the only ornament I had all my life. I had kept
it for you. While I know you will be wearing royal jewellery now,
keep this from your mother.' Shakuntala, who had not displayed
any emotion till now, burst into tears. She hugged Gautami and
wept uncontrollably. There were tears in the eyes of everyone
who was present in the cottage. Shakuntala put on the bracelet
in front of Gautami and smiled through her tears.

Gautami consoled her and said, 'Go, my girl, don't cry. It's
the happiest day in the life of a girl, don't spoil it.' Soon they
were out of the cottage. As soon as they stepped out, they found
Priyamvada standing there. She hugged Shakuntala and said,
'I am sorry, Shakuntala; please pardon me for poisoning your
mind. As usual you are never wrong, and I am so happy for you.'
Shakuntala couldn't say anything and just hugged her. Dushyant
was suddenly feeling odd, amidst all this. He simply stood aside
and watched everybody.

After Shakuntala left, Gautami was alone. She was worried.
Had Shakuntala made the right decision? She had never heard of
anything like this before. A girl from an ashram getting married

to the king of Hastinapur? Even if such things did happen once in a while, what was this great hurry? Why did she not wait for her father? Why did she not consult with anybody? Did she not consider any of them as family? Not even her? Gautami had been a part of Shakuntala's growing up and was privy to all decisions taken for her. Sage Kanva involved Gautami in everything that he did for Shakuntala, while Shakuntala did not even find it necessary to at least inform her before taking such a momentous step. Was this all about Shakuntala being different from her and the other inmates of the ashram? Was this just about being different or was it all about youth, which was always in a hurry? Gautami offered a silent prayer to God to take care of her daughter. Tears rolled down her cheeks while she prayed she was wrong in all her thoughts.

In his cottage, Sage Dhananjaya sat quietly after Shakuntala had left. His thoughts were grave and his face revealed it. A couple of other sages too seemed to share the same emotion. One of them said, 'You look worried, Sage Dhananjaya?'

'Yes, I am,' replied Sage Dhananjaya, 'I think the child has made a mistake.'

'You mean by marrying the king?' asked another sage.

Sage Dhananjaya looked up and said, 'Well, not exactly that. Marrying the king by itself need not be an error. But marrying in haste, without consulting anybody, and not waiting for Sage Kanva, seems out of place to me. Doing anything in haste has poor repercussions, and a life-changing decision of such a nature is too large a step for a child like Shakuntala.'

As if thinking aloud, he said, 'Look at our dilemma. First Shakuntala gets married to a king. Anything we say against the wedding could be construed as going against the king and thus Hastinapur. If we keep quiet, then Sage Kanva might feel that we allowed all this to take place, though I am not sure what he would have done if this had happened in his presence.'

There was a moment of silence as everyone pondered over Sage Dhananjaya's words, till one of them said, 'But sage, now that they are married, what can go wrong?'

'Maybe nothing, and yet so much can,' said Sage Dhananjaya. 'The marriage has taken place here, with no witnesses from amongst us or the royal family. Will the kingdom of mighty Hastinapur accept someone whom the king brings home on his return from an akhet, and that too someone who is not a princess? What if the royal family declines to accept this marriage? How would the other kingdoms see this match? This is not just a marriage of different backgrounds; it is that of a king and a commoner. What the king does is a precendent of sorts. I have never heard of such a thing happen before and I am not sure Shakuntala's marriage will set the precedent.'

'Youth is like a colt that has not learnt to gallop as yet. The colt keeps jumping and running, till it realizes it is out of the confines of the fence but then doesn't know its way back and is soon lost in the big, bad world. Sage Kanva has taken utmost care of this child. He has brought her up like his own daughter, and given her more than what she would have got elsewhere. Needless to say, Shakuntala has measured up to all the expectations of the sage till date. But this? I am not sure this was warranted,' lamented Sage Dhananjaya.

'And besides,' he continued, 'what do we know about the king? Is he married, does he have a wife already? What does Shakuntala know about the king or of life in a court or, for that matter, life outside an ashram? What does she know about palace life and intrigue?' After a pause, the sage added, 'If only she had consulted someone on this,' clearly voicing a worry which loomed large on his face. The other sages agreed with him.

'Is there nothing we can do now?' asked one of them.

'What can we do now that they have got married and we have blessed them?' added another sage, while Sage Dhananjaya continued to be pensive.

Finally, Sage Dhananjaya said, 'Well, for one, let's hope our apprehensions are out of place. Also, we should speak to the king on this tomorrow. Till then, let us keep this discussion to ourselves. Let us make arrangements for a small celebration in the evening, after all there has been a marriage in the ashram!'

The others smiled and left the cottage to make arrangements but Sage Dhananjaya remained pensive.

Shakuntala

After seeking blessings from Gautami, the group reached the cottage of Shakuntala. All the weeping had changed to fun and teasing. Soon the group began to disperse and they were left with only a few, including Anusuya and Priyamvada who had not left Shakuntala's side since morning.

Suddenly, they realized that Sage Dhananjaya and a few more sages had come to invite the newly-weds to have their meal at the sage's cottage and though it would be frugal, as everything had happened so suddenly, they were organizing a wedding feast which would be far better than the lunch. Dushyant tried to explain that his intention was not to bother them, but gave up after a few attempts as Sage Dhananjaya was too senior and would not listen.

After their afternoon repast at Sage Dhananjaya's cottage, a small group comprising Dushyant, Shakuntala, Anusuya and Priyamvada returned to her cottage. Dushyant wanted to go to his cottage for some time, but the girls would not let him go, as his cottage was being done up for the couple to spend their first night together. Shakuntala was embarrassed by this turn in conversation while Dushyant fought hard to keep his expressions under control. He was getting a bit tired of the crowd that seemed to be around them since the two had got married. He was longing to touch Shakuntala and take her in his arms, something he had done very briefly after the wedding at the temple. He couldn't take his thoughts away from that feeling of soft warmth and was longing to be alone with her.

All the celebrations were of no meaning to him. While he did understand the shock and awe in the ashram, he was fretting that he had not spent a single moment in private with Shakuntala. The evening was quite uneventful, except for the aarti which the two performed together, a privilege given to all couples who were newly married or had come to the ashram for the first time after their wedding. From there, they went to Sage Dhananjaya's where a small crowd had gathered for the celebrations. Dushyant was quite amused to see the arrangements, considering the fact that he was used to lavish wedding dinners. However, he appreciated the efforts made by the folks of the ashram, and anyway, he simply wanted it all to end soon.

Soon they were escorted to the cottage that had been occupied by Dushyant since the last few days. The entire cottage was lit up with lamps of all sizes arranged in different shapes. Flowers of all colours had been put all around the room. In one corner, a flower arrangement added to the beauty of the cottage. In the other corner was a small bed-like structure, which was decorated with flowers. The room was heavy with the fragrance of flowers and sandalwood, with the flickering lamps adding to the aura of the cottage.

Dushyant sat at one end of the bed while Shakuntala sat at the other end with her friends, who were chatting and giggling. Soon, an old lady called the girls away.

After some time, Shakuntala got up to close the door of the cottage and came and sat next to Dushyant. By now, quite a few of the lamps had blown out and the room was not as bright as it was when they had arrived at the cottage. She looked ravishing even in the dim light. Her face was radiant, more than making up for the lamps which were fast losing their brightness.

Dushyant touched Shakuntala's hand. He could feel his signet ring under his hand as she turned her face away. Dushyant took her in his arms and the two lay down. He took off his waistband made of heavy gold and flung it aside. The encumbrances were falling off, and the two were coming closer. The lamps were blowing away and the two shadows were merging in the darkness.

The last lamp did not last to say what it saw, except that the two figures had merged into one…one passionate embrace leading to moments of ecstasy.

Departure

The next day, the birds seemed to be singing different songs—songs of joy and celebration. It was a pleasant morning. Shakuntala woke up early to find herself in a dishevelled state. The king was lying next to her, sleeping peacefully like a child. She blushed when she remembered the previous night. She went to the back of the cottage to tidy up and change and by the time she was back, the king had woken up to gaze at her, his eyes full of love and his outstretched arms calling her once again. She smiled and handed him some clean clothes, indicating that he had to rise.

The king rose reluctantly and headed for the river. The water was cold and he was on top of the world. He had never felt so exultant in life. He was in love and he had found fulfilment. A soft drizzle added to the romance in the air.

He was soon back at the cottage to be informed that Sage Dhananjaya desired to see him whenever he was free. Dushyant didn't quite understand the urgency for a meeting as he had met him a couple of times the previous day. The old man was nonetheless very kind and fatherly and had been very gracious about the wedding.

Dushyant walked up to meet Sage Dhananjaya who was waiting for him. He folded his hands and greeted the sage. Sage Dhananjaya rose to bless him and asked him to sit. There were two more senior sages who also blessed Dushyant when he folded his hands and acknowledged their presence.

After a brief lull, Sage Dhananjaya cleared his throat and said, 'My apologies for asking you to come and meet us, instead of our coming to you, but I hope you understand that we didn't want Shakuntala to be a part of this discussion.'

Dushyant replied, 'Please don't embarrass me, you are all my seniors and have been very kind to me. I am sure you would have done the same with your son, so please don't apologize to me. I request you to feel free and tell me your apprehensions, O Sage Dhananjaya.'

Sage Dhananjaya felt a bit reassured and said, 'I am sure you will agree that you have got married in the gandharva style where the parents have not been involved. While I am not worried about Sage Kanva as he would not be too upset about this, except for the suddenness of it all, we are worried about how your parents and the citizens of Hastinapur will take this news when they come to know about it. After all, our Shakuntala is not a princess and does not belong to any kingdom. Have you thought about it?'

Dushyant smiled and said, 'Sage Dhananjaya, please don't worry. No one in the royal family would object to my choice and the people of Hastinapur would be honoured to have Shakuntala as their queen. Yes, while I do agree that everything happened unexpectedly, nothing that has happened is against the laws of nature. I am the husband of Shakuntala and there is no denying the fact. I would be glad to take her as soon as possible with me, except for the fact that it would not be fair to take her in the absence of Sage Kanva.'

Sage Dhananjaya said, 'I am sure you understand that even a gandharva vivaha needs to be sanctified through proper rites, once the parents of both the partners are in agreement. As per the norms, we would need the sanction of your parents too, so it might be well if you seek their concurrence for us to perform the rites before you take her along with you. At least this is what we feel, and if we know Sage Kanva well, he too would have given you the same advice.'

After a brief while, during which there was silence amongst all of them, Dushyant spoke, 'I think I should proceed for Hastinapur and return to take Shakuntala in a few days' time. By then Sage Kanva would have returned and I would be able to take her officially with me after seeking his blessings.'

Sage Dhananjaya threw a glance at him and then looked at the other two sages. He spoke after some moments, 'Wouldn't you like to wait for Sage Kanva?'

Dushyant replied, 'It would be an honour to meet him before I leave, but I have been away from the kingdom for quite a few days now and far from my group which had left Hastinapur with me. They would be worried and in the absence of any particular date of Sage Kanva's arrival, it may not be appropriate for me to stay here doing nothing, so far away from the kingdom and that too for an indefinite period.'

Sage Dhananjaya said, 'I agree with you, King Dushyant. You would also get to speak to your family members and resolve issues in case there are any objections. In the meanwhile, we will wait for the arrival of Sage Kanva. It has been quite some time since he will left and he should be back soon.'

Dushyant smiled and said, 'Sage Dhananjaya, please don't worry, there will be no objection from anybody. The kingdom of Hastinapur is honoured to have Shakuntala as its queen. The only reason I would like to leave is that I have been away from the kingdom for quite some time and my team is waiting in the forest for me. So much of inactivity is not good for us. While I would be glad to take Shakuntala with me, I also understand that she would not like to leave without seeking the blessings of her father.'

So it was decided that Dushyant would leave in the afternoon and come back to take his queen in about a fortnight.

'But we just got married yesterday. And you want to leave now? Why?' protested a disappointed Shakuntala on learning that the king was leaving.

Dushyant repeated the conversation that he'd had with Sage Dhananjaya and the others. While Shakuntala was disappointed, she agreed to his departure, knowing that the reasons were valid. Her eyes filled with tears, but she tried desperately to hold them. Dushyant came close to her and stopped the lone tear from rolling down her cheek with his lips. Shakuntala was touched and didn't know for how long she was in his arms, listening to his heartbeats and feeling the warmth of his body.

Soon it was time for him to leave, as he wanted to reach the camp before nightfall. Shravan and his friend were going to escort him to the camp as they knew the way well. The entire ashram came out to see them off. Dushyant went to meet Gautami before leaving, a gesture that touched both Gautami and Shakuntala. He also sought the blessings of Sage Dhananjaya and the others and after one last look at Shakuntala, who was fighting her tears, he left for the camp.

Shakuntala stood there watching him till he disappeared from sight. Anusuya and Priyamvada were with her till early evening but they too had to leave to finish the chores in their cottages.

Shakuntala was left with Mrigakshi, who had been very patient during the last few days, when so much had happened in such a short span of time. First love, then marriage and the previous night and now he was gone. She went to the bed which they had shared and moved her hands over it trying to feel his presence. Her eyes fell on something in the corner of the bed.

She pulled it out to find the waistband of the king. He seemed to have forgotten to put it on after he came back from the river.

Shakuntala took the waistband and caressed it. It was heavy and beautiful. She brought it close to her bosom, trying to feel his presence through it. She knew that she was going to miss him. Soon it was dark but life had to go on. She cleared the cottage, shut the door and headed towards her own cottage. The sun was setting in the horizon and the cattle were returning from their grazing. She knew this was godhuli, a time she loved. A time when the sun sets in the horizon and the cattle return raising dust; thereby the term go-dhuli, dust raised by the cows. A time when lamps were lit and plants watered and all this before the sun took all light with it and sank in the distance.

Camp

Shravan and his friends left after having some water as they wanted to get back to the ashram before it got dark. All his friends and soldiers surrounded Dushyant as soon as the two boys left. They were amused to see Dushyant in plain clothes, but commented on the radiance on his face.

The moment they reached the camp, Giri fell at the feet of Dushyant and said, 'Pardon me, Your Majesty. It was because of me that you got lost. It was all because of my neglect that...'

Dushyant held him by his shoulders and raised him and said, 'I agree, Giri, it was all because of you...I mean had you not lost me, I wouldn't have reached the pristine environs of an ashram! I must thank you for what you seem to be alluding to as your "negligence"!' Dushyant's cheerfulness was not lost on anybody.

He continued, 'My dear friend Giri, just take this guilt off your mind. It was I who was at fault for chasing a deer blindly. You have never missed taking care of me, but if you did, then this was the best dereliction of duty, if I may add!'

Amish, Bhadrak and Agneya were all very happy to see him. Bhadrak said, 'It might be a good idea for Sage Dushyant to change into something more royal.' The others burst into laughter and it was only then that Dushyant realized that he was wearing the garments from the ashram.

Dushyant went into his tent and changed into silk garments and put on his shoes to emerge looking every bit the king he was. A small feast was organized on the arrival of the king and it was decided that they would leave for Hastinapur at dawn. In the evening, they sat around a fire and all insisted that Dushyant tell them what he did at the ashram ever since he was lost.

Dushyant was hesitant to tell his story, as it meant that he would have to tell them about Shakuntala. He was not sure how these people would react; he needed more time to make up his mind on how to break the news to all. He simply said that he got lost while chasing a stag. Soon he was tired and hungry and saw some cottages at a distance. On reaching them, he realized that it was an ashram. He went in to learn that it was the ashram of the renowned Sage Kanva.

He accepted their hospitality and was moved by the serene and quiet atmosphere of the ashram. Since the sage was not in the ashram, he decided to stay there for a few days and wait for his return. But as time went by, he decided to leave as staying on meant keeping the entire team waiting and it was also necessary to get back to Hastinapur, and thus he came back.

Amish enclaimed, 'That's all? Is that all you did there for the last two or three days? If you knew that the sage was not there, you could have returned immediately. Why did you wait for so many days?'

Dushyant knew that Amish was too sharp to fall for a simple version. 'The other sages insisted that I spend a few days with them as it was an honour for them to host the king of Hastinapur. I didn't have the heart to decline their offer and since I had never had the occasion to spend time in an ashram, I accepted. However, time began to hang heavy and so I made an excuse and left today.' Amish and the others nodded in agreement.

Bhadrak said, 'It was very tough for us on the first day when you went missing. Spending one full night without any news of you was unnerving to say the least. That too after we had sent teams in all directions, but failed to find you. Giri was so sad and disturbed that he did not have a morsel of food till we heard from the ashram. Anyway, we abandoned all hunting thereafter as nobody was in a mood for the same.'

Dushyant said, 'This sure is delicious food after the simple meals I have had at the ashram for the last few days.'

Bhadrak joked, 'A few more days and we would have had a sage return from the ashram, what with the simple dressing and plain food!'

All of them laughed, the first sounds of merriment since Dushyant had gone missing.

A light shower ended the evening and soon all of them left for their respective tents. Dushyant was all alone in his tent reminiscing about the previous night. He was beginning to miss Shakuntala and was wondering what she was up to. He stepped out of the tent to find solace in the rain. Giri was not outside the tent and the fire had been extinguished by the rain. Except for a few lamps which were still burning, it was dark. Dushyant stood in the rain and allowed every drop to quench his thirst. He wished Shakuntala was with him at that moment and both were getting drenched. He knew Shakuntala enjoyed the rain. Was she also out at this hour?

Shakuntala stepped out of her cottage when she heard the rain falling on the roof. The cool breeze was lighting a fire within her, the fire of love, the fire of passion, the fire of loneliness. She was missing Dushyant, the warmth of his love and his body. She wished he had been there for one more day, but would this longing have reduced or would it have been worse if he left a day later? She stood outside her cottage and allowed the rain to cool her.

But the rain did nothing for them. It only added to their

sense of loneliness, longing and love. Both ended up missing each other more. Every raindrop only ignited passion till it became unbearable.

The next day saw a bright and clear sky at the camp. The king and his friends and some soldiers left early in the morning for Hastinapur. The other soldiers were to leave after winding up and clearing the area that they had been occupying for the last few days.

The next day at the ashram was dark and gloomy as the sky was overcast with dark clouds. The ashram was abuzz with activity but Shakuntala's heart was heavy; suddenly she was very lonely.

Sage Kanva

After Dushyant left the ashram, things returned to normal with the inmates going about their work. Priyamvada and Anusuya were the only company Shakuntala had, besides Mrigakshi, with whom she would spend hours talking.

Shakuntala was already feeling that she would miss them all in the palace of the king of Hastinapur. In her own mind, she was wondering what all she would be able to carry with her, her favourite plants, which clothes, which…but all this planning would always end with a question—what if the king's choice was met with resistance? What if Dushyant was unable to convince his parents about her?

Shakuntala went on with life, expecting him to convince his parents and call for her soon.

Sage Kanva returned after a fortnight and knew that his daughter had changed. He could see it in her walk, in her conduct, the moment she gave him some water to drink. Shakuntala didn't have any reason to hide her marriage and told him all that had happened.

Sage Kanva sat still for some time and closed his eyes. Shakuntala watched him, wondering if he was upset or unhappy. 'Did I do anything wrong, Father? Are you angry?' asked Shakuntala.

Sage Kanva opened his eyes and smiled. 'I am not upset with your choice, but I am sad that I was not there when you got married. Your choice of gandharva vivaha is not incorrect and nor is your choice of a partner, after all you do belong to the palaces. I only hope you find your right place and the right honour that you deserve,' the sage paused and then continued, 'These eyes have seen many injustices in life, and I wouldn't be able to bear any of them on you. While I have heard good things about King Dushyant, I have also heard many other things about royal families, so I am just apprehensive, but...' and he stopped.

'But what, Father?' asked a worried Shakuntala.

'Nothing, my dear, I think I am a bit tired after my long journey. At my age, I'd rather stay back at the ashram than travel. But I am happy for you and may you be blessed with a son who will expand the limits of Hastinapur and make you proud!' Shakuntala blushed and lowered her head.

Sage Kanva kissed her head with love and said, 'I will have word sent to the king about my arrival so that he can take my blessings and I may send you with him soon.' After a brief moment, he added, 'I hope that is what you want?' Shakuntala smiled and went out of the cottage feeling elated, but not wanting to show her joy, lest her father feel sad.

Sage Kanva was a trifle disturbed. He was not sure of the cause of the emotion. Was it the choice of the groom, or was it the idea of Shakuntala leaving him? Didn't he know that one day she would leave, like all girls did? So why was this making him sad? Also, for a girl like her, wasn't a king the best choice? After all, the daughter of a king getting married to a king was the best option and honestly, he himself would have never thought of it.

This was destiny! Why else would the king come for a hunt and meet his daughter and fall in love? Besides, Shakuntala was worthy of the king of Hastinapur. She might have been brought up in an ashram, but she was semi-divine and deserved nothing less than a king.

Sage Kanva, the sage renowned for his knowledge, was beginning to think less like a learned sage and more like a father. His emotions were ruling his thoughts and his moist eyes were hampering his vision. He thought it best to confer with Sage Dhananjaya and the others regarding this matter, since they were the ones who had met the king and spent a few days with him.

Sage Dhananjaya and the others came to visit him after the evening aarti. All of them discussed the proceedings at Sage Gautam's ashram and the discourse that had taken place. However, Sage Dhananjaya observed that Sage Kanva seemed to be preoccupied with something else. Sage Dhananjaya said, 'I think we should leave this discussion for tomorrow, as Sage Kanva seems a bit tired today. Perhaps all of us should meet tomorrow morning and take this discussion forward. Should we leave the sage alone now?' Sage Kanva nodded and the rest got up to leave.

Sage Dhananjaya stayed back as he knew what was bothering Sage Kanva. As soon as they were left alone, Sage Kanva asked Sage Dhananjaya, 'What do you have to tell me about King Dushyant?'

Sage Dhananjaya was surprised by the direct question. He said, 'Well, he was here for a few days and we were all surprised by their marriage. Shakuntala and the king got married by themselves, which was not wrong, so we accepted the marriage and allowed them to live together.' Sage Kanva looked up at the last word, taking in its significance.

Sage Dhananjaya continued, 'We met the king the next day and asked him if the sudden wedding, in the absence of the royal family, would in any way hurt our Shakuntala or come in the way of her being accepted as the king's wife. He assured us that it would not and that it was his responsibility to ensure that she would be accepted. He sounded earnest in his words and we felt assured. He decided to leave as he had been at the ashram for quite a few days; away both from his hunting team as well as the kingdom. He has assured us that he will return soon to take Shakuntala with him. Now that you are back, we can send word to the king. He was keen to meet you.'

All the while Sage Dhananjaya was talking there was an expression of doubt on his face, which did not go unnoticed by Sage Kanva. After he had finished, Sage Kanva asked him, 'Is something bothering you, Sage Dhananjaya? Please feel free to share what you have in mind.'

Hesitatingly Sage Dhananjaya said, 'Nothing in particular except for the fact that the way in which these events transpired leaves me slightly worried. Not that I have any reason to distrust the king of Hastinapur, but when something happens in the confines of this ashram, without anybody's knowledge, and without the inclusion of the members of his camp, it does make things a bit complicated.'

Sage Kanva could see his apprehensions being given some shape. 'While I do appreciate Shakuntala's choice, I am only worried about the haste in executing it and that too without consulting anybody, not even her friends,' said the sage.

Sage Kanva looked up, surprised. Sage Dhananjaya nodded. 'Yes, I did check with Anusuya and Priyamvada. They had no idea about the marriage, though from their expressions, I could fathom that both Shakuntala and the king had strong feelings for each other during the short period that the king spent here prior to the marriage, which could not have been more than two or three days.' Sage Kanva was visibly disturbed with the last words, *'not more than two or three days'*.

There was silence between them for sometime, till Sage Kanva said, 'So what would you advise now?'

Sage Dhananjaya tried to smile and said, 'For now let us trust Shakuntala's judgement and let her feel happy. Let our views not be known to her; after all we old people always tend to see things differently. Also, the king has not done anything to warrant distrust in his actions. I think that you should send a message about your return to the king and we wait for his arrival. The rest is God's will and in Him we must trust.'

Sage Kanva always trusted the judgement of Sage Dhananjaya and while his apprehensions were reciprocated by the learned sage, he was beginning to feel better. Sage Dhananjaya did not have any children and always treated Shakuntala as his own and was also an extremely rational person. He thanked Sage Dhananjaya for all that he had done and hoped his daughter would find the peace and recognition that she so deserved and longed for.

Sage Dhananjaya left, leaving Sage Kanva alone. Sage Kanva decided to send word to the king first thing in the morning, and retired for the day. But somehow, sleep eluded him, in spite of the tiredness. At the end of the day, he felt happy about one thing that Shakuntala was married to a Kshatriya, a class she belonged to rightfully. But hadn't he always been apprehensive about the Kshatriyas as a class? Oh well, but this was King Dushyant, whose name itself meant 'one with a strong and unshakeable mind'. He was known for his strength which was capable of lifting the mount Mandara with two arms. He was skilled in weapons and could ride both elephant and horse with equal ease.

He was the king of Hastinapur, the great kingdom. He remembered Sage Gautam praising the kingdom. He had said that in the reign of Dushyant, there were no men of mixed castes and no tillers of soil, since the earth yielded vegetation by itself. There was no fear of famine as Parjannaya showered his blessings regularly. There existed no sinful men and thus no fear of thieves;

and people were fearless. The people were happy under his rule, and a man who took care of his subjects and was loved by them in return must be the right choice for his daughter.

In spite of these assurances, sleep eluded the father whose daughter had married a king.

Nature

The next day brought in more rain. The leaves were all washed and clean in myriad shades of green and the flowers were blooming in all shades of the rainbow. Bees were buzzing around them, waiting to suck all the the nectar from these flowers. While it seemed unfair that the flowers produced nectar and the bees stole them, it was certain that nature wanted it that way. What was not known was whether the flowers loved it or not.

While the rains bring in greenery they also bring in pain and longing for those pining for their loved ones, and who would know this better than Shakuntala who seemed to have lost all cheer and charm from her life. She moved around mechanically doing her chores around the cottage and the ashram. There was no spring in her gait, nor a smile on her lips. It was not lost on her that her father's message to Dushyant had not been responded to and it had been a considerable time since the messenger had left a message for the king.

She was beginning to get worried. Once, while she was sitting with her father, she felt giddy and fainted. When she woke up, she found herself lying in front of a smiling Anandini, the ever-joyful midwife of the ashram. Her father was smiling, and as soon as Shakuntala gained composure, Anandini started rattling off precautions to be taken. She had to eat well, not lift loads, not be sad, feel happy, after all she was going to give birth to a child soon!

Shakuntala stared at Anandini who repeated, 'Yes, my dear, you are expecting the heir to the throne of Hastinapur! Be happy and cheerful. I will leave now to prepare some medicines for you, but I will come again later. Till then, take care.' Sage Kanva was beaming and his eyes had already turned moist with tears of joy. His daughter was soon to be a mother.

No sooner had Anandini stepped out that the loud Anusuya came rushing in and embraced her. One wonders how she came to know of everything! Seeing her, Sage Kanva stepped out of the cottage. Anusuya was giggling, 'Oh my god, so you are carrying King Dushyant's child? I can't believe it. The queen of Hastinapur is expecting, this calls for celebrations of a royal nature...' A sharp look from Shakuntala stopped a surprised Anusuya. 'Why are you angry, Shakuntala?' she asked.

'Don't call me the queen of Hastinapur, I am not one...at least not as yet,' retorted Shakuntala.

Anusuya realized that the word 'queen' was not comforting for her friend. She also knew that this was not the time for anger; her friend had to be happy. She said, 'All right, I will not call you queen, but my dear, stop frowning. Be happy, and I am sure that as soon as the king comes to know about the child, he will come running to take you along with him.' As an afterthought she added, 'Or, he might want to leave you here; after all, aren't you supposed to be here for your first child?'

Shakuntala gave up and smiled. 'When will you stop chattering so much? Now give me a hand, I have work to do. I am sure Mrigakshi is dying of hunger, one more moment and she will be eating my plants.' Anusuya stopped her from getting up, saying she would take care of it.

Shakuntala said, 'That greedy doe needs to eat three times a day, will you be here for the next I don't-know-how-many-months?'

She heard Anusuya's voice from outside, 'Seven months more, I'll take care, don't worry!'

The words rang dully in Shakuntala's ears. She sat down with a thud. It had been more than two months and there was no news of the king! He had said that he would return in a fortnight, and four fortnights had passed since. She felt her stomach and wondered if the child she was carrying would be an abandoned child too. *No it wouldn't*, came a strong voice from within her. She got up; there was a lot to do.

Winter was approaching. Shakuntala's movements were now restricted but that did not deter her from doing most of the work that she was used to. Anusuya was her constant companion, as Priyamvada's wedding date was approaching. Anandini would visit at least once a day, and there was a sense of anticipation in the ashram. They were all aware that this was not an ordinary event. The ashram was going to witness the birth of the heir to the throne of mighty Hastinapur.

Shakuntala gave birth to a rose-hued son whose arrival spread joy in the entire ashram. Sage Kanva was the proud grandfather, fussing over the child much to the amusement of the other sages. The child brought back joy in the heart of an otherwise sorrowful Shakuntala. Tears of joy rolled down her cheeks as she looked even more radiant and beautiful now.

Sage Kanva was happy but concerned as it would soon be a year and there was no news of the king. He had sent word about the birth of Shakuntala's child, but more than a month had passed since then. Had the king cheated his daughter?

Narada Muni

When Shakuntala's son was a few months old, Priyamvada's wedding was solemnized. It was a simple ceremony and the groom hardly spent any time at the ashram. There weren't too many people with the groom, who seemed quite old. By early evening, Priyamvada had left with her husband.

Sage Kanva had asked Shakuntala to request Priyamvada to speak to her husband about Shakuntala's marriage with the king and see if she could reach the king. But Shakuntala did not say a word to her and before Priyamvada left they just hugged each other and wept. Both were concerned for the other; Shakuntala because of Priyamvada's aged husband and Priyamvada because of Shakuntala's fate regarding her husband.

Shakuntala was fully occupied with her son. Soon the newborn was crawling and taking baby steps and even before she realized, her son was already three years old.

One day, when Shakuntala returned after getting water from the river, she was surprised to see her son playing with the celestial sage, Narada Muni. She noticed from a distance that the munivar was teaching her son to play the veena, the musical instrument designed by him. It was well known that Narada Muni was well-versed in music and known for his incomparable knowledge of the precise pronunciation of every word and syllable.

Shakuntala's son seemed to have taken to the sage very

naturally and the sage seemed to be enjoying teaching a child of three.

She approached the sage and sought his blessing. The ever-smiling sage blessed her and said, 'What a lovely son you have. Blessed be the parents of this child, whose future is so bright. He will be known by his name and all before him will be known as *his* ancestors while all after him will bear his name. May God be with both of you and the king of Hastinapur.'

The last words hit Shakuntala, but the sage was smiling as if he knew nothing. Soon Sage Kanva joined them and Shakuntala left to make arrangements for refreshments for the sage.

When she came back with the refreshments, she heard Sage Kanva say, 'What happened then, munivar?' but the moment they saw her, they fell silent. She was about to leave when Narada Muni said, 'Why don't you join us, my dear child. I was sharing an unusual happening with your father.' Shakuntala stayed back and Narada Muni began, 'Let me start again for Shakuntala to follow the story. This is an incident related to a disciple called Galava. Galava was a devoted disciple of his guru and had stayed with him even when the guru was going through difficult times. At the end of his studies, pleased with Galava, his guru prepared to let him go. Meanwhile as per tradition on completion of his studies, Galava offered to pay his guru-dakshina, the fees. The guru was pleased with his services and so decided to waive off the guru-dakshina. Galava, however, insisted that he wanted to pay and that the guru could ask for anything he liked. After repeated insistence, the guru got a trifle irritated and asked Galava to give him eight hundred horses needed to perform an Ashwamedha yagna. However, all the horses had to be white like the rays of the moon but have one black ear.

'While the matter ended there for the guru, it was far from

over for Galava. Though he knew that it was impossible for him to make the payment, he still wanted to do so, lest the world remembered him as a disciple who did not pay for his education.'

Galava meets King Yayati

'Determined to pay his guru-dakshina, Galava set out to look for such horses. He travelled far and wide but could not find them. Sad and dejected, just when he was losing hope, he met Garuda, the magnificent bird with a human body and face and wings of an eagle, and the vahana of Lord Vishnu. Galava stated his problem to Garuda who decided to help his friend. They visited many kings who could have such horses but found none. Finally, they reached the palace of King Yayati.

'King Yayati,' continued Narada, 'was none other than the mighty king who had exchanged his youth with his son, Puru, whose children then went on to become the rulers of mighty Hastinapur. Garuda spoke to the king about Galava's need of eight hundred white horses, each with one black ear. King Yayati, though a mighty king, was not in a position to help Galava with the horses. He expressed his inability to help, but didn't want Galava to leave empty-handed. He suggested a way out.

'King Yayati suggested that Galava take with him his daughter, Madhavi, who was so beautiful that even the gods wanted to wed her. Madhavi, continued the father, was sarvadharmopacayinam, fosterer of all virtues; Galava could set a price for Madhavi and barter her beauty with the kings who had such horses. Her beauty could make kings give up their kingdoms; horses were too small a price for her. Galava saw a ray of hope and thanked the king and went on his way with Madhavi. Garuda, too, went his way, having helped his friend.

'Galava reached Ayodhya whose king was heirless. He offered Madhavi in marriage to the king in return for eight hundred horses that matched the required specifications. The king of Ayodhya expressed his inability to give eight hundred horses, but promised to give him two hundred instead, if he left Madhavi with him and allowed her to beget a son for him. Galava was not sure how to handle this, as two hundred horses wouldn't suffice and leaving Madhavi with the king would not help. At that moment, Madhavi intervened. She said that she was blessed with a boon that she would beget great heroic sons and after every delivery, she would regain her virginity. That way, once she had given a son to the king, Galava could offer her to another king, and get the rest of the horses. Galava found the idea acceptable and left Madhavi with the king of Ayodhya and asked him to keep the two hundred horses for him to collect later.

'After a year, when Madhavi had given the king a son, Galava came to take her. She left her son in Ayodhya and accompanying Galava went to the king of Kashi, who by now knew about Madhavi and Galava's predicament. He, too, had only two hundred such horses and agreed to keep her for a year, get a son by her and release her. Galava agreed and left to return after a year.

'After another year, Madhavi left her second son with the king of Kashi and, with Galava, reached the king of Bhojanagari, who, again, had only two hundred horses. History repeated itself as Madhavi spent a year with the king for a promise of two hundred horses to Galava, and a son to the king.

'After another year, when she had delivered a son for the king of Bhojanagari, Galava came to take Madhavi. Galava now learnt from Garuda that there weren't any more such horses to be had and, therefore, he should return to his guru with the six hundred horses that he had earned and offer Madhavi to him instead of the remaining two hundred horses.

'Galava went to his guru with Madhavi and the six hundred horses. He told his guru that he was short of two hundred horses but the guru could keep Madhavi for a year and have a son by her who would be equal to the remaining two hundred horses. When his guru saw Madhavi, he asked Galava why he had approached the other kings. He could have come to his guru straightway who would have had four sons from Madhavi in exchange of eight hundred horses. The guru kept Madhavi and the six hundred horses and absolved Galava of his guru-dakshina. Galava was happy to have achieved success and thanked Madhavi before leaving.

'The guru spent a year with Madhavi and after she gave him a son, he sent her back to King Yayati. On the return of Madhavi, King Yayati organized a swayamvar for his daughter, so that he could discharge his paternal responsibility of getting her a suitable husband. The swayamvar was attended by all the great kings of the country, including the kings from Ayodhya, Kashi and Bhojanagari, with whom Madhavi had spent a year each. At the swayamvar, Madhavi decided to wed the forest and left to lead the life of a celibate.

'Thus ended an unusual tale,' said Narada Muni, awaiting reactions from the sage and Shakuntala.

Shakuntala's face was red with anger and she seemed to be holding back her thoughts the way a volcano holds lava before eruption. Sage Kanva knew what such a silence meant, but Narada Muni smiled calmly, gazing at them.

Sage Kanva said, 'Well munivar, it sure is an unusual tale. It brings together many aspects—duty, responsibility and sacrifice…'

'And exploitation!' added Shakuntala, before leaving the cottage in a huff.

Sage Kanva got up to reprimand her for her impudence in front of the celestial muni, but a smiling Narada Muni stopped him from following her. He said, 'No, Sage Kanva, don't go, leave her alone. I am not at all hurt by her leaving. She is at an impressionable age and I understand her state of mind. She is like my daughter and I don't feel bad about it.' As an afterthought, Narada said, 'Perhaps we should leave her alone for some time.'

Sage Kanva sat down following the muni's advice resignedly.

Madhavi

Shakuntala was restless for the rest of the day and her mind could not find any peace. Sage Kanva noticed it and knew that he would have to speak to her and let the lava flow. After her son was asleep, she sat on the steps of her cottage and stared at the moon. She wondered if celestial objects were prone to abuse. She remembered her father telling her once how Chandra, the moon, was married to the twenty-eight daughters of Daksha, but he loved Rohini more than the others. Wasn't that natural, that one was loved more than the others, or preferred over the others? Was it possible for a person to love all equally? Later, when the other sisters of Rohini complained to their father, Chandra was cursed by Daksha with a degenerative disease, which led him to lose his lustre and he started to wane. Chandra was worried and he prayed to Lord Shiva, who allowed him to take refuge in his locks and regain his potency.

Later, the curse was reduced to a temporary state, and from that day onwards, Chandra, the moon, waxes when it approaches Rohini and wanes when it moves away from her. On the full moon day Chandra attains his full strength, and then onwards, he loses it gradually till the new moon night, when he has no wife by his side. On the day before that, when he is just a crescent, he takes refuge in Shiva's locks.

Daksha expected Chandra to love all his daughters equally. How was that possible? Why didn't fathers ever get questioned for their irrational expectations from their children? Why did the children have to bear the brunt of their whims and fancies? If Chandra loved Rohini more than the others, then it was the call of his heart. How could he love all the sisters equally? Was it fair on the part of Daksha to curse Chandra with a degenerative disease? Would it not harm his other daughters too? Was it a father or was it a powerful person uttering such a curse? Was it fatherhood or was it the strength of position that made fathers behave the way they did? Did a person cease to have fatherly feelings, if he was a king or a mighty deity like Daksha?

She kept staring at the moon and felt sorry for him. Could emotions be guided by the diktats of elders? Could the elders get away with any order, irrespective of what it did to the mind and body of the child? Chandra's love for Rohini led to his degeneration. When such things could happen to celestial objects then what was the lot of humans?

Shakuntala didn't realize that her father had come and was sitting next to her. 'The moon looks so beautiful, my dear child, but I have never noticed it, as I have always seen the moon in your face.' Shakuntala looked at her father, whose doting eyes said it all. She forced a smile, but her mind was preoccupied and knowing that her father knew what she was thinking, she waited for him to bring up the topic.

Sage Kanva sat silently next to her, gazing at the moon and enjoying the sounds of the night. Shakuntala, too, was engrossed in the silence of the night, but deep inside there was mumbling... the loud and thundering voice of objection.

She heard her father ask, 'Are you thinking about Madhavi?'

Shakuntala replied, 'No, I was thinking about King Yayati, the father.'

'What about him?'

'I was wondering what kind of a father would set a price for his daughter. Wondering what kind of a father would tell an unknown person about his daughter's beauty and how it could be *used*. Wondering what kind of a father would trade his daughter to help fulfil another's duty. Wondering what kind of a father would...'

'What Yayati did was not as a father, he responded as a king' reasoned Kanva. 'It is the rajdharma of a king to help the needy. A king is not worth the title if he cannot help someone who has come to him for assistance. Haven't you heard about King Harishchandra who, as a servant to the chandala, refused to cremate his own son, without the taxes that were due, and made his wife pay for the funeral cloth with her own saree? These are instances when human ideals are raised to a level which every man on earth aspires to or ought to aspire to live up to. These may seem extreme, but how else does a mortal understand the limits of human behaviour? If what is humanly possible is not demonstrated then how will man know his limits and his capacity to earn virtues?'

'And Galava?' asked Shakuntala, 'What exactly was he striving for when he did not even possess an average human's capability? Why promise when one is not capable of giving anything? If it was not in one to give even a penny, then why promise? At the end of it all, who paid the guru-dakshina? He? Or an innocent girl, who had nothing to do with either of the concerned persons, but was used like an animal by all the men around her,' she spat out the words.

Sage Kanva thought it wise to hear out Shakuntala, even if he didn't agree, as it would help her release her bottled-up anger. It was her catharsis.

Shakuntala continued, 'Which ideals are you talking about,

father? Whose ideals…the king's, the guru's or the student's? All managed to uphold their ideals by sacrificing a helpless woman at the altar of ideals. This is ridiculous. Just what is the difference between a woman and an animal? To satisfy their need for milk, humans get bulls to mate with the cow. In fact, the cow is better off; she at least gets to stay with her calf. Madhavi's plight was worse than a cow. She gave the child to the king and renounced all rights to move on to another king to satisfy his need for a child. In all this, Galava's job was to take the woman from one king to another and get six hundred horses for nothing. At the end, when he was not able to get the remaining horses, he simply traded her for horses! And what did the guru do, he kept the horses and the woman till he got a child from her. I guess, the woman and the animals are incidental in this great tale of duty and responsibility! Quite a price for imparting education to his disciple, I must say!

'Father, are we talking about ideals or the lack of them? At the end of it, you want me to think that she gave up her life to uphold the ideals of a bankrupt king, a pauper of a disciple, lusty kings and a guru, who probably forgot to teach his student the most important lesson of not treating women like cattle.'

Shakuntala continued when she didn't see any response forthcoming from her father, 'Are you speechless? That's what all of us should be. I feel nauseated to learn that the ancestor of my husband's family bartered his daughter to uphold his kingly rights. I am not surprised to know that one from the same lineage has no respect for women; why else would he marry and leave his wife alone with a child?' She added, 'But I am no Madhavi, Father, I am no Madhavi.'

Sage Kanva had not expected this, and had nothing to say for sometime. Finally he patted her shoulder and said, 'Every story has something hidden in it, and it might not be possible for us to see that every time. Perhaps we are missing something here. But it's late, my child, go and get some rest and sleep before your son wakes up at dawn and makes you run all over the ashram. Sleep well, my child,' said the sage before he retired to his corner.

Sleep eluded Shakuntala. She couldn't agree with her father that there was a hidden message which they were not able to fathom. She had examined the story thoroughly and she had said what she felt. She kept tossing and turning and couldn't help but think about the trauma Madhavi must have gone through. Her father gave away his only daughter to a pauper to enable him to pay his guru-dakshina and in the process beget children to lusty kings. How terrible must this have been, especially so with the sanction of the sole person, whose prime moral duty was to protect his daughter from such people. She was a woman who could not be a wife; a mother of four but could not express any maternal felings with respect to her children; a beauty who was of the envy of the gods, but reduced to an object of lust and a bearer of children. If this was what being sarvadharmopacayinam, fosterer of all virtues, meant, then a woman was better off without virtue!

However, one thing still disturbed her. Why did Madhavi herself suggest a way to be exploited when the king of Ayodhya said that he could spare only two hundred horses? Why did she bail out Galava by informing him that her virginity could be regained after every delivery? Wouldn't it have been in her interest to keep quiet about it? Was she so disappointed by her father giving her away to Galava that nothing else mattered to her thereafter? Was she so disgusted with the talk about using her and setting a price for her that she simply gave the information as an act of submission? Or was it that she was ensuring that her father didn't lose face and his share of virtues that he would 'earn' by helping a subject who had come to seek his help?

A disturbed Shakuntala dozed off to sleep with many questions in her mind, answers to which she would never find.

Madhavi's Swayamvar

That night, Shakuntala had a dream.

She saw a royal palace, with King Yayati sitting on a throne. It was the swayamvar of Madhavi, which her father had organized after his yet-again-virgin daughter had returned from the ashram of a sage after begetting four sons to four different individuals. A father was discharging his paternal duty, how else would he attain salvation and heaven? Wasn't the act of kanyadaan, the ritualistic giving away of one's daughter to another man, the most auspicious event in a father's life?

On one side were his courtiers and on the other side were kings from far and wide. One by one, the names of kings were being announced. Shakuntala heard the names of three, the kings of Ayodhya, Kashi and Bhojanagari, amongst others. Each of them present was hoping that he would be selected, as the beauty of the princess was known to one and all. They had also heard about how she had spent four years with four different men, begetting each one a child, and was still a virgin. There had to be something about her; why else would the same kings return to wed her?

King Yayati said, 'Kings and princes from different kingdoms, I welcome you all. It is a moment of great pride and honour to host all of you for the swayamvar of my daughter Madhavi, who as you all know is both beautiful and a fosterer of all virtues. For me this is a great occasion and I am proud of having been

·

able to be of service to both sages and people. I am glad that I have been able to help them achieve their objectives, without which they would not be able to walk the path of salvation. I am also proud that I have enabled a student to pay his debt to the sage who imparted him education, the biggest gift to man. I am glad that the world will not remember him as an ungrateful student, who did not pay for his education. Having achieved all this, I would like to perform the last act of a father, that of kanyadaan, the biggest daan for any man. Today, I will be able to discharge all the human responsibilities that God Almighty had entrusted me with.'

After acknowledging the greetings of all, he ordered the ushers, 'Please bring Madhavi here.' He then added, 'Kings and princes, I hope you will understand that I have empowered my daughter with a choice that she will make. Let her decision be respected and the ones not selected by her desist from feeling insulted. Our culture has empowered our daughters with this choice and let us all respect this.'

When Madhavi walked into the court with a garland to select a husband, the men offered a silent prayer. The three kings, with whom she had spent a year each, were hoping that she would select them; after all they knew her worth. The others understood why she was so well known, and why even the gods would give an arm and a leg to wed this woman.

Madhavi stood in the middle of the court with men all around her. In the centre she saw her father, who was basking in the glory of youth and the knowledge of how he had helped a needy student pay his gurudakshina. A proud king was happy to have served the need of an individual. Then she noticed King Haryaswa of Ayodhya. He had told Galava that he needed Madhavi to beget him a child, but he was the same man who had commented about

Madhavi's beauty, saying, 'Here is a woman, six parts of whose body which ought to be high were high, the seven parts which should be slender were slender, and the three parts which should be deep were deep and five parts which ought to be red were red!'ᴰ Was this comment justified in a man who purportedly needed to beget children or was it a blatant display of his kamamohita nature, one who was addicted to sexual brazenness?

Then she noticed King Divodasa of Kashi. This king had enjoyed her to the full and all this in the name of a child which he needed. He was an arrogant man, given to the pleasures of life. His obsession with himself and his looks were his prime concern. He dressed in the most outrageous colours and combinations and was always surrounded by sycophantic courtiers, who would praise him without any rhyme or reason. All he thought of were sexual pleasures and Madhavi had to cater to all his demands.

She then noticed King Ushinara of Bhojanagari. King Ushinara was a much older man, who tried to hide his age with all sorts of potions and lotions. In all the time she spent with him, the king used her no end. She was romanced on the banks of rivers, streams, mountains and plains, in gardens and forests, in palaces and terraces. Such sexual indulgence was nauseating at times for Madhavi, but she bore it without any grudge, after all wasn't that what she was there for? The king never tired and never seemed to have enough, till her tenure came to an end with the birth of a child. Each of the three men had come this day to take her back with them, for the sexual experience that they had enjoyed with her. They wanted a son from her for their 'salvation' but what about Madhavi's salvation?

The others were there because they had heard it all and dreamt of similar experiences. All wanted her for her beauty and body. None saw her as a woman who also had emotions. She stood in the middle of the court, with a garland in her hand, as the kings waited with bated breath. Who would it be?

Madhavi walked around and stopped at the centre of the court and said, 'All you kings have heard about my beauty and how I lived with four men in the last four years and gave each of them a son. So here, in front of you, is a much-used woman and a mother of four, but still a virgin for the next man. My virginity is of prime importance to all of you, but what use is this virginity for you? How is a sexually active woman who delivered four children a virgin? Isn't the issue of virginity just a farce put up by all of you? The three kings, who have sons, never married me when I was brought to them. I was an object of use and abuse to serve their purpose, I was not a wife.

'What do you want—a woman whose beauty is the talk of the three worlds and who can produce sons who will be heroes in their lifetimes, or do you want a partner for your life? I can be your partner and your better half, provided you see a woman in that spirit. In the last four years, I have lived for my father, an unknown disciple of an unknown guru, four men who needed sons and four men who needed a plaything. In all these years, no one has made me feel like a person who has a heart that can cry. I have been seen as a woman who is just a pleasure-giving object, but nobody saw in me a woman with emotions. Not one of you wondered what it must be to give birth to sons and leave them soon after to give birth to another. All saw me as the mother of their child, but none saw the mother in me.

'Each time I attained motherhood, my child was taken away from me. I did not get an opportunity to nurse and feed my children and express my motherly emotions. I was taken from one man to another so that a student could keep his promise of a guru dakshina he could not afford. A man who carries a woman from place to place to barter her for horses is just a trader in flesh and not a student. Just how did he forget that, or was his learning faulty? After getting his first lot of horses, all he thought of was the next lot and then the next. Not once did he find it necessary to check on the well-being of the woman who was enabling him to get the horses. But then why would he, when learned kings and sages had not? And to think that each of these men had mothers! Disgusting!'

She looked at King Yayati and said, 'A father used me to achieve his objective and became a great king. A disciple used me and became a great disciple who kept his word to his guru. I did what I did because it was expected that I agree to my father's wishes, else he would fail in his duty. To save all from failing, I have fallen, and today, the same father is discharging his fatherly duty with such pomp and grandeur. King Yayati is all talk about his achievements and generosity. He even talks of empowerment. What empowerment, dear Father? Has this swayamvar been arranged to exercise *my* choice or for you to ensure that you perform your ultimate daan? If the women in your culture were empowered, then you wouldn't have sold me for virtues to a man, whose only concern was horses. Such a shame—what a charade of fatherly responsibility!'

Madhavi looked at King Yayati who had hung his face in shame, and said, 'Father, I hate men, and I find the very presence of them nauseating. I can't bear to think of any one of those sitting here even coming close to me, leave alone anybody touching me. I have had enough of men making choices for me and leaving me to bear the consequences. I, who have helped all, have decided to renounce the world of men, who are out to use and abuse women like me. I am leaving for the forest. I will now live in the forest, so I pronounce, *Varam Vrivati Vanam*.'E

Saying this, Madhavi left for the forest.

Shakuntala woke up startled and lost her sleep thereafter. She was glad that at least in her dream Madhavi had found her voice.

Priyamvada

Madhavi's story had left a deep impression on Shakuntala, more so, since it dealt with the ancestors of Dushyant. She was worried that such behavioural aspects could show up in her son. She took greater care in ensuring that her son was brought up well and looked upon women as human beings and not as objects. Soon, all her attention was on how to bring up her son as a good human being.

Priyamvada came back to the ashram to deliver her first child and at the first opportunity came to meet Shakuntala. After seeking blessings from Sage Kanva, who left the cottage soon, she spoke to Shakuntala, 'I wanted to tell you something.' Shakuntala looked up. 'I spoke to my husband about you and the king and your child.'

Shakuntala stared at her. 'Why did you?'

Priyamvada replied, 'Why not, Shakuntala? I am your friend, and even if you didn't tell me, it was my responsibility to reach out to him and tell him about you and your son.' Then her face fell. Shakuntala looked at her, waiting for more.

Priyamvada continued, 'My husband was shocked to hear of it and scolded me. He said that he had not heard about it and forbade me from broaching this with anybody. I urged him to speak to the Rajguru, but he declined. He keeps me away from all public gatherings, as he fears that I might tell this to someone and he would get into trouble.'

Shakuntala's worst fears were coming true. Dushyant had forgotten her and she was alone in this big bad world, abandoned once again. First she was abandoned by her parents and now by her husband. Her stern face did not display any sadness, nor did her eyes shed any tears. She was not a weakling. She was the mother of the heir of the kingdom of Hastinapur and she was not worried about what the world would say about her. She was the queen of King Dushyant and had been married to him with God as witness, and borne a child as a testimony to their love. Nothing else mattered; at least not to her.

In the days to come, Priyamvada's movements were restricted as she was not keeping very well. Shakuntala would go to her cottage with her son, but the two couldn't speak much as Priyamvada's mother would always be around and in case she went out for some time, then it was Shakuntala's son who held centre-stage.

Priyamvada gave birth to a dead baby girl and on receiving the news, no one from her in-laws' place came to take her back. After waiting for a few months, her father and mother escorted her to Hastinapur and left her at her husband's home. On their return, Shakuntala learnt that Priyamvada's parents had not been treated with respect. They were not even asked to stay back for a day, so they had to leave immediately. They prayed that Priyamvada would be happy and hoped that she would conceive again.

Shakuntala was hurt on learning about Priyamvada. She couldn't understand why her happiness depended on bearing a son, instead of a girl or a dead child. Wasn't the child a result of love, or was it the cause of love? While she knew that sons were said to be the means to salvation of ancestors, why did people forget that without a woman, there would be no one to bring sons on earth? Was this too complicated to understand for people or was it just a myopic outlook where people were bothered only about their present and not the future of their children?

Even if one would grant that this line of thought was valid, Shakuntala could not rationalize it with reference to Priyamvada's husband, who already had a son from his previous marriage. Just how many sons were needed for his salvation and those of his ancestors? She worried for Priyamvada and was sad for her. Priyamvada had lost her child and had got no support from the one person in her life who mattered most to her.

Wasn't she in the same situation? Even she had not got any support from the only person she had loved. Hadn't she, too, been treated like a discarded cloth, worn once and disposed off after use? Shakuntala wondered what would be the future of Hastinapur, a kingdom where women were not respected and were simply objects of use and abuse, either for physical gratification or for begetting sons. Shakuntala dreaded to think that this was the kingdom her son was going to inherit. In such a scenario, it was imperative on her part to instil respect for women in him. She didn't want a son who only respected his mother and not the other women in his life. She wanted her son to respect a woman as an individual and not as a commodity that could be traded. Shakuntala wanted to ensure that she was able to ingrain such values in her son, so that the generations after him would inherit them.

Achyut

Shakuntala busied herself with her son as he learnt to walk and kept her and the others on their toes. She always felt that extra care was being taken of him and though she didn't quite like the idea she couldn't do much about it. She also noticed that Sage Kanva was not teaching him the scriptures as much as he would relate stories of bravery, morals and principles.

The sage had put him under the charge of Achyut, the imperishable. Shakuntala had known Achyut since he was a child. She knew that he was not interested in becoming a sage even though he was the son of one. He wanted to join the army of the king of Hastinapur. He was athletic and very well-built. He had strong shoulders and had a passion for archery. He would steal into the forest and practice archery as he was not allowed to follow such 'fancy passions' which were very 'unbecoming of a potential sage'. Once when Shakuntala tried to intervene on his behalf, she was asked to stay away from the issue. She was told that they did not want to disturb the established norms of society. It was also subtly added that every time someone had tried to do so, there had been sad consequences. She knew exactly what was being referred to and didn't like her matter being brought up thus. However, she had no choice but to keep silent. Achyut, too, had resigned to his fate and once in a while tried to live his dreams by other means.

Shakuntala's son provided Achyut with ample opportunities

to live his dreams. He would take Shakuntala's son for swimming in the lake, make him run and teach him to climb trees and jump without fear. Sometimes he would wrestle with him in the mud and other times he would be teaching him to fight with sticks. Even all this activity failed to tire out Shakuntala's son who became passionately attached to Achyut. Achyut, too, enjoyed spending time with Shakuntala's son, much to the discomfort of his guru, who felt that Achyut was unwilling to focus on the scriptures and probably taking advantage of Shakuntala's son's increasing demands.

Sage Kanva had noticed that the child would look forward to the sessions with Achyut and feign illness or sleep when it came to lessons. While the sage would be very upset with children who did not take scriptures seriously, he was visibly giving in to his grandson's neglect of the same. And though many saw this as indulgence, Sage Kanva perceived it differently. He knew that it was not in the child's blood to take to scriptures and he had found his calling in the sessions with Achyut. He felt that the heir to the throne of Hastinapur had to be physically active and develop a strong sense of justice and right and wrong.

The child was growing up to be a healthy and handsome boy. He was fair, had sharp features and the gait of royals. He was charming and his smile was divine. It was in her love for him that Shakuntala did not realize that it had been close to five years and they had not heard from the king of Hastinapur.

King Dushyanta

'Your Majesty,' the words startled Dushyant out of his reverie. It was the Rajguru who was standing in front of him. The king looked up and waited for the Rajguru to continue.

'There something that I have wanted to speak to you for some time, and if I have your permission, may I speak about it?" asked the Rajguru. Dushyant nodded in the affirmative.

'Thank you, Your Majesty. The council of ministers and I think that its time you conducted the Ashwamedha yagna, the Horse Sacrifice. A king of your stature and popularity needs to extend his boundaries and win friends and there is no better way to achieve this than conducting an Ashwamedha yagna.'

'Why Ashwamedha yagna?' enquired the King.

The Rajguru replied, 'Ashwamedha yagna is one of the most important royal rituals to assure the prosperity and well being of the kingdom, besides the good fortune of the king and his heirs. Its significance can be traced to the Vedas, where it says that Lord Prajapati was the first to have conducted the Ashwamedha yagna. Besides its religious reasons, the yagna is also the most legitimate way of territorial expansion while maintaining the sanctity and prestige of the king!' He continued, after a pause, 'All of us and the people of this kingdom are keen that you perform this yagna. It will rejuvenate the kingdom and its people and will also herald the power of Hastinapur, which though not in doubt, needs to be reiterated.'

Dushyant found himself smiling. 'Sure, Rajguru, that's a great idea. While I am not for unnecessary battles, an Ashwamedha yagna is a definitely a good idea. I think it would also rejuvenate the people of our kingdom and the army.'

'Exactly,' echoed the Rajguru. 'I am glad you agree with me. If I have your consent, then we should make arrangements, so that we can begin the same in about six to eight months' time.'

Dushyant was a trifle surprised. 'Does it take so much time to organize an Ashwamedha yagna?'

The Rajguru smiled. 'The arrangement for the yagna takes just about a month or two, what will take more time is your wedding, Your Majesty!'

'My wedding?' asked a bewildered Dushyant. 'What has my wedding got to do with the yagna?'

The Rajguru said. 'You cannot conduct an Ashwamedha yagna without a wife, Your Majesty, so first we will have to find a bride for you and select an auspicious time for the solemnization. All this will take about six months to complete and only then can we conduct the yagna.'

The words startled Dushyant. Marriage? Wife? The words had an ominous ring to them. Over the last few years, he had not been able to tell the Rajguru and his friends about him and Shakuntala.

'Why?' Dushyant heard himself ask.

'I beg your pardon, Your Majesty? You mean, why should you get married? Is that what you are asking?' asked a slightly amazed Rajguru, since he had never had to answer such a question from anybody, least of all a king!

Dushyant muttered, 'No that's not what I meant. I meant, what's the hurry?'

The Rajguru couldn't contain his bewilderment, 'Did you

say, *hurry*, Your Majesty? Rather, the general opinion is that it is already too late. The kingdom is ripe for a queen and an heir soon after.'

The Rajguru noticed that something was amiss with the king. He realized that the subject had unsettled the king, which was surprising. While there was no dearth of princesses from the neighbouring kingdoms, each more beautiful than the other, the king seemed a trifle disturbed with the idea of a wedding.

'Is everything fine, Your Majesty?'

Dushyant heard the Rajguru through the turmoil raging within him. 'Oh yes, Rajguru. I am fine. Allow me to think over the matter,' he said, indicating that the discussion was over.

The Rajguru bowed and left the court.

That night Dushyant retired early. He asked his guards not to disturb him, no matter what. He had all the lamps extinguished except one near his bed. The lone lamp failed to do justice to the huge chambers of the king, but Dushyant wanted it that way. He sat at the edge of his bed and kept staring at the lamp, which was stirring up memories. He could see Shakuntala in the flame of the lamp, staring at him. He could see her sad face asking him why he had forgotten her. Pain and disappointment were writ large on her face. He kept staring at the lamp.

The flame began to flicker, heralding the end of its life. It reminded him of the last lamp that had witnessed them embracing each other on the night of their wedding. Soon all that was left was the smoke from the burnt wick of the lamp. The smell left Dushyant disturbed. He headed towards the window in search of fresh air.

From the window he could see the stars. It was a clear night. What was not clear though was his mind, within which a war was waging. Why was this bothering him so much?

Why was this one instance disturbing him in such a manner? After all he was not in love. What he'd felt at the ashram was probably the environment which worked on him. There was something in the air, the serene beauty, the onset of monsoon, the birds, the rivers; it seemed that nature had conspired against him and set a trap.

And above all, Shakuntala—she was amidst it all. He had never come across a girl like her before. She had the lustre of fire and beauty which was beyond words. The way she stopped him from shooting the doe and the reprimand that she had unleashed. Nobody in his life had ever had the audacity to stop him from doing what he wanted to, but Shakuntala. She reminded him of a sandalwood tree surrounded by snakes. To possess her was a challenge and to win her over became a mission. The unachievable was the quest, and the moment she agreed, no promise was big enough in return...even the commitment of their first-born to be declared the heir apparent of Hastinapur. The wedding simply followed, even if it was gandharva-vivaha.

But wasn't the wedding his idea?

Of course it was, but at the ashram, a union without exchanging wedding vows would have been unthinkable and sacrilegious. He would have been accused of misleading a simple girl. The kingdom of Hastinapur would have been blemished forever and his ancestors would never have forgiven him for this act.

But wasn't he in love with her?

Dushyant was unsure. Was it love? Or was it a conquest? To have a girl like her say yes to him was the task. He wanted to win her over without force, for force was easy. He wanted her to bend emotionally. She was different. She was the daughter of a powerful Kshatriya, and the most beautiful of all celestial beings.

She was different from all the women he had ever known or wanted. He had to have her, but only after her consent.

Then why couldn't he forget her?

Dushyant did try to, but always failed. Just when she seemed to receding from his mind, there would be a missive from the ashram of Kanva, which fortunately was always delivered at his chambers. Once Amish noticed it and asked him about it. 'Oh nothing of your interest.' he had parried. Amish had joked, 'So what are you interested in at the ashram of Sage Kanva?' Dushyant had replied, 'I had sent them some grant from the treasury for building another ashram and buying some cows. Sage Kanva has just acknowledged the same.'

Amish found it odd as any grant from the treasury was an official matter and delivering such messages at the chambers was strange, but did not pursue the subject as it did not warrant discussion.

If he informed the others about Shakuntala, there would be no harm. He could bring her to the kingdom as a queen. There should be no objections.

Dushyant was unsure about this. He had tried to break the news of Shakuntala to his friends and even to Rajguru. But Shakuntala's parentage bothered him. Vishwamitra was both a feared and a revered sage who was once a powerful king. In many quarters, people felt that his challenging the order of society was out of place while some felt that he had been justified in questioning the order of Manu. Wouldn't his daughter have a streak of this rebel in her? Menaka was an apsara and all and sundry knew what apsaras meant to mortals. What kind of character traits would her daughter carry and would such a person be acceptable to the people of Hastinapur as a queen?

Further, he had promised Shakuntala that their first-born

would be the heir-apparent. What if the council of ministers and others questioned him about this decision? Did Dushyant, the as even king, have the right to grant that? As a husband, he could grant anything that was within the domain of the family or within his physical prowess, but thrones were not in the ambit of personal property. A wedding which was not solemnized in public and which had no witness could not be the basis of any commitment which could have political ramifications. What if this was challenged? What if people objected to this commitment as Shakuntala was not a princess of some kingdom? Would the people accept the son of a commoner as their heir-apparent? Who would he side with, the kingdom or Shakuntala?

It was this turmoil that would grip Dushyant and stop him from talking about Shakuntala. Many a time, he had tried to speak to Amish about it, but he felt that Amish was used to following the rule book. He would definitely object to this alliance. Once he thought of talking about it to the Rajguru, but he was of a different generation. He would never understand Dushyant's views and would perhaps resort to a discourse on ethics and morals! He had never been able to reconcile with the subject and as time passed, it was becoming more and more difficult. Now, after so many years, he would be confronted with 'Why now?'

But today, with the subject of the Ashwamedha yagna and his wedding being brought up, he was in a quandary. Now what? Should he tell them about Shakuntala, or should he let them make arrangements for his wedding?

Would it be best to simply forget the matter and look forward to a new chapter in his life?

Questions, questions and more questions. Why did life pose so many questions and not provide answers?

Sarvadaman

Shakuntala's son was now about five years of age. He was growing up with all the boys in the ashram and was undoubtedly the leader of the pack. Children loved him and the seniors adored him; no one made him feel that he was different from them, though all the elders of the ashram could see the difference. He not only looked divine, his mannerisms, too, were different from the other boys of the ashram.

One day when everyone was busy, Shakuntala's son went missing. Soon there was panic in the ashram and a massive search was initiated, headed by Achyut who was aware of all the probable places where he could be found. Shakuntala and the others stepped out of the ashram to look for him, thinking that he could have gone out to seek some fruits or chase some bird. Shakuntala had an uncanny fear that he could have gone to swim in the river, as that was his latest passion. She decided to head for the river with Achyut to rescue him, if he had got into any trouble, God forbid.

Shakuntala, Achyut and some of the boys got together and headed for the river. The way to the river was through a forest, in which a path had been beaten by the regular walking of the inmates of the ashram.

While they were walking towards the river, immersed in silent prayers, Shakuntala noticed something glittering in the rays of the sun on the ground. It was one of the anklets worn by her son which had been given to him by Gautami when the child was born. Panic beset everyone except Shakuntala—she knew that nothing untoward could befall her and her son, till she achieved her objective.

They stopped and started looking around. When they heard some sounds from deep inside the forest Achyut gestured all to keep quiet and followed the sounds with Shakuntala a step behind him, though Achyut had asked her to stay put. One by one, everybody joined them. And what they saw took their breath away.

Shakuntala's son was sitting playing with some tiger cubs with the tigress watching them benevolently. The child, happy to see his mother, ran towards her to show her and the others his new friends. But the tigress retreated deep inside the forest with her cubs, seeing a crowd approach. Her son tried to follow and stop them, but by then, he had been lifted by Shakuntala.

Shakuntala and the others heaved a sigh of relief and looked to see if he had been hurt anywhere. No one had ever seen such a sight, where a child of five was fearlessly playing with tiger cubs as the tigress watched them. The child was not scared, rather he seemed to enjoy the company of the wild cats as if they were his friends.

When the news reached the ashram, all the inmates were relieved that he was safe. Sage Kanva took the child in his arms and proclaimed proudly, 'From today, this boy will be known as Sarvadaman, the subduer of all! A boy who is not six as yet playing with tigers is straight from the tales, but this child has also proven that he is someone who is going to be remembered for long and forever. May you make the name of your parents and your ancestors shine like the sun!'

Sarvadaman ran to his mother, while all around him people chanted, 'Sarvadaman, Sarvadaman.'

That night, when Sarvadaman had gone off to sleep and Shakuntala was sitting quietly, Sage Kanva approached her and said, 'I want to speak to you about your son, my dear.'

Shakuntala was jolted out of her reverie, something that she would very often slip into. 'Yes, Father, what is it?' she asked.

Sage Kanva said, 'My dear, your son is growing and is at an impressionable age. What he has done today, comes to me as no surprise as such acts of bravery are characteristic of his clan and his calling. Whatever he had to learn in the ashram has been taught to him, and now we have nothing more to offer. As the future king of Hastinapur, he needs to get training that we are not equipped for; and neither should we deprive him of the same. It's time he started martial training and study of political policies.' The sage paused and then continued, 'Maybe it's time that you visit the king, since he hasn't in so many years. It is not fair to deprive the kingdom of Hastinapur of a such a deserving prince.'

Shakuntala knew that the defining moment had come and she had to face this by herself. Sage Kanva was saying, 'While I understand that this might not be very comfortable for you, you need to do it for the sake of your child. He cannot grow up here, which would be unfair to him. He has been asking about his father; how long will you keep telling him that his father is a king? He has to meet his father now and I am hoping that the father will accept him. After all, Hastinapur is a kingdom that is known for upholding dharma and the royal family has never been found wanting in this. While I don't want to force this on you, I want you to give it a thought. It is time you went there with Sarvadaman.'

Shakuntala was quiet for some time and said, 'When should we leave?'

Tears swelled in the eyes of the old sage as he left saying, 'I will make arrangements for you.'

Shakuntala leaves for Hastinapur

The morning was gloomy as if heralding the sadness of the day. The ashram had seen the child brought up on its premises, but now had to make peace with the idea that Shakuntala was moving on. Mrigakshi refused to budge from the spot that she hated, as if to lodge a silent protest on her being left alone, which she had never been in her long life. The plants woke up in tears and the birds declined to chirp.

Shakuntala went to meet Gautami who was inconsolable that she would breathe her last in her daughter's absence. She repeatedly told Shakuntala to make sure that she returned for her funeral. Shakuntala broke down.

One by one, she met each of the families in the ashram, as they were all part of her larger family. Shakuntala could feel all the birds and animals of the ashram shedding tears of sorrow. She was going to miss all of them, as all her life she had not known another place and other people. This was where she belonged and this was her home.

Sage Kanva was making great attempts to hide his tears. A celibate ascetic was sad at the departure of a child he had brought up. A man who was more than a father to the child was distraught at her leaving him. He was not sure if he was hiding tears of joy or sadness. Was he happy that she was at last going to be united with her husband, or was he sad that she was leaving him and his home? It was the dilemma of every father. Nurture the daughter, hold her hand and show her the way, keep her safe from the evil world, and one day, let her go to an unknown place, amongst unknown people and into an unknown culture. Would she be fine, would she be comfortable, would she be loved the same way, if not more, would she be happy as she was in the ashram…there was no end to his worries. Was that the reason why celibacy was considered a greater joy? But much to the horror of many sages, he had found more joy in this child. He had seen her from the time she was born, or soon after, and had never known a moment when he was not thinking about her, in the last few decades. As a daughter, she was sheer joy and her child simply divine. Possibly, God wanted him to be her father and the sage silently him thanked Him for that. The silent prayer caused a tear to trickle down the wrinkled face of the old father.

Shakuntala bent to touch her father's feet and his hands moved to bless her. 'May you find peace, my child, and may you get what is your due. Go my child, may dharma be with you.'

Shakuntala embraced her father and sobbed her heart out. She was not sure if she would ever get to see him again. She wanted to thank him for everything he had done for an abandoned child, but she couldn't find words to express her gratitude. She realized that by thanking him, she could demean his love for her which was nothing short of a love of the father. She decided to let her silence say it all.

Sarvadaman couldn't quite fathom why people were so sad. He was stepping out of the ashram for the first time and was made to wear new clothes. They said that he was going to meet his father, then why was everyone so sad? Moreover, Achyut was also with him, besides Anusuya, so there was no reason to worry.

Sage Kanva thought it necessary to send Achyut and Anusuya along with Shravan, who had been to Hastinapur a few times with missives from the sage to the king. Achyut could keep company with the child and Anusuya could stay with Shakuntala.

It was decided that they would reach Priyamvada's abode and leave Shakuntala and Sarvadaman with her and return. From there it would be Priyamvada and her husband who would take care of them.

Shakuntala left the ashram leaving everyone sad and depressed. Mrigakshi, shedding silent tears, remained immobile, expressing her solidarity with all the members of the ashram. Sage Kanva stood at the gates of the ashram, watching them leave, till they disappeared from sight.

Menaka was watching her daughter leave for her husband's home. Her heart was heavy…heavy with sadness and a dark foreboding about the future. Over a period of time, she had become wary of men on earth and was worried that her daughter would have to bear the brunt of her birth. She knew that the world was not as forgiving to a woman as it was to a man. A man was seldom blamed for his sins and if at all he was, it was passed off as an oversight. But a woman was blamed, shamed and made to suffer for the misdemeanours of men around her and for no fault of hers.

She was worried about the reception her daughter would get at the palace of the king of Hastinapur. If the king had not called for her in the last six years, would he accept her now? Menaka's heart was beating loud, betraying her apprehensions.

Hastinapur

Shakuntala and the others reached Priyamvada's house by late evening. She was very happy to see them. Priyamvada's house was very different from the houses in the ashram. It was made of bricks and had ornate windows. It had furniture which looked very royal and different from what they were accustomed to in the ashram.

Priyamvada's husband didn't seem too happy to see them and went out of the house after the customary greetings. Priyamvada explained that he had some work and would come back soon, but everybody understood the reason for his leaving.

As was planned, all except Shakuntala and Sarvadaman would leave, but since it was too late, they would leave the next day. Sarvadaman was tired as this was the first time he had travelled out of the ashram, for that matter it was the first time for all of them, except Shravan, who had travelled to Hastinapur carrying Sage Kanva's messages to the king.

They had dinner and retired for the day. Shravan and Achyut slept outside in the courtyard and Shakuntala, Anusuya and Sarvadaman slept in one of the rooms cleared for them. The three friends sat together till late, but without any major conversations. Each was trying her best not to broach the subject of Shakuntala meeting the king the next day.

It was very late when Priyamvada's husband returned. As soon as he arrived, she excused herself and left them to tend to her husband. After some time, Shakuntala could hear the loud voice of the husband. She knew that her arrival was not welcome, but she had no option. She decided to overlook it, feeling sorrowful that her entry to Hastinapur had started a war of words between the couple.

The night was interminably long and it seemed that the rooster had decided not to herald the arrival of the morning. The sun, too, had decided to be lazy that day. Soon nature had to give in and the first rays of dawn could be finally seen in the distance.

Shakuntala got up and stepped out of her room to find Priyamvada up and attending to household chores. She offered to help, but Priyamvada told her not to worry and freshen up.

One by one, they all woke up and soon, Shravan, Achyut and Anusuya were ready to leave. Anusuya was uncontrollable and could not be separated from Shakuntala. Achyut was sad and they had to tell Sarvadaman that they were going out to buy some new clothes for him, else Sarvadaman would not leave Achyut. Both Achyut and Shravan were devastated when they took their leave along with Anusuya.

Priyamvada's husband did not come out to see them off. Priyamvada feigned some excuse. However, just when they had reached the threshold, she whispered to Anusuya, 'Please do not say anything to my parents. It would only make them sad. Tell them I am very happy at my husband's home and convey my regards to them.' Anusuya embraced Priyamvada and wept again.

Soon Shakuntala was left all alone with Sarvadaman, thinking about what the day had in store for her and her son.

At the Court of Hastinapur

'Where are we going, Ma?' asked Sarvadaman. He could sense something important was in the offing, but couldn't fathom what. The last few days had been adventurous for him. He had seen life outside the ashram for the first time. What he didn't know was that it was a first for his mother too. People dressed differently here; they lived differently too. He could see different kinds of people and different dressing styles. Animals were made to work—he saw a horse pull a carriage, a donkey carrying bales of clothes and on the way to Hastinapur he noticed a pair of bullocks tilling the land. But there was no sign of tigers, lions or deer.

He noticed that his mother was tense and asked her, 'Where are we going, Ma?'

Shakuntala looked at him, as if she was rehearsing the words that she was going to say. 'We are going to meet your father.'

Sarvadaman stopped. 'Father? You mean the king?'

Shakuntala said, 'Yes, your father. He is the king of Hastinapur.'

Priyamvada and her husband looked at each other. They had almost reached the palace. As planned, Priyamvada stopped at the gates. Her husband was to leave Shakuntala at the entrance of the sabha, lest he got into trouble. Shakuntala had accepted the suggestion and was grateful for all the help provided so far.

Priyamvada embraced her and said, 'Go, my friend, you have endured enough. May God be with you.' Priyamvada stopped there and her husband escorted the two past the guards at the palace. They knew him and didn't stop them.

Sarvadaman was staring at the palace as they walked towards the main entrance. He had never seen anything like that before and was awed by the very magnificence of it all. Shakuntala too had not seen anything like this, though she could not see the entire structure, she could only see the entrance to the sabha.

They approached the sabha and Priyamvada's husband slowed his steps. Shakuntala realized that she was alone from here. She looked back at him and said, 'Let me thank you for everything that you have done so far. If I see good days, then I will meet you again, and if I don't then I won't mention a word about you. You can trust me.' Priyamvada's husband managed to smile and bowed his head and turned around to leave. But no sooner had he gone a few steps that he turned around and joined Shakuntala.

Shakuntala gave him a surprised look. He smiled and said, 'If you have the courage and determination to speak for yourself and your rights, then I, as a subject of Hastinapur, have the right to hear every word of yours. Let me escort you till the sabha. May God be with Hastinapur!'

Shakuntala was pleased for Priyamvada and happy that her husband had finally displayed strength of character. She followed him.

They entered the sabha, and suddenly she found herself standing right in the centre of a big gathering. Priyamvada's husband found his voice and said, 'Your Majesty, I have someone with me who wants to say something.'

All eyes were on the lady with the child. Priyamvada's husband stood aside. Shakuntala lifted her gaze towards the king of Hastinapur, sitting on a magnificent throne in front of her. He looked much the same except that the royal regalia made him look more a king than the man she had fallen in love with at the ashram. Even in her dreams, she had not visualized him in such finery. For her, he would always be the same dhoti-clad Dushyant of the ashram.

She suddenly realized that all eyes were on her. She looked straight at Dushyant and said, 'I am Shakuntala.'

'What can I do for you, lovely maiden?'

'Lovely maiden? Do you not know who I am, O King Dushyant?'

'No, lady, I don't remember having seen you before,' said Dushyant

'You don't remember or you don't prefer to remember? In any case, let me introduce myself to you. I am Shakuntala, your wife and the queen of Hastinapur.'

There was a hushed silence as the court reeled with shock. Then the courtiers started discussing and one by one all eyes turned to the king when Amish spoke up, 'Just what sort of a joke is this, lady? Do you know who you are speaking to and where you are standing at the moment?'

Shakuntala shot him a look and said, 'Yes, I know who I am speaking to. I am speaking to my husband and this is the court which my husband presides over and that makes me the queen of this court. Besides, I would rather have the king speak to me, instead of his minister. He didn't need one when he courted and married me, so I presume he doesn't need one now too.'

Amish's face glowered with anger but he kept quiet when he noticed firm confidence and surety of purpose on the face of the woman. She didn't look like an ordinary woman and the child radiated a mien of royalty which was beyond his comprehension.

Shakuntala turned to the king and said, 'Rise, O king, and welcome your wife. Doesn't the family of the Kurus know how to welcome women when they come to their in-laws' place for the first time? Is this the family of the great Puru who sacrificed his youth for King Yayati?'

The courtiers were visibly surprised by the king's silence and were looking at him curiously. It was then that the Rajguru spoke up, 'Just who are you, my girl, and do you realize what you are saying? You are accusing the king of having married you.'

Shakuntala looked at him and bowed with folded hands. 'Pranam, Rajguru. I am not here to accuse the king of anything. I am here only to remind the king of his duty and what is due to me as the rightful wife of a man, more so of a king. As for my identity…I am the daughter of Sage Kanva and was brought up in the pristine environment of his ashram; the same place where the king stayed for a few days and married me about six years ago.'

Amish shot a look at the king and stuttered, 'Sage Kanva's ashram?' Many more faces in the court recognized the name of the famous sage and shot a questioning look at Dushyant, just as did the Rajguru.

Dushyant was not affected by any of the looks, and simply said, 'So you claim that you are my wife; are you also going to tell me that the child with you is my son?'

Shakuntala said, 'Should I be thanking you for remembering or should I think that you are being sarcastic?'

'Lady, will you stop this nonsense? This is the royal court of the king of Hastinapur, not a stage for theatrics. We do not assemble here for entertainment, we conduct serious business here,' shouted Dushyant, beginning to lose his temper.

Shakuntala opened her mouth to respond when she heard Amish speak. 'Wait a minute. You said that you are the daughter of Sage Kanva. But all of us know that the sage is not married, so how are you the daughter of the great sage?' Amish continued as an afterthought, 'Unless you are also casting aspersions at the character of the sage…'

'Mind your words, young man,' Shakuntala retorted. 'You haven't seen the world enough to raise a finger at the sage, and don't you dare do that, lest you lose the finger that is raised at him. Even the gods wouldn't dare do it!'

The Rajguru intervened and said, 'Amish, please do not speak such words about Sage Kanva. My dear girl, I apologize on his behalf, but he is also true when he says that the sage is celibate, so how do you call yourself his daughter? Pray, if you could please explain.'

Shakuntala softened her voice as soon as she looked at the Rajguru and said, 'He is right when he says that the sage is a celibate. Sage Kanva is my foster-father and the only father I know. I am the daughter of Sage Vishwamitra and Menaka of Indra-lok. I was found by the sage, after my parents had abandoned me, and he has brought me up since then.'

Dushyant laughed. 'Oh, so you are the daughter of Sage Vishwamitra and Menaka? Menaka, the celestial apsara, who was *used* to lure a man away from his chosen path to a life of lust? Menaka, the divine apsara, who is at the beck and call of the great lord of the gods, Devendra? Menaka, the entertainer at the Indra-sabha? Some credentials to show, my lady! A daughter of an apsara lands at the sabha of Hastinapur and says that the king is her husband and all of us ought to believe her and recognize her as the queen. What more can we expect from a person of such origins? The same deceit, I guess.'

Shakuntala was shocked by the king's words. By now a few in the court had started to wonder who to trust, the king or this simple woman who seems to be absolutely unfazed by the surroundings.

There were some sneers at the last statement of Dushyant.

And then Dushyant growled, 'Are you out of your mind, lady? How dare a woman of such lowly birth come to my court and weave yarns? I would have you thrown away had it been anybody else.'

Shakuntala met Dushyant's eyes and said, 'Then why don't you do so, O mighty king of Hastinapur? What stops you from doing so? The truth, isn't it? And who gave you the right to pass judgements on my mother, Menaka? She was only obeying orders and, for all we know, she did it against her wishes. But mortals like you might not understand such divine compulsions, this would be beyond you, especially you, who are devoid of morals, and when questioned use the same morals as a shield. My mother was divine and being her daughter makes me semi-divine. Remember, you walk on the grounds but I fly the heavens! The difference between you and me is not small; it is that of the Meru mountain and a mustard seed. It is that of the rushing Ganga and a drop of water in a stagnant pond. It is that of the sky and a solitary bird in it! And as far as my father is concerned, well he was a Kshatriya, one of your kind, except much larger in stature, for you can't even dream of what he achieved. O king, don't question my birth and parentage as the constructs and the designs were divine. It is something beyond mere mortals like you and the likes of your ministers.'

The court was shocked into silence. Shakuntala said all this with quiet poise, but the sternness in her voice was not lost on the listeners. Amish was beginning to wonder if she was right, as he had never seen anybody with such dignity and confident fearlessness, which only came to those who had truth on their side.

The Rajguru was spellbound. He knew everything about the king-turned-sage Vishwamitra whose achievements were the subject of lore by now. He had never seen such radiance in any woman before and the child with her seemed to be naturally endowed with calmness and composure. His eyes were roving all around the court and he was listening to every word attentively as if he understood everything being spoken and could comprehend the significance of it all. A rare trait in someone who had been brought up in an ashram, which only went on to prove that probably Shakuntala was…

Dushyant snapped, 'One more word and I will have you thrown out and put behind bars. You have taken enough advantage of my civility, but no more. I hate to think that a woman in the guise of an ascetic is capable of such mischief and untruth. You will leave right now and take this mistake of yours who you refer to as my child.'

'Mistake? Did you call your son a mistake? Mistake by whom, O mighty and *virtuous* king? By me or by you? Nobody dare call him anything other than his name and address him as nothing but "prince". That is what he is, the prince of Hastinapur.

'O King Dushyant, you don't recognize me, but I have recognized you well. If you were not a human, then you would have been a bee who forgets the flower after depriving it of its nectar. If you were not a human then you would have been any lowly animal who uses the female of its species to satisfy its bodily need and leaves once its hunger is appeased. But O king of the kingdom which takes its name from rock-steady elephants, I am no flower who simply cries over its lost nectar and nor am I an animal which allows its male to leave after giving in to his need. I am Shakuntala and I am not someone who suffers in silence and sheds tears in isolation. I am like the snake that opens up its hood, and strikes, strikes the fear of life and God in men like you. I am the lightning, the sound of which reverberates the world over and not just at the place it strikes. I will not leave without ensuring that my son gets what is his right. I am not here to become the queen of Hastinapur, that's too small a compensation for cheating on me. I am here to ensure that our son gets the recognition that he deserves, first, since it was promised by you and second, so that no one thinks that lust was the cause of our child's birth and laughs at his parents, the way you and your courtiers have made fun of my parents.'

The court was shocked into silence. No one moved or said a word. At that moment, one could have heard the sound of a pin fall. But Shakuntala had not finished. She continued, 'O king of impeccable birth but the one who questions others' birth, don't forget, ridiculing a woman of noble birth is nothing short of inviting trouble, both on oneself and on one's kingdom. But I am not here to curse you as you are already cursed by your unwillingness to recognize me—the woman who is your wedded wife. A marriage whose witnesses have been none less than the gods in heaven, and I call them to testify for me. If there be gods in heaven and if I speak the truth, then may they make their presence felt, else the world will lose all faith in them.

'O mighty king, the Supreme Creator doesn't spare even one evil, and not in least, the spurning of a woman, who has left everything to be with one man. You dare to speak ill of me because I have come on my own without your invitation. But I waited for you to call me for more than six years, ever since you left the ashram of Sage Kanva after your hunting expedition. I have come on my own because you failed in your duty of sending for me, your wedded wife. I have come on my own to show the people of Hastinapur the folly of their king. I have come on my own to show your mighty ancestors what their descendant has fallen to. Their successor is insulting and ill-treating his wife and that too in public. I can hear the elephants trumpeting in agony, seeing what has been done to the kingdom that they have lent their name.'

Shakuntala paused and Dushyant tried to say something, but the burning rage on her face stopped him. She continued, 'You say you don't know me, your wife? What is a man without a wife? Till he doesn't get a wife, he can do nothing. A king without a wife is no hope to his kingdom. A wife is a man's best friend even when all friends have left him. A wife is a companion in all ages. A wife is like a father who holds one's hand and participates in yagnas, and at the same time, she is like a mother who nurses him when he is sick. A wife plays both these roles with equal ease. A wife is a partner in life. She walks before him when she sees death or danger approaching him; she walks with him when he needs an equal companion to share his success and dreams and she walks behind him when she sees fame approaching. A wife is the stability in a man's life; she is the pivot of dharma in every man's life. A wife is a path to salvation, even of an evil man. A wife is the path to the salvation of his previous generations, for only she can give him a son. On his own, he can do nothing, even for his own ancestors. Without a son, his ancestors would be languishing in the hell called put. A son is referred to as put-ra as he is the one who rescues his ancestors from hell.

'A wife can show him heaven on earth, and if spurned can show him hell on earth. A wife, when treated scornfully, can become the terrible Kali who kills all who are evil, not only in deeds but also in words. I who am chaste and honest have the power in me to curse you for your behaviour. I who have thought of no man other than you, I who have given myself wholeheartedly to none but you, I who have loved none but you, have dharma at my behest. If I have faltered in any one of the above-mentioned attributes, may I be struck dead right now by all the celestial objects, elements and the gods who are watching this murder of dharma by the one who is supposed to be the upholder of dharma himself. But, for you, O liar of a king, I don't need to invoke the gods. My chastity is enough to ensure that another word of evil against me, and your head would burst into a thousand pieces. But I am not done yet. I have not proven to the august assembly of the Kuru court my pristine position and the pious birth of my child, the prince of this kingdom!

'With me, I bring life's most joyous creation, your own child. Can there be any happiness other than the joy of seeing one's son running towards him to play on his knees and climb on his shoulders? In a child, a man sees his own childhood. A child is a mirror of his past and the only way to relive his childhood. A man longs to have his child hold his finger and learn to walk and talk. A man longs to have his children follow him, love him and carry forward his name. They say that even ants take care of their eggs; what kind of an example are you setting by questioning the birth of your own child in this court, O king?

'God has been kind enough to give you a son, why are you not accepting His kindness instead of insulting him in public?'

Shakuntala's eyes were blazing and she seemed to be the child of Lord Agni when she spoke. No one in the court had any doubt about what she was saying; fire never needed to prove its own worth and capability. While the king was beginning to feel the heat of Shakuntala's words, for some reason, he could not bring himself to accept his guilt. It seemed to be too late to stop Shakuntala…she had gone too far to be stopped. Her anger seemed as dangerous as her warmth that he had experienced at the ashram. The divine beauty that had attracted him had now changed to a raging fire which was bound to burn him to ashes, but not before she had poured out all that she had been provoked to say.

Shakuntala continued, 'This son of yours is no ordinary child, O king. He is destined to change the course of history. On his birth, the gods had prophesied that he would perform a hundred Ashwamedha yagnas, and you, O grand Kshatriya of the Puru clan, know the meaning of performing a hundred Ashwamedha yagnas. You are spurning your own child who is destined to make the entire lineage proud. Have you forgotten the chant during the consecration rites of infancy? They say, "Thou art born, O son, of my body! Thou art sprung from my heart! Thou art myself in the form of a son. Live thou to a hundred years! My life dependeth on thee, and the continuation of my race too, on thee. Therefore, O son, live thou in great happiness to a hundred years."[F] He is your mirror image and he has your blood in him. Just as the fire for sacrifices comes from one's home, he has come from you. Look on him, O king, and you will find yourself in him. Don't spurn him, for he is you and in him live the aspirations and dreams of your ancestors. Look at him, and you will see in him the future of Hastinapur. Look at him and you will see in him...'

'Stop, you wretched liar!' shouted Dushyant from his throne, to the utter shock of the gathering. 'You have spoken enough and I will hear no further. A child of lust, born of deception, an impious purposeless life, is quoting the scriptures in the court of Hastinapur? The rotten fruit of a liar of a mother and over-ambitious father now brings forth her fruit and tries to hang it on the chaste tree of the Purus? Go away, woman, go find a father for your child elsewhere, for all the scriptures cannot change my path of righteousness and truth. Your words and curses have no meaning for me, for I know that I have never met you and know you not and have seen you never before. You will leave before I have my guards throw you out of this palace of the great Kurus.'

Shakuntala stood there like the banyan tree in a storm, steadfast and strong. She was an image of strength and piousness. Her eyes blazed and fire emanated from every pore of her body. Not a soul in the court had any doubt regarding her words, even though they had not seen her before or heard about her. The child, though in the garb of an ascetic, looked more royal than royalty.

Shakuntala was quiet for a moment and then extended her hand to the king, and said, 'And this, O mighty king? Don't you remember this signet ring that you left with me before you left with a promise that you would send for me as soon as you reached Hastinapur?'

There were murmurs in the court. Dushyant was quiet. The Rajguru came closer and saw the ring of the royals of the Puru clan and then looked at the king, who just hid his hand under the cloak. If there was one person in the court, who till this moment was in doubt, he too was now convinced that Shakuntala was speaking the truth. She continued, 'I could have shown this the moment I entered the court, but O king of this kingdom, I wanted you to atone for the last six years by accepting the truth without any proof. I wanted you to walk the path of truth on your feet without the help of the crutch of the signet ring. But you remain crippled and unable to stand for yourself.'

Dushyant found the Rajguru staring at him, just as Amish and the others were questioning him with their silent stares.

'O you vile woman, that was the same ring I lost during one of my hunting expeditions. You, who roam the forests, could have found it and kept it for this day. The ring bears the symbol of the kingdom and for wily women like you, it is not unimaginable to make such claims by bringing it here. Let me tell you, lady, such things will not make me change my mind. You have no proof and

I need none to be convinced that you are behaving according to the blood that runs in your veins, so leave before it's too late!'

Shakuntala said, 'I will leave, O King Dushyant, for I hate to spend any more time in this court of deception, but not before I have told the people the truth of my child and reminded you of yours. Six years ago, you were at the ashram of Sage Kanva and got married to me with the gods as witness. At that time, my being the daughter of an apsara and a Kshatriya was acceptable to you as that made me worthy and apt for you. At that time, my birth out of lust didn't bother you, and what I thought was love was nothing but the lust of another Kshatriya in my life. Needless to say, my life is full of coincidences and repetitions of sorts. First my father, a Kshatriya, fell in love with Menaka and called it lust and then you, another Kshatriya, fell in love with me, which I now see was nothing but a moment of lust for you. First I was abandoned by my parents and now I am abandoned by my husband, the man who should have been my sole protector, at least as they ordain in the scriptures. You spend a night with me and leave the next day for your kingdom, with the promise of sending for me as soon as you reach your kingdom.'

Shakuntala paused and brought out what seemed like a waistband from her potli, and said, 'Was this, also lost during some hunting expedition, O king who seems to be losing too many things? This is not something that comes off anywhere, except in the inner chambers of one's home, right, King Dushyant?'

Gasps were heard from the court as she held the waistband aloft which was undoubtedly royal. Shakuntala hurled it at the feet of King Dushyant to the shock of everyone present in the court. The waistband lay mockingly at his feet and a few emeralds fell out, scampering away to hide in shame, for being part of the adornment of such a man.

'It is a shame to bring this out in this manner, especially since it reminds me where this could have come off and why. But I hope the generations to come see this as an insult to you and not to me. I have been insulted enough by the man who should have risen to accept me; thereafter, nothing can be worse. I am not here to claim my position as the queen of Hastinapur, but for the rightful place of my son, who has been with me and has been brought up to be the future king of this kingdom. But I now realize that he will not grow up to be a good king under the guidance of his father who is a liar and has no moral strength of character.

'But let me tell you, O King Dushyant. Sarvadaman, my son, will be one of the greatest kings on earth, who will prove all his ancestors worthy and will expand the kingdom to all sides only to be stopped by the mighty oceans and mountains and nothing else. His name and fame will surpass all others in the clan, and that I promise, will happen, you notwithstanding!'

Menaka was watching her daughter's reputation and life being sullied in the same court which was known for upholding the traditions of civility and establishing many rules of life and laws. She had kept quiet through all the injustices heaped on her, but would not allow this to go on any further. She ran to Indra to seek divine justice for her daughter.

When she entered the court of Indra, she found Narada Muni with him. Seeing her rush in unannounced, they were shocked. But Narada knew the cause.

Menaka said, 'Lord of the gods, there is nothing unknown to you and not a leaf moves without your knowledge. I have never said a word till date, but today my daughter is being ill-treated on earth and the world is keeping quiet. Before she turns into a destructive feminine force and rightfully so, please stop and do something. I want justice for my daughter. She is being insulted and called all sorts of names as a result of the acts and designs of gods. I am not worried that I am called names, but not my daughter, Lord Devendra, please, I beg of you, you have to intervene. It's now or never. Never will people have faith in love and every act of love will be known as lust. Never will women be able to decide for themselves what is right for them, for every decision will be seen as erroneous. Never will people trust a man, for every gesture of a man will be seen with doubt and intrigue.'

Menaka looked at Narada. 'Munivar, you know how much I loved the sage and that he, too, was in love with me. While I agree that lust was the cause of our meeting, you know that my child was not the result of lust. I don't want my child to be remembered as the result of an unholy union and nor should her child be seen as a child of deception, even if that was the case from the king's end. Munivar, please stop this insult of women on earth. You know what happens when women are wronged. We have seen the scorn of a woman wronged, I dread to think what would happen if my Shakuntala becomes a Kali on earth. Please, lord, please.'

Indrani had entered the court by then and was sad to see the plight of Menaka. She went to her and said, 'Blessed are you who have felt the pain of humans. Blessed are you who have felt the love of a child in the human way, for only humans cry out of joy during the most painful moment of their lives, that of giving birth to another life. Blessed are you who are able to cry in pain for your child, as only a mother can do so. My dear, yours will be done.' She then looked at Indra and said, 'While I am not too concerned with your motivations to start it all, I feel that your intervention is needed, lest people laugh at the lord of the rains in future. If you want to be associated with the spring of life by unleashing the rains, let your presence be felt today as the breeze of justice. Here is an opportunity to save a child who is being wronged by the institution that should be most faithful on earth, the monarchy. They say that when a man is a king, he is God's incarnation on earth. Are you going to let someone sully the name of gods and the faith placed in them? No, my lord, you cannot let this happen. Do something my lord, before the bounds of faith are broken forever.'

Indra saw all eyes on him.

Shakuntala was saying, 'Sarvadaman is your son and will remain your son and for that I don't need your acceptance. He will prove his claim under the sun, irrespective of you. I am leaving your court, O king of Hastinapur. You have made a grave mistake by spurning your wife and child and the gods are a witness to this, just as they were during our wedding. Just as your character has been tested today, so have been the gods in heaven. It is for people to maintain their trust in you and the divinity that is supposed to rest with you on earth.'

Saying this, she turned to leave the abominable atmosphere of the court of Hastinapur. Just as she was stepping out of the sabha, there was a huge thundering sound, which seemed to shake the entire earth. Everyone stopped wherever they were, as a bodiless voice pronounced: 'O King Dushyant, stop your wife from leaving. Don't insult the woman who has given you a son, a son who will bring fame to your lineage. Shakuntala is your wife and we were witness to your wedding. A kingdom which doesn't respect women cannot be saved even by us. When famines and floods strike a land, it is not at the whims of us gods; it is because the land has been unfair to women. We don't visit a place that doesn't respect women, and nor do we accept offerings if a woman is not accompanying the man. The child with her is your son, and the deliverer of your ancestors. He is part of you and born from Shakuntala. There can be no greater misfortune than to disown one's own son and that too with full knowledge of the same. A woman is the receptacle which accepts and nurtures the son who has been begotten by the father. O King Dushyant, you have been blessed with a wife like Shakuntala and twice-blessed with a son. Stop them and accept them.'

अभूतिर एषा कस तयज्याज जीवत्र जीवन्तम आत्मजम
शाकुन्तळं महात्मानं दौ:षन्तिं भर पौरव
भर्तव्योऽयं तवया यस्माद अस्माकं वचनाद अपि
तस्माद भवत्य अयं नाम्ना भरतों नाम ते सुत

abhūtir eṣā kas tyajyāj jīvatra jīvantam ātmajam
śākuntalaṃ mahātmānaṃ dauḥsantiṃ bhara paurava
bhartavyo 'yaṃ tavayā yasmād asmākaṃ vacanād api
tasmād bhavatya ayaṃ nāmnā bharato nāma te sutaḥ

Therefore, O thou of Puru's race, cherish thy high-souled son born of (Queen) Shakuntala and because this child (Bharat) is to be cherished by thee even at our word, therefore shall this thy son be known by the name of Bharat ('the cherished').[G]
(Adi Parva, Mahabharat)

The court rose in unison and chanted, 'Bharat Bharat'. The prince of Hastinapur was named Bharat by the gods.

Dushyant was shocked and knew that he was left with no alternative as all eyes were on him. The courtiers, Shakuntala and the child were all staring at him. His sin had been exposed and for a moment he wondered why he had lied and been so rude when he knew it all, all this while? Why had he not welcomed her the moment she entered the court? He stood up and said, 'People of Hastinapur, please welcome your queen and the crown prince of Hastinapur. The lady is my wife and the child is my blood.'

He got up from his throne and came down to Shakuntala.

She looked at him; the pain visible for all to see.

Dushyant embraced Bharat who was elated to find his father. He was happy and so was everyone present in the court. Dushyant approached Shakuntala and said, 'My dear, I am sorry, but I had to put up the pretence. I recognized you the moment you walked in, but couldn't accept you straight away. O queen, I hope you understand. Our wedding and our union was held in private and there were no witnesses to it. All that we spoke about and all that we had for each other was in private.'

Shakuntala, snapped, 'Private? What is private on earth? When you were with me and when I was with you? Even in the moments which were private between us, there was someone watching. Did you ignore the presence of Surya during the day and Chandra at night? Did you ignore Vayu and Agni which are all-pervasive? Did you ignore the fear of Yama which is with every mortal all his life? And above all, even if any one of them were missing, how could you ignore Lord Dharma, who should be by the side of every man, and more so, of a king? Not for a moment is a man alone, O king of Hastinapur, and don't forget that if the gods do give up on you and decide to remain absent from the universe, man still has his soul with him even in his loneliest moment.'

A rather shocked Dushyant tried to explain, 'My dear Shakuntala, I don't deny the presence of all of them in the universe, but the world is made up of human beings. History has never been fair to women when there have been no witnesses to their weddings or when they have been away from the eyes of the majority for a long time. All sorts of aspersions are cast on women. I was only echoing the words that could have been hurled at you if I had accepted you unconditionally. With all the harsh words spoken, I have ensured that no one can question your conduct in the future,' and added softly, 'even if history paints me as a poor character.'

He continued, 'More importantly our son would not have been recognized as the legal heir to the throne if I had accepted you at your sole behest. Even if people had not objected, they would have cast aspersions on him. My promise to declare him the heir to the throne of Hastinapur was made by a husband to his wife. What I assented to was a personal matter between two individuals who were in love. While matters of the heart should have been separated from matters of state, I yielded to your condition, but that was the call of my heart. Once I returned, I was a king and realized that such matters of state needed the acceptance of all the courtiers and subjects. A marriage which was not solemnized in public would have led to hushed discussions in the kingdom, which would have been counter-productive both for our son and the kingdom. Such kingdoms where the royalty is in question are vulnerable to attacks by enemies, who wait for such issues. My dear, I wouldn't want all this, would I? But now with the sanction of the gods, I have no problem. People have accepted you and Bharat and so have I. Come my dear, let me take you with me and introduce you to your family.'

Saying this, Dushyant lifted his son and turned to leave for the inner quarters.

Shakuntala

Dushyant realized that Shakuntala was not following him. He turned around and repeated, 'Come, my dear, why have you stopped?'

Shakuntala looked at him calmly and said, 'I am not coming with you. I am leaving.'

Dushyant was surprised, 'Leaving? Leaving? Why? For where?'

'I am leaving you, O king of Hastinapur,' said a cold Shakuntala.

'But why?' asked Dushyant, 'I have accepted you now and have no hard feelings. I have even pardoned you for all that you said to me…'

'Pardoned me? Pardoned me, did you say?' shot Shakuntala. 'I haven't asked for pardon from you, O king of Hastinapur, and pardon for what? I have not said anything wrong and stand by all of it even after your magnanimous acceptance of our relationship.

'You didn't hear me well, O king. I didn't come here for myself; I came here only to ensure that our son gets his rightful due. Having done that, I have no urge or need to stay here. One more moment and it would mean compromising with my self-esteem. I can't imagine spending my life with a man who loved me not for what I am, but for my body. All that you said to me six years ago were lies and had I not come here, you would have forgotten it all. I hate to think that I allowed you to touch me without love. I hate to think that what I thought was love was in fact lust and nothing more. In the last six years, you never thought of me once and that is a proof of your feelings towards me. All that you now say are mere excuses.

'I need no forgiveness, on the contrary, it is for you to seek pardon, O king of Hastinapur. But I will spare you the trouble, as I don't intend to forgive you, so ask not for pardon, O great king. You came on a hunt and hunt you did and that is the truth. But I am not an animal who will succumb to injuries. While I extract no price for the injustice, I do not accept it either. Having established the rights of my son, I don't absolve you of the crime of deserting the one person who had left all behind and walked with you. A woman walks with a man leaving everything—her friends, family and surroundings—in the sole anticipation that she would need nothing but the love of the man for whom she has left everything. And when the same man cheats her, there can be nothing more heartbreaking. The six long years that I spent waiting for you, the six long years it took me to realize that you would not come on your own, have been the longest years of my life. In these six years, I have waited, but now I have accomplished the main objective of my life.

'When you wanted to marry me, there was no conflict between the king and the man in your mind. When you touched me, no conflict arose in your mind, then why is that when it came to accepting me, you were torn between the two roles? When you promised me that our first-born would be the heir to the throne of Hastinapur, there was no conflict, but once you were back to your kingdom, how did such a conflict arise?'

'But…' Dushyant tried to protest, but piped down when he saw Shakuntala brush aside his feeble protest.

Shakuntala raised her hand and said, 'I am not done yet, O

mighty king of Hastinapur.'

She continued, 'I leave Sarvadaman with you, as he is your responsibility and the heir to the throne and thus, the hope of Hastinapur. But, from today onwards, he will remind you of all the wrongs heaped on me. Every day, he will remind you of my existence and refusal to bear the injustices meted out to me. O king of Hastinapur, it's your turn to feel the pain of love, if there was any, and separation, which is for sure. From today, you will feel the pain of being abandoned, with a difference though… because in your case, you will know the cause of being abandoned.'

Dushyant was shocked, 'But where will you go?'

Shakuntala looked at him through bloodshot eyes. 'Is that all that you are concerned about? Well don't worry, I will find a place. Whoever has asked Ganga where will she go? She finds her place, the world is large.'

Sarvadaman had tears in his eyes, and said, 'But Ma…'

Shakuntala looked at him and a tear escaped her eye. 'Don't cry, my son, I am here. But from today, work to ensure that you become a good king and worthy of the throne of Hastinapur. Before you become a king, make yourself a good man. Never discard scruples and principles for anything, however alluring it be. Bring strength to your character first, the rest will follow. Don't forget the basics of humanity and never hurt or spite a woman. A woman is earth who can beget and allow continuity to humanity. Respect her and love her, don't despise her, and above all, never abuse her.

'Remember, my son, it is a woman who brings you on earth and it is the same woman who holds your finger and teaches you to walk. Later another woman befriends you and journeys the world with you and makes your life heaven on earth. At every stage of your life, respect the woman for who she is to you. The earth tears herself to allow the sapling to sprout, but if man hurts mother earth, she opens her mouth and swallows all in her bottomless pits. The world comes to an end when a woman is wronged. Don't ever become a cause to end the world.'

All eyes were on Shakuntala, who was oblivious to the people around her. She added after a pause, 'Son, you will see worse times ahead. Stand up to the oppressors and oppose the tormentors. Women of later generations might not have the courage that I have; they will need more help from men as one of the major perpetrators of violence and injustice will be men. Give them that courage and be a man among men. Grieve not for me, and remember, your mother is alive. Every mother is alive, till mother earth continues to bear mankind.'

Sarvadaman touched her feet and Shakuntala gave him one last look before she turned to leave.

The court rose, but none had the courage to stop her. They knew that she would not stop, just as the blazing rays of the sun cannot be stopped and gushing water cannot be contained. The courtiers had just witnessed a lightning of a woman, who was nothing short of divine, endorsed by the gods. Divinity had its own manifestations and they knew that there was no match for her in the palace, or the kingdom.

Shakuntala stepped out of the palace and started walking out of Hastinapur.

Dushyant and Bharat kept gazing at Shakuntala, watching her leave them forever, till she disappeared into the horizon.

Menaka saw all and her tears just wouldn't stop. She was proud of her child and wished women on earth had the courage of her daughter. She was glad that her daughter had the courage to say—I am Shakuntala, no less!

Epilogue

The court of Hastinapur was quiet. It was quite a contrast to when the court was in session. The regal throne, the seat of King Bharat was unoccupied, as were the seats of the courtiers. The few oil lamps that were burning threw long shadows on the walls of the massive hall. The ornate design of the chandelier was occasionally visible when a slight breeze brought its crystals into the line of light. Except for the tinkle of the chandelier and the gentle rustling of the curtains, there was no other sound in the empty hall.

There were no one at the large court, except for the king of Hastinapur, King Bharat, who stood in a corner looking at the large court in its empty darkness. The darkness seemed to be a reflection of his state of mind. Each was challenging the other, as if to ask which was darker.

He looked all around; there were portraits of all the past kings who were his ancestors, King Yayati, King Puru and his father, King Dushyant. All of them seemed to be questioning him as the erstwhile kings of a great kingdom. Each wanted to know why it was taking him so long to declare the heir-apparent to the kingdom, when he was the proud father of nine sons?

Proud?

'Did you call for me, O benevolent king?' a known voice brought King Bharata back to the court of Hastinapur. It was the voice of the Rajguru.

'Yes, Rajguru, please be seated. My apologies for calling you at such an unearthly hour, but I needed to confer with you immediately, and so...' said King Bharat.

'You embarrass me, Your Majesty. Please tell me what I can do for you. If you have called me at such an hour, then it must be of importance for the people of Hastinapur,' replied the Rajguru.

Bharat nodded his head and said, 'You are right, Rajguru. It is important and it does concern the people of Hastinapur.'

For some time they sat in silence. Bharat looked in the direction of the lone guard on duty and gestured to him to leave. Now they were absolutely alone in the court, except for the ancestors on the wall, waiting eagerly to hear what the king of Hastinapur had to say.

Bharat began to pace the huge hall while the Rajguru waited patiently for the king to say something. He had observed that the king seemed worried lately; very often he was lost in thought. He knew that it was something that had serious ramifications; else he wouldn't have been summoned at such a late hour. It also meant that the matter could not be discussed with anybody and needed secrecy.

'I have been thinking about declaring the heir-apparent to the throne of Hastinapur,' the voice of Bharat jolted the Rajguru from his thoughts. However, he waited, knowing that there ought to be more to the statement. 'But I have a dilemma,' Bharat continued looking at the Rajguru.

The Rajguru favoured him with a look which seemed to ask 'what dilemma'?

Sensing the question, Bharat said, 'The dilemma is regarding who should be declared the next king of Hastinapur.'

The surprised look on the Rajguru's face was back—what was the confusion?

Bharat continued, 'I am not sure who should be declared the next king, as none of my sons are eligible for this great responsibility!'

The Rajguru's jaw dropped. 'Your Majesty...'

Bharat continued, 'You heard me right, Rajguru, I don't find any of my sons eligible for the enormous responsibility that my forefathers have left me. That is the cause of my worry. I am unable to arrive at any decision.'

'But...' the Rajguru said, 'but what do you intend to do? Out of your nine children, you don't find any one eligible? On what counts do you deny them this right?'

'Right?' Bharat shot a look at the Rajguru. 'What right? Right to the throne of Hastinapur? The throne of Hastinapur is not the personal property of Bharat. It is the legacy of the previous kings and their rule. The previous kings found their offspring eligible, and handed over the throne to their sons to rule, but I don't seem to find the same qualities in my sons my forefathers found in their sons and my father in me! Do I still hand over the throne to one of my sons? Is this fair to the legacy of my ancestors? Will they pardon me for doing so?' Bharat looked up at the portraits of his father and grandfather.

'But what choice do you have, O Majesty?' asked a bewildered Rajguru.

'That's exactly why I called you here, Rajguru. Tell me, should I install an ineligible son of mine, simply because he is my son, and bring disrepute to the mighty kingdom of Hastinapur or should I install someone else, who might not be my blood, but could be far more eligible for the throne?' Bharat asked.

'If we go by the rules, then your son should become the king, but then...' Rajguru stopped, as if he was thinking or searching for words.

'Then what, Rajguru?' asked an impatient Bharat.

'But then,' continued the Rajguru, a trifle hesitatingly, 'you can exercise any other choice, except that it might not be fair to the princes.'

Bharat looked at the Rajguru steadily. 'Not fair to the princes, but fair to the people of my kingdom. To be fair to my blood, I can't be unfair to my subjects. Aren't my subjects my children too? You have always advised me that all decisions should be taken keeping the subjects and ethics in mind. How come today you are going against your own suggestions? Installing my son on the throne would be unethical besides being unfair to my subjects.'

An exasperated Rajguru said, 'Then what do you propose? There is no precedent to what you are trying to do, nor do we have anything in the rule book.'

'If there is nothing in the rule book, does it mean it doesn't exist?' asked Bharat.

The Rajguru said, 'Your Majesty, I am unable to understand your words. Let me assure you that I have always trusted your judgement. If you say that your sons don't deserve to sit on that throne, I am not disputing you, but I still have not understood what you propose to do. I am willing to hear your judgement on this and, if it is in the benefit of your subjects, rest assured that I will be the first one to commend it. I pray, Your Majesty, please tell me what you have in mind.'

Bharat said, 'If the rule books do not say anything about who should be the crown prince in the absence of an eligible person, can't the king declare someone he considers worthy as the crown prince? There will be no father on earth, who would not like to see his son taking his place in future; rather, that is the dream of all fathers. But I am a father to my subjects too, and that makes my decision all the more critical. In the absence of an eligible candidate amongst the royalty, can't I declare a commoner or someone who is not royal to be the king?'

The Rajguru was surprised, but decided to keep his counsel.

Bharat continued, 'I have met Bhumanyu, the son of Sage Bharadwaj, and in him I find all the qualities of a great king. For the sake of my subjects and for their well-being, shouldn't I overlook my own sons and allow a worthier person to become the king? Would this be against the laws? What rule am I breaking? If the well-being of my subjects is the reason behind my decision, then I see no crime in that. I want my descendants to realize that I have made a change in the institution that will go a long way in establishing the law of succession. Let my descendants make use of this as a precedent, where the ineligible is sidelined even if he is of royal lineage to let the deserving ascend the throne.'

The Rajguru could sense heaviness in the voice of King Bharat. He could sense the father in him taking a back seat to the king of Hastinapur. He could hear the choked voice of the father being made to lie low by the fearless and just voice of the king. The Rajguru's eyes blurred and it was only then that he realized the true meaning of Chakravarti. It needed a lot of strength and high standards of ethics to say what the king had just stipulated. No wonder they called him Chakravarti Bharat!

The Rajguru nodded in approval of the king's suggestion and left the court feeling proud that he had the rare honour of being an advisor to such a king who had set a precedent that no one had seen or heard before. Such kings were a rarity and praised be the parents of such a king.

Bharat stood tall amongst the portraits of his ancestors. He could feel all of them smiling at him and blessing him. Bharat offered a silent prayer to his mother Shakuntala and said, 'Mother, I hope I have taken the right decision. I hope I been able to live up to your expectations and have done justice to all that you had taught me as a child.'

Bharat sat in the court in solitude till late, waiting for the first rays of the sun. Today, the rays of the sun were rays of hope—hope for his kingdom, hope for his subjects and hope for his ancestors; and, above all, the rays epitomized the smile that he could sense on the face of his mother, Shakuntala.

Many say that it was King Bharat who sowed the first seeds of a vibrant democracy where merit was given precedence over lineage. Tragically, the next few generations forgot about this, and later, the likes of Dhritarashtra reverted to the practice of anointing their sons to the throne as a birthright, making dynastic succession a norm.

Unfortunately, not much has changed in the modern-day Bharatvarsh, the Land of Bharat!

Glossary

VRITRA: In the Vedas he is the demon of drought and unfriendly weather, with whom Indra fought a major war and released the waters of the skies withheld by Vritra. Sometimes called Vritrasura.

MUNIVAR: A generic way of addressing Narada Muni.

APSARAS: The apsaras were the celebrated nymphs of Indra's court. The name signifies 'moving in the water'. The Ramayana and the Puranas attribute their origin to the churning of the ocean. It is said that when they came forth from the waters neither the gods nor the asuras would have them for wives, so they became common to all. They also bear the appellations of suranganas, 'wives of the gods', and sumad-atmajas, 'daughters of pleasure'.

GANDHARVAS: Gandharvas were singers and musicians in the court of Indra who attended the banquets of the gods. Chitraratha was chief of the gandharvas and the apsaras were their wives or mistresses.

VEDA: Root, *vid*, to know. 'Divine knowledge'. The Vedas are holy books which are the foundation of the Hindu religion. They consist of hymns written in an old form of Sanskrit, and according to the most generally accepted opinion they were composed between 1500 and 1000 BC. But there is no direct evidence as to their age, and opinions about it vary considerably. There are four Vedas, Rig, Yajur, Sama and Atharva.

It is believed that the Vedas were arranged in different forms by the renowned Maharishi Ved Vyasa, the author of the epic Mahabharata, which is often referred to as the pancham-ved or the 'fifth veda'.

ASURA: Demons and enemies of the gods.

MANTRA: An incantation, a spell.

YAGNA: A sacrifice, a ritual to achieve some objective.

DEVENDRA: A name of Lord Indra, meaning lord of the gods.

KAMADHENU: The celestial cow which grants desires. She emerged from the churning of the ocean.

KSHATRIYA: The regal and warrior caste.

BRAHMIN: The learned class, the members of which may be, but are not necessarily priests.

MANU: The primordial man and also the author of the lawbook, known as Manusmriti, which lays down the laws of behaviour for mankind.

SOMARASA: The juice of soma, a milky climbing plant (*Asclepias acida*), extracted and fermented, forming a beverage offered in libations to the deities. In mythology, its exhilarating qualities have been seen to be enjoyed by gods.

RAGA: The ragas are the musical modes or melodies personified; they are six or more in number. Musical notations.

RAGINI: Personified consorts of the ragas.

UPA-VEDA: The subordinate veda.

SOMALATA: The soma shrub, which is a climber.

RISHI: Sage.

INDRA-DHANUSH: The rainbow, or the bow of Lord Indra.

KAMDEV: God of love.

KARTIKEYA: The god of war and the planet Mars. Also considered to be the handsome son of Lord Shiva and Goddess Parvati.

MAHENDRA: A name of Lord Indra.

RUDRAKSH MALA: A necklace made up of rudraksh beads. Rudraksh are the seeds of an evergreen tree (*E. ganitrus*) found in the foothills of the Himalayas. In mythology, rudraksh beads are supposed to be the teardrops of Lord Shiva.

ASHRAM: Hermitage.

SAPTARISHI: The seven great sages.

SHAKUNT: The Blue Jay bird.

MUHURTA: Auspicious moment in a day.

PARIJAT: A plant which has white flowers and an orange stem. The tree was supposed to have emerged during the churning of the ocean and was planted in the garden of Lord Indra.

TULASI: The basil tree considered to be holy by Hindus.

MALATI: The Chinese honeysuckle, a vine with red flower clusters.

VARNA: Class or caste.

KARMA: Actions.

DHARMA: Religion, code of conduct.

MANASA-PUTRI: Mind-born daughter of Lord Brahma.

BRAHMA-MUHURTA: Brahma-muhurta is known as the time of Lord Brahma. It is the pre-dawn period—one and a half hours before sunrise and is recommended in all practices of yoga. This time is traditionally considered most apt for meditation, worship or any other religious practice.

BRAHMA-KUMARI: The daughter of Lord Brahma.

SARASWATI: Goddess of learning and also the wife of Lord Brahma.

AARTI: A religious ritual during worship in which wicks soaked in ghee are offered to deities, accompanied with the singing of hymns in praise of the deity.

VYAYAMSHALA: An traditional gymnasium.

NEELGAI: An antelope, also known as the blue-bull.

AKHETA: A hunting expedition.

VAIDYA: A doctor who practices Ayurveda.

HAVAN: A religious ritual in which offerings are made into a consecrated fire.

SINDOOR: Vermilion.

Saree: A traditional garment worn by Indian women.

PARJANNAYA: A Vedic rain-deity or rain personified. In later times, it became another name for Lord Indra.

VAHANA: A vehicle. Most of the gods in the Hindu pantheon are represented with animals as their vahanas or carriers.

SWAYAMVAR: A gathering of kings and princes, where the girl gets to choose her husband.

SABHA: Court.

AGNI: Fire god.

POTLI: Cloth bag.

CHAKRAVARTI: A universal emperor. He who rules over an extensive territory and is well known for his justice.

References/Explanations

A: Pradip Bhattacharya, *Shakuntala*, Schubert and Sarabhai.

B: It is said that the piece of iron goes on to become the head of an arrow accidentally used by Jara to kill Lord Krishna. The Yadavas fight among themselves and after the Mahabharata war, Krishna, the last of the Yadavas, is killed too.

C: The Mrigavyadha myth is from Aiterya Brahmana.

D: Mahabharata—Udyog Parva, Section CXVI; K.M. Ganguli version.

E: Mahabharata—Udyog Parva, Section CXX; K.M. Ganguli version.

F: Rites of consecration.

G: Mahabharata—Adi Parva.

Bibliography

The Mahabharata of Krishna-Dwaipayana Vyasa, translated into English from the original Sanskrit text by K.M. Ganguli (1883–1896)

Classical Dictionary of Hindu Mythology and Religion, Geography, History and Literature by John Dowson (1888)

Indian Myth and Legend by Donald A. Mackenzie

Sakoontala, translated into English prose and verse from the original Sanskrit of Kalidasa by Sir Monier Monier-Williams (1855); Project Gutenberg eBook.

Shakuntala, translated by Arthur C. Ryder

Puranic Encyclopaedia by Vettam Mani

Essays

'Shakuntala: Flaming Indian Womanhood' by Satya Chaitanya

'Shakuntala, Schubert and Sarabhai' by Pradip Bhattacharya

'Vashishtha—Vishvamitra Katha' by Pradip Bhattacharya

'Shakuntala' by Pradip Bhattacharya

Acknowledgements

First and foremost, I would like to thank Prof. Satya Chaitanya for his brilliant essay, which introduced a different Shakuntala to me. The essay, an eye-opener for me, made me dig deeper into the subject, the result of which is in your hands. I would further like to thank him for agreeing to write the foreword for this book.

I would also like to thank my wife, Viki, without whom this book would not have become a reality. It is thanks to her faith and belief that this book has taken shape. Besides being the first critic, and often a harsh one at that, she was also the sole reviewer of this book. She was also the sole participant in debates that I undertook with her on many a topic and characterization, the result of which you have read. I can't thank her enough for her contribution!

Finally, I would also like to thank the entire team of Rupa Publications for giving my manuscript the final shape of the book and enabling Shakuntala to tell her version to each one of you!

However, any errors or discrepancies are solely mine and no one else is to be blamed for them.